The Potent Perfume

THE LADY MORTICIAN'S VISIONS SERIES

HELEN GOLTZ

The Potent Perfume – The Lady Mortician's Visions, book 5.

PUBLISHED BY: Atlas Productions

First published 2024.

Copyright © Helen Goltz

Cover design, as always, by the wonderful Karri Klawiter, Art by Karri.

PLEASE NOTE: This book is written in British-Australian English.

Chapter 1

Tuesday 3 February, 1891. Brisbane, Australia. Clear skies, 32 degrees daytime.

Miss Phoebe Astin tapped the top of her powder tins, her fingers trailing along their lids until she selected the right glow for the gentleman lying on her workbench. It was a serene picture as she worked quietly in the large room at the bottom of the stairs of *The Economic Undertaker* on Tribune Street, South Brisbane. Phoebe could hear the hum of business upstairs—voices, footsteps, the street noises when the door occasionally opened and closed—but in her room, it was peaceful.

Light streamed in from the top windows, and tasteful mahogany furniture with burgundy or pale pink cushioning was placed around the room. A large fern named Florence added a burst of green, and a fresh bouquet of dusty pink roses from the gentleman who only recently asked to court her, Detective Harland Stone, held pride of place. Phoebe's pale pink dress matched the roses today, although that was not planned. It was her third bouquet from the detective in as many weeks, and he always surprised her with his flower and colour choices.

'Mr Tate, I believe warm gold is your colour,' she said quietly, holding the brush close to the young gentleman's cheek and giving a small nod of satisfaction before wiping the dust on her apron.

'I've always thought of myself as pure gold,' a smooth male voice said behind Phoebe. She turned in haste to see the very man on her table before her, now in spirit form.

'Mr Tate!'

He gave a low bow. 'Edward Tate, at your service, if that is at all possible, given I am now the dearly departed,' he said with a cheeky grin that made him look a little roguish and most striking. 'May I enquire after your name, if it is not beauty?'

Phoebe gave a small laugh. 'Mr Tate, you are as charming as you are handsome.' She glanced at his body on the table. He had the looks of a leading man on the stage and undoubtedly had caused many a lady's heart to flutter. Not hers, though.

'Miss Phoebe Astin, at *your* service, as it so happens.'

'Indeed. Well, the pleasure is all mine, Miss Astin.'

'But the honour is mine,' she said most sincerely. 'I am sorry you have departed this world so young.'

He nodded his thanks. 'Some might say three decades on this earth is better than a poke with a burnt stick, Miss Astin.'

Phoebe gave a small laugh. 'Perhaps so.' But it seemed a shame that Mr Tate, with his sunny nature, was gone so soon.

He wandered close to his body. 'My, I am looking peaky.'

'Not for long,' Phoebe assured him. 'May I ask how you departed, Mr Tate?'

'You may!' he pronounced theatrically. 'Please call me Teddy. Well, it was a most extraordinary death,' Teddy announced as if he were proud of the manner in which he turned up his toes.

'Do tell, and please call me Phoebe.'

'Phoebe is a beautiful name for a beautiful young lady. I do love that you wear your golden hair loose, most becoming,' he said, admiring her. 'But to answer your question, I am or rather, I was, a travelling perfume salesman and, if I may say, a very good one.'

'Of that, I have no doubt,' Phoebe said firmly.

Teddy laughed. 'Was it my appearance or delivery that gave me away?'

'Perhaps both – the straight back, voice slightly projected and confident, I am sure I would buy your wares,' she said, guessing Teddy did not need compliments from her to keep his confidence up, especially as he was dead, after all.

'Funny you should say that, Phoebe, because it was during my sales speech that I met my end.'

'Goodness gracious,' Phoebe exclaimed. 'How terrible for you and the recipient of your sales delivery.'

'I imagine so; she was a beautiful young lady by the name of Amy. I am sure it was terribly melodramatic,' Teddy agreed. 'I gave my best and last performance that day.'

'I am so very sorry, Teddy,' Phoebe said. 'I didn't see anything about it in the newspaper.'

'I imagine Mr Higson, proprietor of Higson's Quality Perfumes, whom I worked for, did his best to hush it up. No one wants a salesman dying on their doorstep or thinking that our perfume is cursed.'

'Cursed, that is interesting,' she said, frowning. 'But I suppose people can be superstitious.'

'My word,' he agreed. 'Especially as Mr Higson has had a few calamities of late, including a lady who claimed she broke out in a terrible rash from his perfume, but it turned out to be from some crustacean she had eaten the night before. Of course, the damage was done by then.'

'Poor Mr Higson. Running a business is fraught with danger,' Phoebe agreed.

'Even burying the dead?' Teddy asked.

'Especially so. One has to be sure you have the right body, bury quickly in this terrible heat, and provide affordable services with dignity. It is a time when emotions are raw; thus, people are inclined to be a little more impatient than they might ordinarily be.'

'Yes, I see, fraught indeed. Speaking of the dead, which I am, may I ask a favour of you, Phoebe?'

'Of course, Teddy. What may I do for you?' Phoebe stopped working to give the salesman her full attention. Perhaps he wanted to deliver his last sales presentation for her benefit or request a message be delivered to a person of importance to him.

'I am hoping you might bring the matter of my death to a head. To shine some light on it, so to speak. You see, I have learnt that it was a broken perfume bottle that brought about my death. I collapsed onto the bottle; it shattered and pierced my heart.'

'How dreadful, Teddy. Shall we see?' she asked in a quiet voice, usually reserved for the delivery of bad news. Phoebe pulled back the covering on his body to reveal the jagged flesh wound on his chest.

'Ghastly,' he groaned. 'But why would I collapse?'

'So, you were not ill or prone to fainting spells?'

'Not a day in my life!' he proclaimed proudly before lightly clearing his throat and adopting a sheepish look that appeared most out of character. 'The lady I was selling perfume to was a very beautiful woman, and I am rather embarrassed to have fallen at her feet, so to speak. But she was not mine to have, even though I admired her ardently.'

'I see.'

'Good, I'm glad you do. I hoped you might tell several young ladies I held them in high regard and am most sorry to cut our acquaintance short.'

'Several!' Phoebe exclaimed.

'Yes, Isla, Sophia, and Rose were all so dear to me; I am torn between who holds my affections the most. Thank you, Phoebe, I am most grateful. They will be distraught that something sinister happened to me.'

'Will they?' she asked, unsure they would be upset, especially if they learnt of each other. She returned to the matter of his death. 'Did you drink or eat something that morning that might have caused you to collapse?'

'Not that I recall, lovely Phoebe. If I were not so convinced of the quality of the perfume I was sampling and selling, I might consider it brought me to my knees, but I know better.'

'Did the young lady with you at the time sample that very same perfume?'

'An excellent question, but she did not get the chance to do so. I inhaled it first, several times. I always do that in my presentations so that by the time I hand it to the ladies, they are desperately keen to sample the fragrance I have been admiring some time before them.'

'That's very clever,' Phoebe said.

'I know. I learnt it from Mark Twain.'

'How so?' Phoebe asked.

'In his book, "*The Adventures of Tom Sawyer*", Tom is painting a fence, a terrible and tedious task. But he makes it look so desirable that soon everyone wants to do it. It was so clever that I declared I would do the same. Thank you, Mr Twain. I create this desire for the perfume, and when the ladies finally get their turn to smell it, consider it sold.' He tapped his nose knowingly.

Phoebe laughed. 'Goodness, I must be careful of you, Teddy. You know all the tricks.'

'Maybe I do,' he teased. 'But I assure you, Phoebe,' he said in a serious voice, 'my death is not natural. Someone has done me in, and I am most grateful for your attention to the matter.' With that, Teddy bowed and disappeared, and Phoebe stood staring at the space where he once stood, eyes wide, mouth open.

'Oh, but—' She looked around. Teddy was definitely gone. 'Well, what am I supposed to do with that?' she mused.

Chapter 2

BROTHERS JULIUS AND AMBROSE Astin of *The Economic Undertaker* looked dignified and respectful in their dark suits as they stood to the side of the funeral proceedings on the humid February day. Despite Julius's engagement being widely well known—to Miss Violet Forrester, the manager of his mourning-wear dress store—several women succumbed to heat distress and required his assistance.

'Surely it is your turn?' Julius whispered to his brother, who shook his head.

'I just helped that elderly lady, who patted my cheek when she recovered and said I reminded her of her husband before he grew whiskers.'

Julius gave a small huff of laughter and went to assist a young lady into a chair, followed by another who caught his eye before fluttering her eyelashes and swaying slightly.

On returning and ignoring his brother's nudge and teasing, Julius gratefully stood in the shade; the calm before the storm was oppressive, to say the least. A loud rumble of thunder saw both men glance to the skies, as did many of the parishioners, and a nervous energy ran through the gathering. The storm was building fast, and Julius wanted to have the horses safely undercover before the lightning spooked them. He did not care that he might get wet; both men would have happily shucked their jackets and let the rain soak them through to cool off.

Father Morris took his cue from the skies and sped up his blessing as much as possible without being irreverent. Mourners twitched, looked above, and seemed ready to depart the moment Father said "Amen". A huge gust of wind blew half a dozen hats off the ladies' heads, and Ambrose, along with several able gentlemen, took chase, returning the hats to the owners.

'Amen,' Father Morris said.

Like scurrying ants, the funeral party rose and broke up. Those not family or related by marriage were first out the gates, making haste to beat the pending storm as the wind continued to rise. The sea of black-wearing mourners weaved their way to where their carriages, or hansom cabs, awaited to take them to the local hotel for the wake. Very few were armed with umbrellas, as the day had started fine and hot.

The Astin brothers and Father Morris stood beside the coffin as family members filed past for their last farewells and departed just as quickly.

'Dying in summer should be forbidden,' Ambrose muttered when no one remained to hear his moaning except his brother and Father Morris. 'It's just bad manners.'

'Amen to that,' Father Morris agreed, mopping his brow.

'If gravediggers were not in danger of falling into the graves, I would offer funerals at twilight,' Julius said.

'You've got connections, Father,' Ambrose said, indicating above. 'Can't you at least request it be a little cooler when a funeral is in progress?'

Father Morris laughed and tapped his nose. 'You're right, Ambrose. I may have an inside advantage. Leave it with me, gentlemen.'

With all the mourners departed, the brothers were safe to enjoy the joke with Father Morris.

'You best go, Father; you don't want to be soaked through or risk lightning hitting the metal hanging around your neck,' Julius said, with a glance to the large cross Father Morris wore.

'That would be divine intervention,' Father Morris agreed. 'There'll be a wait for a hansom or omnibus by the looks of it.'

Julius looked towards the gate, noting the funeral party still snaking along the road to hail hansom cabs; a full omnibus seating sixteen had just departed. The driver was also keen to get his horses to safety.

'Ambrose will take you, Father; it is on the way,' Julius suggested. 'You go, Brother. Drop Father off at the Presbytery and return the horses to the stable. I shall stay to see the coffin buried, pay the gravediggers, and return when the storm abates.'

'I will happily accept your offer. God bless and save you, Julius,' Father Morris said.

'I hope so,' Julius said with a nod and a smile at the priest.

The gravediggers approached, pulling their small cart loaded with tools behind them and looking skyward.

Ambrose started, 'We can wait another ten—'

'No, best you go now,' Julius cut him off.

Ambrose needed no encouragement. He was sweltering hot and only too happy to get moving and get the horses to shelter. Julius watched as his brother and Father Morris stepped up to the hearse.

'Don't go too fast; remember, we are a dignified funeral business,' Julius warned. 'But if you think no one is watching, speed up a little.'

'I never thought I'd live to see the day I would get to gallop in the hearse,' Ambrose said in jest and, turning the jittery horses, headed off with a wave, keen to move as the sound of rumbling thunder and the wind swell increased.

Julius turned to greet the two gravediggers as they arrived beside him. Father and son, the Redford family was respectable folk and had been in business for decades.

'Hello there, Mr Astin,' the senior Redford said in return greeting. 'I love a good summer storm. Come on then, Son.' The elder of the gravediggers threw the first clump of dirt on the coffin, and a crack of lightning made them all jump.

'Perhaps we should do this later, gents, and you should seek cover,' Julius suggested.

'We can't leave a gaping hole,' the younger man said. 'Some idiot will fall into it. You go, Mr Astin, we can finish this.'

'I shall wait with you,' Julius said, never one to cut corners. He had heard of other funeral directors not seeing jobs through and gravesites being robbed, not that the Redford men would do such a thing, but it was his job to see it done. Julius removed his jacket and laid it on the grass. Seeing several other shovels on the men's cart, he grabbed a shovel and helped.

They heaped the dirt quickly. Fifteen minutes passed, and the storm was dark and menacing. Julius looked up to see two funeral guests re-entering the grounds and huddling under a large tree near the entrance gates while they awaited a ride that may not return. It was quite a walk to the nearest shelter, and he guessed they had weighed up their chances of staying dry.

As he returned to shovelling, a movement caught his eye, and he saw in the distance a lady on her knees beside a grave praying, a sorry spectacle.

Mr Redford followed his gaze between throwing spadefuls of dirt in the hole. 'She'll be struck by lightning and join her loved one if she doesn't get a scurry along.'

'Common sense is not so common,' the young Redford added, obviously parroting a saying he had heard from his father on many occasions, and Julius and Mr Redford senior exchanged a smile.

The men increased their labour and quickly finished the job. Mr Redford Senior compressed the earth before hurriedly cleaning up the dirt surrounding the gravesite's border. His son filled the indents his father made.

An almighty crack of lightning made them all quake.

'We're done now; thanks for your help, Mr Astin. I'd say she's close by,' Mr Redford Senior said, nodding to the skies.

'I counted the seconds between the thunder and lightning, Pa,' Young Redford said, raising his voice over the wind. 'Less than a mile.'

Julius paid the gentlemen, including a generous tip, thanked them, and retrieved his jacket from the grass.

'They're nearly all gone now,' Mr Redford senior said, looking at the half dozen outside the gate as large raindrops began to belt down upon them.

A loud lightning flash seemed to crackle to the earth, and the men turned in time to see lightning strike a large branch.

'It's falling!' Young Redford yelled in alarm.

Senior Redford waved his arms frantically, trying to get the attention of the older couple huddling beneath the branches.

'Get away from the tree,' Julius yelled, but the wind and rain carried his voice away.

The couple under the tree's shelter looked up in time – but not in time to get away. They were standing, and then they were not, the weight of the branch leaving no doubt they could survive the crushing.

Young Redford swore, saying, 'Seen nothing like that before.'

Julius and Mr Redford Senior stared in shock before Julius hurried them off to find shelter in the groundsman's shed. They threw the spades onto the cart and began to pull it. The skies opened fully now, and the rain bucketed in sheets large and heavy. It was just under two miles from the South Brisbane Cemetery to *The Economic Undertaker* office on Tribune Street, and Julius hoped Ambrose had covered that distance in the nearly thirty minutes since he departed, and that he and the horses were high and dry. He was fairly confident his little brother would have moved the hearse along at a pace unbecoming but necessary.

'Thank you, Mr Astin,' Mr Redford yelled over the beating rain as the three men pulled the tool cart. 'We'll be back to clean the site up properly later.'

'Thank you, Mr Redford,' Julius said, panting as they fought against the rain and the wind, cowering at the lightning in case it regarded them as targets; the shed was now in sight.

Julius glanced behind him at the tree, and there was no movement below it. He heard Mr Redford Senior loudly say, 'Got yourself a few more customers, I'd say.'

'Sad to lose your life at a funeral,' Julius yelled above the wind.

'Life and death, all entwined,' Mr Redford Senior yelled back philosophically, and they entered the shed, immediately enjoying the quiet reprieve from the wind and rain and picturing the gruesome work to follow when the storm abated.

$$Chapter\ 3$$

Detective Harland Stone glanced out the window and moved back slightly as the lightning flashed across the sky.

'I believe you are quite safe, Sir,' his protégé, Detective Gilbert Payne, said from his desk. 'I have never heard or read of anyone being struck by lightning within a building, but if you were outside on the front steps, you might not be so fortunate.'

'Thank you, Gilbert,' Harland said, knowing Gilbert's store of facts covered vast areas of interest. 'Good to know.'

A knock on the door had them both turning as Sergeant John Henderson entered. 'Here's the file you've been waiting on detectives, with the boss's compliments.' He chuckled at his own joke; the boss rarely offered compliments, although Detectives Stone and Payne were his golden pair. Since Harland Stone had won the posting in Brisbane, one of the youngest detectives to do so—in exchange for partnering and mentoring the inexperienced Detective Gilbert Payne—the men had solved every case they had been assigned.

They made a formidable odd couple. Harland was rugged, dogged, physically strong with a boxer's nose, but with a polished education that gave him a genteel way of speaking. By contrast, Gilbert was a neat, fastidious, and poetic soul who stored facts voraciously and had a church-going upbringing. It was fair to say that Harland's analytical mind and Gilbert's fact-storing nature gave criminals a run for their money.

Harland thanked the sergeant, accepted the file, and sat down at their joint worktable, where Gilbert joined him with his pad.

'Right then, what have we got?' Harland said, halving the file of its dozen or so sheets and slipping them to Gilbert. They read silently for a moment, then exchanged sheets and began reading again. When they had both read the file, Harland sat back.

'I'd say if the lady and her family were not known to the top brass, this would have been ruled an accidental or natural death and not have seen the light of day,' Harland said.

'I have to agree, Sir. But, having recently found a lady who may be my future,' he said of Miss Phoebe Astin's friend – the clever, beautiful Miss Emily Yalden of the *Miss Emily Yalden School of Deportment,* 'then I confess should anything happen to her, I would use all my influence to have her case investigated.'

'Yes, I believe I would do the same, Gilbert,' Harland conceded, his mind going to the lady mortician who had him in her thrall and who crossed his mind every moment of the day that he allowed his thoughts to stray. 'You are right; we should not show a bias against this case or this young lady just because her family has the status to pull rank.' Harland looked at the file to check her name. 'Miss Sophia Beaver.'

Gilbert removed her illustrated portrait from his half of the paperwork and put it on the desk between them. 'She is an attractive lady and accomplished; it says here that Miss Beaver spoke three languages.'

'Sadly, all that talent is going to the grave with her. So, what have we then?' Harland read some statements from people who knew Miss Sophia Beaver. 'She's a good girl, would never knowingly meet a man for a liaison—'

Gilbert read some statements from his paperwork. 'She cared for her elderly grandmother, volunteered for the church committee—'

'And her manner of death was not suspicious,' Harland said matter-of-factly. 'Septicaemia – blood poisoning. A slight cut can cause that if not treated well.'

'It's very common,' Gilbert agreed. 'Sadly, it's been a few weeks since her death, so I'm assuming Miss Beaver has been buried, and we won't be able to see her body.'

'Most likely, but we shall catch up with Tavish, regardless. He may recall something of interest or discreetly share information that his superiors told him to suppress,' Harland said, referring to Dr Tavish McGregor, the resident coroner.

'Does that happen, Sir?' Gilbert asked naively, rising to grab his hat and follow his superior.

'I can't say it happens with Tavish, but it has been known to happen. We all have pressure to bear and have had to follow orders, even if they go against our principles.'

'Have you personally, Sir?' Gilbert asked, surprised.

The men strode down the hallway like two detectives with purpose; a new case always gave them a rush of energy.

'We can be found at the coroner's office, Sergeant,' Harland called, passing John at the desk. Exiting the building and coming into the light, he suggested they walk. The storm had abated, and the humidity was lifted, replaced with the smell of fresh air and earth.

'Have I?' Harland repeated the question now that they were out of earshot of the station. 'I've been directed to prioritise cases, release prisoners because they were connected to someone of importance, reduce charges, and yes, I've followed orders. But every man has their limit, or they should.'

Gilbert thought about this for a considerable time, somewhat out of character for a man who often said what was immediately on his mind. Harland glanced at him.

'Have I rendered you speechless?'

'No, Sir,' Gilbert laughed. 'I am just considering my limits.'

'I suspect they would be stricter than mine. You are God-fearing of nature, Gilbert, whereas I find myself unsurprised by wickedness and thus resigned to some degree.'

They arrived at the building housing the coroner and thanked the gentleman exiting who held the door for them.

'I think you are a man of firm principles, Sir. You sell yourself short.'

Harland gave his protégé a brief nod of thanks. 'Well, let's hope I live up to your estimation of me.'

'I have no expectations, Sir. Only to live up to yours.'

They entered the coroner's office, and Harland felt immediate relief from the chill in Tavish's room. The red-haired, bearded Scottish coroner had been sitting quietly doing paperwork and was presentable in a dark suit; no corpse in sight. He exclaimed with delight at seeing them.

''Tis the living, how grand!'

Harland laughed. 'Tavish, how are you on this fine Monday afternoon?'

'Dry, I am pleased to say. What a storm. How many people have died from being struck by lightning, young Detective Payne? You are the fact guru.'

Gilbert flushed with the praise. 'I believe it is less than three per cent, Doctor. You have more chance of dying from a tree falling on you, or suffocation, or drowning or—' Remembering his superior's advice about the importance of brevity, he concluded, 'There's a lot to choose from,' making the men laugh.

'There you go then, spoilt for choice,' Tavish announced. 'Still, one doesn't want to be counted in the less than three per cent. So, gentlemen, why do I have the pleasure of your company?'

'Miss Sophia Beaver,' Harland announced.

'Ah,' Tavish nodded. 'I remember the young lady as I didn't expect that was the last I would hear of Miss Beaver.' He tapped his nose as if he were a source of secret information. 'The acting commissioner's niece.'

Tavish indicated the meeting table in his room for the men to sit while he rifled through a large filing cabinet, pulling out the file for Sophia Beaver.

'And your diagnosis was that it was not a suspicious death?' Harland asked as Tavish sat with them.

'It was a difficult one to diagnose because the family would not allow an autopsy, and the family doctor signed the death certificate. It came to me at the acting commissioner's insistence. The young lady had symptoms consistent with blood poisoning, but I could not find any wounds or cuts. I did, however, find several injection marks where a small area was inflamed.'

'Did she have any illnesses that might require her to receive a needle or syringe, Dr McGregor?' Gilbert asked.

'None I could see without an autopsy and none that the family claimed to know about. However, she did not have the look of a morphine or drug user. She was a rather pampered young lady, attractive, well-endowed, well-fed, and well-groomed.'

Harland's fingers tapped the table with frustration. 'The family believe foul play may have had a hand in her death but then prevent you from undertaking an autopsy and expect us to prove it.' He shook his head. 'Might she have been injected with or drank poison?'

'She might have, but as the family found her dead the next morning and cleaned her up—'

'No!' Harland exclaimed.

'Yes,' Tavish nodded. 'So, if she vomited or had a fever, we'll never know. There were no visible signs of discolouration, but there was a small rash around the injection area. You have your work cut out for you – no corpse, nothing but a few needle marks and a handful of character references to lead the investigation. Good luck.'

'Thanks ever so much,' Harland responded drily, making the coroner laugh. 'I am assuming our good friend, Julius, did not bury her?'

'Oh no,' Tavish shook his head. 'No economic funeral for this one. Miss Beaver's family spent a small fortune seeing her off, or so I was told.'

'It would help assuage their grief, I imagine,' Harland said. 'Did anything strike you as odd, Tavish?'

'Well, yes.'

Both detectives perked up as the coroner rose, returned to his desk in the corner and retrieved a black leather diary from a drawer before returning to the men.

'I keep personal notes and don't put them in the case file if they are just my thoughts and not clinical observations. They can be useful should I be called to court.'

'I can imagine with all the bodies you see, remembering one from another would be tricky, Doctor,' Gilbert agreed.

'Very true, Detective Payne, especially if I'm inclined to have a tipple and memory does not serve me as well the morning after,' he said with a laugh. He flicked through the diary until he found the date of Miss Beaver's death and the entry related to her.

'Tell me it will help solve the case,' Harland said optimistically.

Tavish exhaled. 'Knowing you two, it just might. She was wearing a white lace dress and white lace underwear. I noted it because it was similar to what a bride might wear. When I asked the family if her ring was missing, they claimed she was single, but this was her favourite dress; hence she was found in it.' He looked at his notes again. 'She had a slip of paper in an inside pocket of the dress.'

He flipped to the back of the diary, where a leather pouch held documents, and fished around in it until he found the note, which

Harland thought was quite a feat given the state of the coroner's papers. Harland accepted the scrap of paper, unfolding it to read: "Beauty is only skin deep". Harland handed it to Gilbert as Dr McGregor continued.

'I noted the white dress in particular because about two months ago, there was another young lady in a similar dress with blood poisoning.'

'That is significant,' Harland said, leaning forward. 'And you mentioned this to the detective?'

'Only to the police officer who came to get my findings. It was never assigned to a detective. I went as far as to offer him the file, but he said that wasn't necessary. This other young woman was located in another town, Toowoomba. I only learnt of her because the Toowoomba Coroner was here for the day on business and called in on me. I had Miss Sophia Beaver in-house that day, and on seeing the similarity, he sent me a copy of his victim's file. A lucky coincidence.'

'It was indeed. Did she have the same line of verse on her as well?' Harland asked.

'A record of it was not in the Toowoomba Coroner's files, but I shall ask him the question and let you know.'

'May we have the Toowoomba victim's file, Doctor?' Gilbert asked.

'Of course.' Tavish rose again. 'I remember her name; a lovely Scottish name.' Tavish found the file and returned it, placing it on the table where Harland reached for it.

'Gentlemen, meet Miss Isla Barr.'

Chapter 4

THE HEAD OF THE Astin family, Randolph Astin—silver-haired, handsome and the perfect front man for *The Economic Undertaker* business—had been pacing since Ambrose returned on his own.

'I shall go back out and collect him as soon as the storm passes, Grandpa, so that the horses won't be spooked,' Ambrose promised.

'Not before,' Randolph agreed. 'I still hear some rumblings and don't need two grandsons to worry about.'

The backdoor opened, and Julius strode in, removing his hat and shaking himself of water like a dog with a wet coat.

'Thank God, lad, you had me worried,' Randolph exhaled, studying the eldest of his grandchildren whom he and Maria Astin raised after his son and daughter-in-law met a tragic end. 'You're drenched.'

'It's raining,' Julius said matter-of-factly but with the hint of a smile for his grandfather. 'Ambrose, did you get Father Morris and the horses back before it broke?'

'With five minutes to spare,' Ambrose boasted, helping Julius strip off his wet jacket.

'You should have come then too, Julius,' his grandfather said sternly. 'The dead are already dead, and no one expects you to be out there in this weather.'

Julius thanked Mrs Dobbs, their kind office lady, who hurried up the hallway to reception with two large towels. Taking them, Julius patted himself down as she departed to make him a cup of tea.

'I think they do, Grandpa. If it were my loved one, I would expect the job to be seen through to the end, and the coffin wasn't abandoned or left uncovered just because of a storm.'

Randolph conceded the point.

'There was a problem, though; I have advised the police at the station nearest to the cemetery that—'

Violet Forrester ran past the shop windows and rushed into *The Economic Undertaker* office moments later, closing the door quickly behind her.

'You're back!' she exclaimed with relief and hurried to Julius, kissing him on the cheek and making them both flush with embarrassment. 'And you are soaked,' Violet grimaced, backing away.

'I waited it out in the groundsman's shed but just caught the edge of the storm,' he assured his fiancée while patting down his hair with a towel, the dark locks sticking up at odd angles.

'I saw you both depart and Ambrose hurrying home without you. I would have come in earlier, but I was with a client,' Violet explained. 'I am sure I stabbed her with pins in my panic, but she was most tolerant.'

'Julius!' Phoebe exclaimed, appearing at the top of the stairs. 'Ambrose, why did you not tell me he was back?' she asked, scolding Ambrose. 'Hello, Violet, you must have been so worried.'

'I was.'

'I just walked in the door minutes ago,' Julius said calmly, 'and there was nothing to worry about. What did you tell them, Ambrose? That I was holding a lightning rod?'

The group chuckled.

'Yes,' Ambrose said, 'and that you were standing out in the open chanting something about being Zeus, the god of lightning.'

The laughs broke the tension, and in her usual well-timed manner, Mrs Dobbs called out, 'The tea is made.'

Randolph herded the gathered group from the reception area into the large meeting room, where they usually took morning and afternoon tea when no customers were in the house. Mrs Dobbs had wasted no time putting cake and biscuits out, along with the cups, and was pouring; she knew how each person liked their brew. Phoebe moved to assist her.

'You are a godsend, Mrs Dobbs,' Julius said, making her smile with pleasure. 'I'll change and be straight back.' He headed to the small room where spare suits were hung for situations like this or if the stable staff needed to fill in for Julius or Ambrose. His hand brushed Violet's as he departed, bringing a flush to her cheeks as she watched him leave, his wet shirt clinging to him.

'Perfect timing as always, Mrs Dobbs, thank you,' Randolph said, relieved. 'Violet, can you stay for tea, dear? Julius was about to elaborate on a problem that had occurred.'

'I would be pleased for the break, thank you, Mr Astin. My staff is working, and we have no customers in-store.'

The group spoke about the severe weather as they sat around the table. Ambrose regaled them with stories of Father Morris saying the service as speedily as he had ever heard, the mourners continuously glancing to the sky, and the hurried "Amen," and Julius soon rejoined them.

'What has happened then?' Randolph asked as Julius thanked Mrs Dobbs for the cup of tea.

'A tree fell on a couple while they sheltered from the storm inside the cemetery gates. They are deceased.'

The table guests gasped, and Mrs Dobbs made the sign of the cross, which she often did in the presence of the Astin family.

'We did have grounds to worry about you, lad!' Randolph said, grateful his grandson was not a victim of the storm.

'Did you see it happen?' Violet asked with her hand on her heart.

'Yes, as did the gravediggers, Mr Redford senior and junior. We were levelling off the grave when we heard the almighty crack. The couple had been waiting for a hansom and decided to re-enter and wait in the grounds.'

'How dreadfully sad to die at a funeral,' Phoebe said, quite shocked.

'It is a shame you could not bring them straight back here, Brother,' Ambrose said. 'Two new clients and all in a day's work.'

'Ambrose,' Randolph said with a sigh. He gave his grandson a shake of the head, trying to hide a smile as did all around the table.

'If the family was pleased with our services, we might get them yet,' Julius said; he rarely joked about business. 'I believe the victim was an uncle of the deceased whose funeral we were hosting.'

'Goodness, what a terrible time for the family,' Phoebe said, reaching for one of Mrs Dobbs' jam-drop biscuits. The Astin family rarely let grief affect their appetite; they were well used to it.

'They might ask for a family discount, which I think would be justified,' Ambrose continued, and even Mrs Dobbs, who tried to stay reverent when it came to talking about the dead, could not help but give a little smile.

'We only have one client in-house at the moment, don't we?' Julius asked his grandfather.

'Yes, a gentleman with a viewing booked for tomorrow. He was a bachelor with no immediate family, but his uncle would like to host the viewing here for his work colleagues and friends. Plus, we have several bodies to collect late today or early tomorrow.'

Phoebe spoke up. 'The client present is Mr Edward Tate, Teddy.'

All eyes turned to her.

'Teddy? Uh oh,' Ambrose said. 'He has appeared to you then?'

Phoebe nodded. She was safe in the present company; all knew about her ability to converse with the deceased. Julius could also see the deceased, but he had never admitted it; only Phoebe was in his confidence.

'Teddy believes his death to be untoward, and he wants me to do something about it, heaven knows what, as he was brief on detail.'

'Good Lord,' Mrs Dobbs said and blessed herself again with the sign of the cross.

'He is such a congenial man, so positive and charming, but I don't know how to help him.' Phoebe said.

'How did he die, do you know, Phoebe?' Violet asked.

'Yes, he was selling his wares—perfume—and fell. In doing so, the perfume bottle broke, perforating his heart. Or that is the accident version, which Teddy does not believe.'

'Good heavens!' Randolph exclaimed. 'It is a day of oddities!'

'A very odd way to go, Grandpa,' Phoebe agreed. 'Teddy said his collapse was most out of character. He wants to know what brought him to his knees and claims he did nothing to bring about the fall, nor did the lady customer he was with at the time, as far as he recalls.'

Julius offered, 'If you wish, Ambrose and I could swing by and ask Tavish if he thought anything was odd about the death of Mr...?'

'Tate, Edward Tate,' Phoebe reminded him.

'Right, Mr Tate. Unless you wish to send a note to your detective, of course?' Julius asked.

'He is not my detective,' Phoebe gave her brother a look. Julius was not usually the brother who teased her, but she had to expect it, given his friendship with Harland. 'And you can all stop with your little smiles,' she scolded the group, smiling herself now. 'Yes, please. Perhaps ask Dr McGregor first, and then we can inform Harland if need be. Teddy might return if I am lucky.'

Violet shuddered. 'You are very brave, Phoebe. I would never wish that on myself.'

Julius and Phoebe exchanged a quick look that did not go unnoticed by their grandfather.

'Nor I,' Mrs Dobbs agreed. 'Your generous heart makes you open to such things, I imagine, Phoebe dear.'

Phoebe smiled at Mrs Dobbs's kindness.

Julius finished his tea. 'I shall walk you back,' he said to Violet as she rose, and he shot to his feet.

'Thank you, Mrs Dobbs,' she said, accepting the small bundle of jam-drops to take to the ladies in the dressmaking store.

'It's much quicker via the front way,' Ambrose teased as the pair headed to the back door.

Randolph smiled at their shenanigans. 'Love is grand,' he said to Mrs Dobbs.

'That it is, Mr Astin, that it is.'

Chapter 5

Reporter Lilly Lewis wrinkled her nose in disgust, making her writing partner, Fergus Griffiths, laugh. It was a pretty nose on an intelligent face, but today, that face was scowling.

'It is so disappointing that there have been no great mysteries for several weeks.'

'Our run of good stories could not have gone on forever,' Fergus said, giving her a nudge as they left a most unsavoury sight at the wharves where a load of rotten vegetables had been dumped. 'We have been fairly consistent, but let us hope it will not be a feast or famine. I would always like to have something of interest bubbling away.'

Lilly gave Fergus a wry look at his attempt at humour. 'Your food references are most apt when we are surrounded by rotting vegetables from a feast that never was. But I agree with you; occasionally we must tread water, I suppose.'

Before continuing, she accepted his hand to step over a muddy ditch made by wagon tracks and the recent storm. 'It is frustrating that even my sources have nothing of interest,' Lilly continued to complain, lifting her light blue dress skirt as they left the putrid area and returned to the main thoroughfare. 'Bennet is investigating a boring insurance fraud claim,' she said of the private investigator whose attention she had captured, 'and Phoebe has no bodies that have been murdered. Even Detective Stone is working on some dull case at the whim of his superior. I am sure I will die of boredom.'

'Or melodrama,' Fergus grinned, dodging her friendly swipe. 'Come then, we'll write up this feud, and you can make your rounds again. I shall make mine and let's see what we can dig up. It has only been a matter of weeks since our deathly dolls exposé.'

Lilly smiled and cocked her head to the side as if thinking of a distant memory. 'That was amazing. But I'm sure our next story is just around the corner, Fergus.' She brightened. 'Here comes the omnibus now, so our wait will not be too long.'

The pair stood enjoying the post-storm atmosphere. They were like-minded of nature but as different physically as colleagues can be – Lilly being fair, brunette and blue-eyed, and a head shorter than Fergus with his mop of unruly brown hair that framed a face full of character with dark eyes and full lips. He recently became a father, which explained the weariness that donned his countenance.

'Perhaps because of the heat, everyone is taking time off, including the criminals,' Lilly pondered as she watched the omnibus approaching.

'Maybe. But it does make for short tempers. I am sure there will soon be plenty to report,' Fergus said.

Lilly's blue eyes lit with renewed enthusiasm; she was not one to wallow. 'You are right, Fergus. Let us write up this silly feud between the shipowners and the export company, and I shall go sniff out a story. I do so hope someone has died an interesting death.'

Fergus laughed again and shook his head at her as they stepped onto the omnibus stairs and searched for a seat.

'Detectives!' Lilly exclaimed, delighted at the sight of Detectives Harland Stone and Gilbert Payne near the rear of the omnibus. She plopped down beside them before the horse and carriage started again. 'Clearly, your budget is as limited as ours.'

'Hello Miss Lewis, what a coincidence,' Harland said drily and shook Fergus's hand, as did Gilbert.

'We do our best to cut costs,' Gilbert said, smiling happily at the sight of Miss Lewis, a good friend of the woman he strongly admired, Miss Emily Yalden. Any reminder was most welcome.

'It is at times tiresome, but I don't mind having the opportunity to observe people,' Fergus said, and they all braced as the omnibus stopped unexpectedly to let an insistent passenger on board.

'We are reporting on the dumping.' Lilly said. 'What finds you out this way? Please tell me it is something exciting. We're desperate for a good story.'

'A case, but it is early days for us,' Harland said. 'A file has just landed in our laps, and we are not convinced it is a suspicious death.'

Gilbert opened his mouth to speak, and Lilly leaned forward keenly, but remembering himself and his superior's warnings to be discreet, he added, 'The victim's family is inclined to think it is suspicious.'

'Excellent!' Lilly proclaimed. 'If we promise to abide by our agreement of past cases, Detective Stone, will you tell us, even if you are dubious of your case's merit?'

'It has been an honourable agreement,' Harland said, acknowledging their successful working relationship. He glanced around and, seeing no one was likely to overhear, leaned forward, his hands webbed between his knees, and offered a précis of what he knew.

'We have two young women dressed in white—not a bridal dress, but not dissimilar—both dead from blood poisoning but with no obvious addiction or illness.'

'Most odd. And where are you going now?' Lilly asked as the detectives' stop was only a short distance away.

'We have been to the coroner and then to the records office, and now we are heading back to our office. I have nothing more to tell you as yet.' He sat back in his chair, having delivered all he had to date.

'Thank you, Detective. May I ask a few quick questions?' Lilly said with a glance at Fergus, who nodded his encouragement.

'Our stop is before yours, so fit in as many as you can,' Harland said, smiling on issuing the challenge.

Lilly looked excited; the challenge accepted. 'Were the undergarments white and of similar quality to the dress?'

'To the best of our understanding, but that requires further investigation. Why do you ask?'

'A woman will wear her best garments when meeting a suitor,' Lilly said as if the answer was obvious. 'Do the ladies know each other?'

'We don't know.'

'Are they from the same area?'

'If you consider eighty miles between them to be proximity enough.'

'I see. Are they of the same age?'

'Three years apart.'

'Who buried them?'

'If you are asking if it was *The Economic Undertaker*, it was not for the first victim. I could not say for the second lady yet, but it is unlikely as she was based in Toowoomba.'

'Could you please tell me their names, Detective? I will discreetly enquire who buried them.'

Harland looked at Gilbert, who recalled their names without checking his notes. 'Miss Sophia Beaver of South Brisbane and Miss Isla Barr of Toowoomba.'

'Thank you, how exciting,' Lilly said as the detectives' stop came into view, and all three gentlemen could not hide their smiles at her enthusiasm. 'I shall ask Phoebe this evening; the *Vexed Vixens* are meeting.'

'Ah, thank you for reminding me,' Harland said, and Lilly looked surprised.

'Are you expecting your ears to burn, Detective?' she teased, and he laughed.

'No. On occasion, when I can, I walk Phoebe home. I recall her saying she was leaving early today, so I shall not delay her.'

'You are meeting at Miss Yalden's, are you not?' Detective Payne said, enjoying the sound of her name on his lips.

'Your sweetheart?' Fergus asked, having been informed of all the latest romances by his reporter partner, Lilly.

'I hope to claim that title soon, Mr Griffiths,' Gilbert said sincerely.

'Yes, dinner at Emily's this evening,' Lilly said hurriedly as the horses began to slow.

'May we call on you tomorrow, Detective, for an update?' Fergus asked as the driver brought the horses to a stop.

'Yes, I shall see you then,' Harland said, farewelling them both, Gilbert doing the same as he rose and descended.

Once the omnibus recommenced its journey, Lilly turned to her colleague.

'What luck to find them on board. Although I suspect they regularly traverse the coroner's office and South Brisbane.'

'We should remember that. It is one way to secure a story if needed,' he said in jest.

'Fergus, I am sure this will be our next investigative piece,' she said. 'We must hurriedly write up the dumping story and be ready to go tomorrow.'

He smiled at her renewed zeal. 'We should notify Mr Cowan so he does not allocate us anything else.'

'Yes,' Lilly agreed, thinking of her editor. 'We will promise to pitch it to him late tomorrow to give ourselves some time.'

And with that, the two young reporters awaited their stop near the offices of *The Courier*, the smell of a story in the post-storm air.

At dusk, in the day's last light, with everything feeling balmy and clean after the storm, the *Vexed Vixens* met at the townhome of Miss Emily Yalden.

'You are very kind to host again, Emily dear,' Phoebe said as she and Violet arrived together, Julius dropping them off at Emily's abode. It was Lilly's turn to host, but one of her five brothers had come down with a bad cold, and now the whole family seemed to be home sniffling and not going out as planned.

'Thank you, Phoebe, but as you are all bringing a dish, I can hardly claim to be a good hostess. Ooh, is that your grandmother's peach pie?'

'It is,' Phoebe offered the pie for the dessert table. 'I intended to make a dessert, but Grandma was making one for the family, so she made two!'

'Please thank her, how delicious. I can never get my pastry right; I will ask your grandmother to teach me if she has the time.'

'And I have ham and potato puffs as promised; I made some for my brother as well,' Violet said, handing over her baking dish covered in a secured towel.

Emily inhaled the spicy scent. 'Delicious, thank you, Violet! When did you get the time to do that?'

'Before work this morning. Fortunately, Julius collected me, so I didn't have to go on the omnibus with my baking dish.'

'Is that not out of his way?' Emily teased, and Violet blushed.

'Very much so; it is good of him to make the time.' She hurried on. 'There are a couple of my puffs missing as Nellie and Mary were looking at them hungrily, and I had to offer them a taste,' she said of her senior dressmaker, Mrs Nellie Shaw and the young seamstress, Miss Mary Pollard.

'I cannot blame them,' Emily said, eyeing them with equal longing.

A noise at the door told them that Lilly and Kate had arrived. Only after the ladies admired the dinner spread, the party was seated at the table with beverages, and their meal served, did Emily call the gathering to order.

'I am handing this meeting to Lilly as it is her turn, even if the venue has changed.'

'Oh, thank you, Emily,' Lilly said, fork suspended as she was about to taste Kate's Irish stew. 'It is most tiresome having five brothers who still live at home; my apologies for not hosting. Nonetheless, I call the monthly meeting of the *Vexed Vixens* to order. Would anyone like to start with what is vexing them, or shall we talk about what has unfolded with our potential suitors since Emily's dinner dance party?' she asked with an enthusiastic giggle, most unlike herself. The look in Lilly's eyes indicated she wanted to speak of the latter, and the suggestion received enthusiastic support, except for Emily, who did not like the meetings to be all about men.

'To appease you both, let's combine them,' Phoebe said, being diplomatic. 'Why don't you start, Kate? Is my brother still annoying you?'

Attractive, fair-skinned, auburn-haired Kate laughed. 'Yes, thank goodness. He is very handsome, and we are going to take some photographs together on Sunday. Ambrose dropped in on his way to the morgue to suggest the outing.' Her eyes widened. 'Goodness, do not tell your eldest brother, Phoebe, I was sworn to secrecy.'

'Not much gets past Julius, and I'm sure he would not mind Ambrose diverting off course on his way to do collections,' Phoebe said with a laugh. 'Are you not alarmed to have a hearse out the front of your office?'

'Only if it brings me more death portrait requests, which I don't do.'

Emily shuddered. 'Awful. Please do not let anyone photograph me when I am dead! So where are you going for this photography session?'

'Ambrose has picked out a picturesque location but intends to surprise me. So, it is fair to say he is not vexing me at all.' Kate proclaimed happily.

Phoebe smiled. 'Excellent.'

'But I had a most vexing client this week,' Kate continued. 'I thought she was a dear, sweet old lady when she came in to get her photograph taken for her 70th birthday. She looked very respectable, and the shot was quite beautiful, even if I do say so myself.'

'Then what happened to make the experience vexing?' Violet asked. 'Did she refuse to pay?'

'Oh no, she paid after insisting I do the shoot again! She said she looked too old.'

The ladies all looked at each other and then burst out laughing.

'Did you tell her she was old?' Lilly asked.

'Definitely not. I said she looked charming and that the camera does not lie, nor can I alter her image, which appeared to offend her even more.' Kate sighed. 'I confess I am not keen on my appearance in photographs, but I know my age! I nominate you, Emily, to go next. What of Detective Payne then, and what has you vexed?'

'Well, Gilbert and I had an outing last Sunday after church. We enjoyed a walk in the gardens, and I received a large bouquet this week. He is so interesting and genuine. It is most refreshing.'

'He is that and very clever,' Lilly agreed. 'Have you met his mother? I understand he holds her in high regard.'

'No, and I do not look forward to that; I imagine she is quite formidable, especially regarding who wins her only son's heart.' Emily shuddered. 'But I believe he wishes to court me and will state as much very soon. As for what has vexed me this week, where do I start?' She looked skyward as if asking for strength, and the ladies laughed at her theatrics.

'I love hearing about the ladies at the *Miss Emily Yalden School of Deportment*,' Violet said.

'If you marry Detective Payne, will it become the *Mrs Gilbert Payne School of Deportment*?' Lilly asked.

Emily sighed. 'Thank you, Lilly. I was going to say it was a week of silly questions, and you have led me to that perfectly.'

They playfully teased Lilly and her reporter habits, even though Lilly insisted it was not a silly question; Emily chose not to answer it.

'Do tell us about the students,' Violet prodded as she offered her plate of potato puffs for a second serve.

'I will give you my two favourites.' Emily adopted the whiny voice of one of her students and said, '*Miss, can we stop pretending we have good manners if we are just with friends and family?*'

The ladies laughed.

'Imagine if we did that,' Kate said with a shake of her head. 'My mother would chase me around the house with her rolling pin.'

Emily continued. 'Silly question number two: *Miss, what if we realise the man we are trying to impress is stupid? Can we say so and leave?*'

The ladies laughed heartily.

'Oh, I wish,' Lilly sighed.

'That is a good question,' Phoebe said. 'What did you advise, Emily?'

'I told my students it is best to extract themselves from the conversation politely. But I confess, I have been guilty of thinking the same on many occasions. I even made it a compliment once,' Emily said, lowering her voice as if someone might overhear.

'How?' Violet asked, fascinated.

'I suggested it was refreshing that intellectual thoughts did not overburden him, and he thanked me with a smile as I departed.'

'Emily!' Phoebe laughed. 'I am shocked.'

Emily laughed. 'I know; keep that to yourself. I nominate you, Phoebe.'

'I have had a delightful few weeks. Harland walked me home three times last week but declined to stay for dinner as he always returns to the office. But we are going to the theatre this weekend.'

'Alone?' Violet asked, keen to know what the Astin family thought of that, given she was often with Julius alone.

'It is a matinee, but my grandparents trust him. As for vexing,' she hurried on, wanting to keep details of Harland Stone all to herself at this early stage in their romance, 'I have had a visitor.'

Lilly clasped her hands. 'Please tell me it is a lady in a white dress who has died of blood poisoning?'

'No.'

'Oh,' Lilly slumped, 'what a pity. The detectives possibly have a new case.' Lilly filled them in on the details. 'I was coming to see you, Phoebe, to ask if you buried the second victim.'

'We may have. What was her name?'

'Miss Isla Barr,' Lilly asked, her voice hopeful.

'Isla. No, but that name—Isla—sounds familiar,' Phoebe mused. 'I shall think on it, Lilly. My visitor is a gentleman, Mr Edward Tate—Teddy—who is most handsome and charming. He worked as a salesman and fell on the perfume he was selling; the bottle broke and perforated his heart.'

The ladies looked appropriately shocked.

'Good grief!' Emily exclaimed. 'And what does he hope you can do, Phoebe?'

'He misguidedly believes I can find out why he was impaled on it, as Teddy does not recall a great deal or understand why he collapsed but believes something is amiss. So, I must somehow.'

'I am seeing the detectives first thing, Phoebe. Would you like me to mention it to them or to suggest they call on you?'

Phoebe happily agreed. 'Yes, please do tell them, Lilly. It maybe nothing, but I feel compelled to try. Edward Tate was his name. Will you come to see me after?'

'Indeed, and I would be grateful if you could recall why the name Isla is familiar. This is bound to be my next story!' she said enthusiastically.

Emily smiled and shook her head. 'What is becoming of the *Vexed Vixens*? Murder and men.'

'What a grand combination,' Lilly said, and Phoebe silently agreed. Somehow, that seemed to sum up her life of late.

Chapter 6

TUESDAY WAS NOT ONE of the days that Julius collected Violet from her home to share their morning ride to work. Thus, he sat in the morning meeting thinking of her. It was the day she had breakfast with an elderly neighbour and then caught the omnibus; the relationship was important to Violet, who had lost her mother and grandmother, and important to the lady she called Aunty Viv, even though she was no relation.

'We have the viewing this morning of Mr Edward Tate,' Mr Astin senior, Randolph, was saying at their usual morning catch-up before the doors to *The Economic Undertaker* opened. 'Phoebe has that under control.'

'I do, although I expect Teddy to return and instruct me on solving the mystery of his death. It is most peculiar,' she said, sipping from a cup of tea in her favourite china cup.

'Too much perfume inhalation, perhaps?' Ambrose joked.

'Can one die from that?' Phoebe asked.

'Possibly, I believe some scents can overwhelm. I am sure Detective Payne would know; he is often abreast of the most obscure knowledge,' Randolph said. 'What do you think, Julius?'

Julius snapped to attention. 'I beg your pardon, Grandpa, what were you saying?'

Ambrose shook his head. 'On the mornings that Julius does not collect his betrothed, he is of little use until he sees her.'

Julius rolled his eyes at his brother. 'I was thinking of matters of business, not listening to you prattle on about... whatever you were prattling on about,' he said with a wave of his hand. 'Are we ready to go?'

'Don't you want to know the schedule for the day?' Randolph asked with a hint of a smile as he teased his grandson.

'Have we not done that yet?' Julius frowned. 'Sorry, do go ahead.'

'Attention, please,' Ambrose said, slapping the table and making Phoebe laugh. 'The floor is yours, Grandpa.'

'Yes, thank you, Ambrose,' Randolph said drily. 'Julius, Ambrose, you have two bodies to collect from the morgue and one from the hospital, and this afternoon, a body to collect from a home address and bury at South Brisbane Cemetery. Father Morris is officiating again.'

'Thank you,' Julius said, rising.

'Why don't you drop in next door, Julius, before you leave,' Randolph suggested. 'I am sure Miss Forrester will have arrived by now. Phoebe, I will get the stable lads to bring Mr Tate from your room to the viewing room if he is ready. Ambrose, please ensure the hearse has the correct number of shrouds for the collections.'

'Aye, aye, Grandpa,' Ambrose said, hurrying to his feet.

'Mr Tate is ready to be taken; thank you, Grandpa,' Phoebe confirmed.

Julius hesitated; no one noticed. Phoebe went downstairs; his grandfather went to the stables with Ambrose; and Mrs Dobbs removed their empty tea cups with her tray and disappeared into the kitchen.

'Right then,' he muttered, and checking his appearance and looking around for some legitimate reason to visit, came up short, so departed nevertheless to say good morning to his fiancée at the *In Mourning – Attire for the Family* store.

'Oh! Your fiancé is coming, Miss Forrester! He is early today!' Mary Pollard exclaimed from her dressmaking desk, well placed to see all coming and goings. She busied herself with the pattern she was pinning on black fabric and did not see the smile exchanged between Violet and Nellie Shaw. Young and shy, Mary was most uneasy in the presence of the men of the Astin family and most gentlemen, truth be known.

'Thank you, Mary. He did not collect me this morning, so he may wish to say hello; I had breakfast with Aunty Viv.'

'How is she?' Nellie asked.

'In good health, thank you, Nellie. She is always busy with her charity work,' Violet said.

'Volunteering gives as much as it gets,' Nellie agreed. 'It's important to keep busy.'

The door opened, and the very handsome business owner hesitantly glanced in, removed his hat and swept a hand through his dark locks.

'All clear, Julius,' Violet said, rising and feeling self-conscious using his Christian name amongst her staff. He looked somewhat uncomfortable, as Julius often did when calling on three ladies, but more so today.

'Miss Pollard, Mrs Shaw, Violet, I hope you are all well this morning?' he enquired, stepping inside and closing the door behind him, blotting out the noise of the street.

'I could not be better, thank you, Mr Astin,' Nellie answered, greeting him with a smile.

'I am very well too, thank you, Mr Astin,' Mary said, making hasty eye contact with Julius and then looking away.

'As am I,' Violet said, her smile showing her pleasure in seeing him.

Julius sighed. 'I tried to find a purpose to visit, but I confess I am running out of them. So, I am here to see your face before I start my day.'

Violet flushed with pleasure, as Julius was not prone to public romantic gestures.

'So romantic,' Mary said and then, embarrassed, hurriedly started pinning again, and Nellie laughed, exclaiming, 'Be still my beating heart.'

Violet joined him at the door and took his hand, appreciating his vulnerability and smiling at the ladies' reaction. 'Would you like a cup of tea?'

'Yes, but I must decline. We have a busy day, and I cannot stay. Good day to you then.'

Violet laughed. 'Oh, you really are just seeing my face.'

'That should tide me over,' he joked. Julius prepared to exit when two customers entered the store – a mother and daughter.

As Violet was already on her feet, she was about to greet them when the woman exclaimed, 'Mr Astin! Can it be? We have not seen you in such a long time. Hannah dear, look who is here.'

Mrs Reed had taken considerable time and planned numerous visits to *The Economic Undertaker* to select her husband's headstone – a ruse for putting her daughter before the then-eligible Julius Astin. Now, she looked to her daughter, who seemed equally pleased to see the senior brother in the flesh.

Julius's reaction did not go unnoticed by the ladies in the store, but he hurriedly schooled his features as Mrs Reed turned back to face him.

'Mrs Reed, Miss Reed, what a pleasure. Is this your first visit to the store?'

'Yes.'

'Allow me to introduce you—'

Mrs Reed cut him off as they moved into the store, closing the door behind them.

'Mr Astin, we cannot tell you how devastated we were on hearing of your engagement and pleased for you, of course. What a catch that young lady must be. I always fancied you and my Hannah might get together. Is your brother still single?' she asked with no attempt at discretion.

Violet did her best not to laugh. Nellie was not as successful and disguised it as a cough, rushing to the kitchen and calling back, 'I shall make tea.' Young Mary's eyes were as wide as saucers as if watching an exciting stage drama.

'Ah, Ambrose is courting,' Julius said.

'Oh, the pity,' Mrs Reed said. 'And Hannah is such a good catch.'

'Indeed. I am afraid I must hurry as business calls, but allow me to introduce you to our store manager and my fiancée, Miss Violet Forrester, and Miss Mary—'

'Your fiancée! My word, Mr Astin.' Mrs Reed looked at Violet from head to toe. 'Well, you are a beauty; I can see how you would have caught the handsome Mr Astin's eye.'

'I shall depart and wish you both a good day,' Julius said again, his hand on the door handle. He was gone with a quick glance and a flash of a smile at Violet.

'Mrs Reed, Miss Reed, how may we be of service then?' Violet asked, secretly vowing to get Julius later for creating a stir and departing so hurriedly.

'I need several new mourning dresses,' Mrs Reed said.

'I am so sorry,' Violet said.

'Thank you, Miss Forrester. My dear husband passed away some years ago, but I will never love another,' she said melodramatically. 'Do you have a brother of marriageable age, dear?'

Detective Harland Stone had just walked into his office, hoping to have some time alone to organise his thoughts for the day ahead, when Detective Gilbert Payne entered.

'Good morning, Sir.'

Before Harland could respond, reporter Lilly Lewis entered, and the sergeant waved as he left her at the door. Lilly knew the way, but it was frowned upon to let guests wander around the large Roma Street headquarters, especially reporters.

'I know it is early, Detectives, but I am keen to get to it,' Lilly said enthusiastically, looking most becoming in a pale mint dress and oblivious to the looks of admiration she received from members of the police force as she wandered down the hall.

'Good morning to you both,' Harland said. 'Mr Giffith is not with you then?'

'No. Phoebe told me something I wanted to share, and Fergus is not privy to her visions. He has gone to speak with the coroner and glean more information about the two young ladies.'

The small party looked to the door as John, the desk sergeant, entered again, waving a piece of paper.

'Detective Stone, a message for you delivered by the younger Mr Astin.'

'Ambrose? Is he still here?' Harland asked.

'No, he was on the hop,' the sergeant said and departed after handing over the note.

Harland read the note and looked at Lilly. 'Phoebe says she recalled where she had heard the name you mentioned to her last evening.'

'Your victim, Miss Isla Barr. So, did they bury her after all?'

'No, it appears Miss Barr is connected to another recently deceased client, Mr Tate,' Harland said, pocketing the note. 'Phoebe said you might elaborate?'

'Yes,' Lilly said. 'I saw Phoebe last night at our *Vexed Vixens* dinner, and she confirmed *The Economic Undertaker* buried neither of your two victims, Detectives. However, she had something she wished to discuss with you.' Lilly glanced at the door to ensure they were alone, and Gilbert rose to close it.

'She has a client, a young deceased man who died the oddest death,' Lilly told them of Edward 'Teddy' Tate and how he claimed foul play in his manner of death.

'So, is it Mr Tate who is connected to Miss Isla Barr then?' Gilbert asked, writing Edward Tate's name on the board next to the two deceased ladies – Miss Sophia Beaver and Miss Isla Barr.

'I believe so, but how, I don't know,' Lilly said.

'Phoebe has invited us to call in should we need clarification. Shall we do so and talk on the way there?'

The young detective and reporter needed no encouragement, and all three were out the door and on their way in minutes to hear what the dead had to say at *The Economic Undertaker's* premises.

Chapter 7

PHOEBE JUMPED AS TEDDY Tate appeared beside her at his viewing. She gave an apologetic look to the two mourners, who were surprised by her sudden movement, and pulled her delicate pink shawl around her shoulders, hoping they would believe her shudder to be chill-related. Phoebe rarely attended viewings but stepped in as her brothers were delayed and due back any moment from collections.

'Sorry, lovely Phoebe, I didn't mean to startle you,' he said and crossed his arms, looking at his body lying in state. 'You have done a very good job, young lady; I look most handsome.'

Phoebe's lips twitched, but she could not allow herself a smile at a viewing or talk to him, given that mourners were filing through to pay their respects.

'Ha, there's Harry. We work together and are partnered on a project. He'll be rubbing his hands together with glee to get my territory. I've done all right with that South Brisbane to Toowoomba area,' Teddy said and softened as he watched Harry. 'He's not a bad chap, though; we had fun and great plans for the future.'

After ten minutes, when the room was empty for a few moments, Phoebe said in a low voice, 'He seemed genuinely sorry to find you departed, Teddy, as did all your guests today.' She turned toward him. 'I need your help. I don't know where to start.'

Phoebe stopped talking as two ladies entered the room with white lace handkerchiefs pressed to their faces.

'Oh, dearest Teddy,' one said, which started a fresh bout of tears.

'Darling ladies,' Teddy said, which they could not hear. 'I wish I could console them; they were loyal customers,' he explained to Phoebe. 'But onto matters of business, or rather, matters of the heart, Phoebe dear. I did not get a chance to give my love to Isla, Sophia, or Rose. My sales area is so large that I may not see them for months, but they have remained loyal and held a flame for me.'

Phoebe thanked the ladies, farewelled them, and returned her attention to Teddy in spirit form.

'I am not sure how I will convey your love to them unless I tell a little white lie and say their name was on your lips when you passed.'

'Oh, Phoebe, that is very good,' Teddy said, impressed.

'Except, that might make them very melancholy and unable to move on, and I am sure you want them to move on in time.'

He thought about this but was not quick to answer. Phoebe recognised that might be a desirable outcome for Teddy, so she added, 'I believe you to be a thoughtful and kind man, so perhaps think on their anguish.'

'You are right,' he said, bending to her flattery.

'Perhaps if you have some perfumes I can access, I could wrap them and gift them to the ladies, saying they were found in your possessions and marked to them.'

'What an excellent idea; thank you, Phoebe. Goodness, you are very good at this business of consoling.' He reached for her hand but could not hold it. 'That gives me great relief.'

'Will you tell me their names and where I might find them?' she asked hurriedly, reaching for her small notebook and a pencil.

'Did I not already?'

'You mentioned them only by their Christian names, as I recall.'

'How remiss of me. There is Miss Isla Barr of Toowoomba, Miss Sophia Beaver of South Brisbane, and Miss Rose Ward of Ipswich.' He choked a little at the mention of Rose. 'Oh, here is my uncle, coming to bury me, no doubt.'

Phoebe pocketed her book and greeted the distinguished senior man; she mused good looks run in the family. Phoebe looked away to afford him some privacy so he could say a few words to Teddy.

'I'll miss you, young man,' the older gentleman said, touching Teddy's cold face. 'You were as dear as a son to me, dearer than my own son.'

Teddy in spirit form, made a sniffing sound. 'He was the best of the lot. Goodbye Uncle.'

The senior man turned to Phoebe. 'May I close the lid now and prepare for the funeral?'

'Of course, Sir. We are ready to assist.'

Teddy hurried, realising his time was limited. 'Phoebe, the challenge now is to find my murderer. I am convinced it was a plot – a jealous woman, a cuckold husband. I am not much help as I can't recall any display of outward hostility toward me, but I know something sinister led to my downfall. You will help me, won't you, Phoebe?'

His last words faded as the lid on his coffin closed, and Teddy's body vanished from sight, as did his spirit.

'I will have our staff load the coffin now, Sir,' Phoebe said, masking her distress, and as if on cue and well managed by Randolph, Ambrose—just returned—and Will entered in their dark suits, acknowledged the gentleman present and solemnly removed Teddy's coffin to take it to the hearse where Julius would be waiting.

Randolph led the gentleman away, and now alone, Phoebe stood for a moment, gathering herself before leaving the viewing room and returning to her workroom.

The external door to *The Economic Undertaker* opened, and Harland peered around the corner. Randolph gave a nod of greeting but put a finger to his lips, indicating a viewing was winding up as he ushered a senior man to another room where two ladies were taking refreshments. Harland nodded, pointed to the staircase to Phoebe's room, and once granted permission, warned Detective Payne and Lilly. They entered, following him downstairs in silence.

Harland's eyes found Phoebe instantly; he was sure he could find her in a crowd in a heartbeat. She was standing by the window, removing her shawl, the light warming her hair to a golden colour.

'Phoebe!' Lilly said in a loud whisper. 'Can we enter?' she asked, even though they were halfway down the staircase.

Phoebe's eyes went first to Harland, then to his entourage, and she smiled.

'Of course, perfect timing. Hello Lilly, Harland, Detective Payne.' She hugged Lilly as the three entered the room. 'I am always a little melancholy after a viewing, and now I feel much cheerier seeing you all.'

'We knew that and arrived accordingly,' Harland said in jest.

'And I am desperate for a story,' Lilly added.

'We got your note, Miss Astin, thank you,' Gilbert said, the most serious of the three and respectful of the undertakings happening upstairs.

'Oh, thank you for coming, Detective Payne. Let's sit,' Phoebe said, and the party moved towards her small table. Footsteps above them indicated the viewing party was departing, and the Astin brothers would take Teddy to be buried.

'Is that the gentleman who claims to have been murdered departing for burial?' Lilly asked.

'The very same. Nothing untoward occurred at the viewing, not that I am a detective or journalist trained to read an audience,' she hurriedly added.

'I imagine, given you see faces in all their states of emotion, you are a very good judge of character, Phoebe,' Harland said generously.

'Thank you,' she said, and the pair held each other's gaze for a moment longer than conventional before footsteps on the steps had them both turning.

'Ah, Mrs Dobbs, you are so thoughtful,' Phoebe said, rising as their kind office lady appeared with a tray and sliced cake.

'I assumed you had time for tea and cake; I hope I am not wrong,' Mrs Dobbs said.

'Allow me,' Gilbert said, standing and hurrying up the stairs to accept the tray from Mrs Dobbs.

'We would love refreshments, thank you, Mrs Dobbs,' Lilly said, and Harland thanked her, happily agreeing.

Seated again with the tray placed before them, Phoebe poured with Lilly's assistance. To any outsider, the picture was a pretty one of four young people taking tea. But the business was a matter of murder.

'Would you care to start, Phoebe?' Harland asked.

'I hope I have not wasted your time, gentlemen,' she said and glanced at Lilly, 'or your time, Lilly, but I know you can cleverly sniff out a story from anything suspicious.'

Lilly beamed, 'Thank you, dear friend.'

'We are currently burying Mr Edward 'Teddy' Tate. He is, that is, he was a very debonair young man and a travelling salesman.'

'What were his wares, Miss Astin?' Gilbert asked, between bites of Mrs Dobbs' fruit cake.

'Ladies' perfume.'

'Ah,' Harland said, indulging in the cake Mrs Dobbs knew was his favourite. 'And was he a man of integrity?'

Phoebe thought momentarily and answered diplomatically, 'He was well-intentioned and harmless from what I could gather, but I suspect he left a trail of lady admirers behind.'

The detectives and Lilly listened astutely as Phoebe told of Teddy feeling faint but not prone to such feelings or weakness and his collapse and death, impaled by a perfume bottle.

'How ghastly. I shall verify his death with the coroner,' Gilbert said, taking notes. 'Pierced through the heart by a broken perfume bottle, what misfortune.'

'It is certainly a novel way to die,' Lilly agreed.

'He believes he was attacked or the like, but cannot remember how or by whom. Is that not most odd?'

'There are documented cases of men who sustained head injuries and found on recovery that they had no recollection whatsoever of the happenings before they sustained the severe shock to the brain,' Gilbert offered.

'That is interesting, Gilbert,' Harland said.

'Yes, perhaps Teddy sustained a head injury before death or at the time of his fall then,' Phoebe mused. 'He insists a jealous suitor or a scorned woman somehow brought about his death.'

Harland could not explain his irrational anger at Phoebe, referring to the deceased by his nickname, Teddy. It was as if the man had wooed his sweetheart even if he was in spirit form, and Harland felt a raw green shot of jealousy.

Phoebe continued, 'He also wants me to pay his respects to three ladies he visited in his territory, and I believe he was romancing them all.'

'Despicable,' Gilbert said, shocked.

'So, they would not know about each other?' Lilly asked, not at all surprised by Teddy Tate's actions.

'Goodness, no. Well, I can't say for sure. But that is why I requested your company, detectives,' Phoebe said. 'When Lilly mentioned your victim's name to me—Miss Isla Barr—I recognised it as one of Teddy's ladies.'

'Is that so?' Harland asked with interest. 'She was dressed as if expecting a suitor.'

'Did he give you the other ladies' names, Phoebe?' Lilly asked.

'Yes, he gave me the three names and asked me to pass on a message to them, but I said that would be distressing and suggested I gift them a perfume on his behalf. Do you want the names?'

'Yes, please,' Gilbert said, pencil at the ready.

Harland tried to stay focused on the case and not on Phoebe. He knew he was not asking enough questions or pushing the interview along, but he was happy to have a few moments in her company and claim them for work purposes.

Phoebe reached into her skirt pocket and withdrew a very small diary. She flipped a few pages and read, 'Miss Isla Barr of Toowoomba, Miss Rose Ward of Ipswich, and Miss Sophia Beaver from South Brisbane.'

Harland's eyes widened in surprise.

'Sir!' Gilbert exclaimed.

'What is it?' Lilly asked, taking notes.

'Two of those ladies are already deceased,' Gilbert said.

'And both found in similar circumstances,' Harland said with some urgency in his voice now.

'They were the ladies who died recently of blood poisoning and were both wearing a white dress and undergarments of quality,' Lilly told Phoebe, having learnt the fact from the previous discussion on the omnibus.

'One and the same,' Harland agreed.

'Bridal wear?' Phoebe asked.

'No, but similar, like graduation dresses,' Harland said. 'Do you have graduations here? I recall going to several balls up north in my police capacity, and the young ladies wore white.'

'It is also done here,' Phoebe agreed.

'But Mr Teddy Tate must not have known they were dead if he was asking you to call on them,' Lilly said.

'Teddy told me his territory was from South Brisbane to Toowoomba, and he would cover the region thoroughly once a month. He also said the ladies were loyal to him. So perhaps he was not due to visit them yet. Or perhaps because he had not completely passed over yet, he did not know Miss Barr and Miss Beaver were on the other side,' Phoebe suggested and gave a small shrug. 'But now that he is buried...' her voice trailed off; they were all at a loss as to what happens after one dies.

'Yes, perhaps.' Harland agreed, 'That leaves just one of his three ladies alive.'

'Yes, Sir,' Gilbert agreed, 'Miss Rose Ward of Ipswich.'

Harland sat back, thinking. 'Mr Tate had three ladies that he admired,' he said tactfully, 'but there might have been more, given he believes a scorned woman or her jealous suitor brought about his demise.'

'True,' Lilly said. 'Oh, this is so exciting and coming together nicely. There could be a lot of suspects, Detectives – even people who didn't like the product!'

'Possibly,' Harland agreed, not as keen to jump to conclusions. 'Or perhaps he just collapsed and fell on his sword, so to speak.'

'Except for the odd coincidence of Mr Tate being connected to two recently deceased ladies,' Gilbert said.

'I think we have our next case, Gilbert,' Harland said.

'Can I report exclusively on it, Detective Stone? I promise to abide by our usual terms,' Lilly said.

'As you and Phoebe made the connection between the ladies and the perfumer, I can't see how we could deny you that,' Harland said with a small smile.

'Thank you,' Lilly gushed. 'Where to now then?'

'Back to the station for us and then possibly a visit to Mr Teddy Tate's workplace,' Harland said, implying Miss Lewis would not accompany them. 'We will also call on the families of the deceased young ladies.'

'That will mean travelling to Toowoomba, Sir,' Gilbert stated the obvious.

'Yes. And Ipswich if we call in on the other young lady who is hopefully still alive,' Harland said.

'I shall go brief my editor and then start with a story about a strange connection and two deaths, and if I can meet the deadline, file a piece.'

'Please do not mention the deceased ladies' names in your article yet,' Harland requested. 'It will unnecessarily distress their families, and we are not yet certain of a connection. It is tenuous at best.'

'Agreed,' Lilly said. 'I shall tell the story from Mr Tate's perspective, mentioning two victims may be connected pending further investigation by you both. Will that suffice?'

Harland nodded. 'Yes, thank you.' He turned to Phoebe. 'You have done us a service, thank you, Phoebe. We might not have connected Mr Tate with the ladies if not for your insight.'

Phoebe coloured with pleasure. 'I hope the information will be of value.'

'I shall see you out, Miss Lewis,' Gilbert offered as the pair took to the stairs, leaving Harland alone with Phoebe for a moment.

'You are not in danger from this man, Mr Tate, who claims to be murdered?'

'Oh no, not at all. In fact, I may not see Teddy again. But I need three bottles of perfume from his sales bag to gift the ladies, I promised him. Goodness!' Her hand went to her throat.

'What is it?' Harland asked, alarmed, looking around, expecting a threatening spectre he could not see.

'Two of those ladies are dead. What am I thinking? I need only supply one bottle of perfume.'

Harland breathed a sigh of relief. 'Perhaps allow us to check on the young lady first to ensure that perfume is still needed.'

Phoebe nodded. 'I do hope she is alive and well.'

'As do I. May I call on you this evening, Phoebe? Perhaps I can walk you home from work?' His eyes searched her face, hoping she would read of his affection as he was not a man adept at voicing emotion.

'I would like that very much, Harland,' Phoebe said, 'but do not be concerned if you find yourself unable to attend me; I shall see myself off at five-thirty but won't hold you to it.'

'I will do my best to get here.' He reached for her hand, placed a kiss on it and, on straightening, wanted to kiss her lips. 'I need to leave.'

'Of course.'

'Right now,' he said without moving, and made her laugh.

'Then you must unhand me, Sir,' she teased.

'Yes, that would make it easier,' he said with a grin, reluctantly releasing her small hand from his rough one. Harland withdrew to the stairs, and it took all his willpower to climb them. He didn't look back, not once, in case he turned and rushed back to her.

Chapter 8

HIGSON'S QUALITY PERFUMES WAS located in a small two-story office block wedged between two similar buildings on Duncan Street, West End. Like the building itself, George Higson was thin and nondescript. He did not have the gift of the gab to sell his own wares, nor the handsome face or twinkle in his eye to charm the ladies, but he was very good at management and hiring staff that made up for his deficiencies.

'Thank you, Miss Jones,' he acknowledged the attractive young secretary, who placed a cup of tea in front of him and moved her trolley to serve the other gentlemen. His eyes automatically went to her departing form – the hourglass shape, the blue gown fitted over a shapely bottom, travelling to the dark hair neatly tied back in a bun and her creamy neck and shoulders slightly on show. George Higson cleared his throat and waited to address his team at their Monday meeting. Six men of varying ages sat around the eight-seater boardroom table; one chair was vacant.

'Thank you, darling,' Harry Beaumont said with a wink.

'Don't waste your charm on me, Harry,' she reprimanded him saucily, getting a round of laughs from the gents at the table.

George Higson hired Miss Jones because her references mentioned she was capable and did not put up with any sass. The young lady was the perfect fit for a perfumery business with numerous salesmen who could charm the birds from the trees. The mature and debonair Joseph Collis was the only salesman who didn't openly flirt with the office ladies. In his fifth decade, he was the eldest of the salesmen, respectful of his wife, and a father of four. The office ladies and his older lady customers adored him.

'Thank you, Miss Jones,' Joseph Collis said, accepting the cup of tea with a nod. She slipped an extra biscuit on his saucer because Mr Collis had asked about her health earlier and wished her a good day.

Once Miss Jones had departed, George Higson took a sip of tea and tapped the desk for attention.

'Shall we begin?' he said, surveying his sales team.

'Where's Teddy then?' one of the men enquired. 'Are we starting without him?'

George Higson cleared his throat. 'Harry has informed me of some distressing news,' he said with a glance at his second-best salesman. 'I am sorry to report that Edward, that is, Teddy, met his death on Friday afternoon. I thought it best to wait until we were together at our weekly meeting to share the unfortunate news.'

Harry Beaumont drowned out the shock and murmurings of sorrow by proclaiming, 'I heard of his death from a mutual friend, and I have had several days to mourn for Teddy privately.' He turned to George Higson, 'Can I have his territory?'

'Steady on, Harry, the man's not cold in his grave,' Mr Higson said, more impressed than appalled. Harry was a man after George Higson's heart, putting business first and foremost.

'I'll put my hand up for it too.'

'Me too.'

Mr Higson held up his hand. 'Righto, gents, I get the picture. I've already given this some thought and come up with several options,' he said and began to relay them. 'I could offer it to our best salesperson.'

'That was Teddy,' the mature Mr Joseph Collis reminded him.

'Yes, you are right, Joseph, so the second highest salesman, I believe, is you, Harry,' Mr Higson said. 'Or, I can appoint a new salesperson to Teddy's round, or I could reshuffle all the zones to share the load.'

'And which one did you decide upon?' Harry asked, keen to hear he would get the zone as the second best-selling salesman. 'I could manage both my zone and Teddy's.'

Some men around the table snickered or ribbed him, and Harry grinned good-naturedly.

'Alright, Harry, I'd say you've earned it. I'll give you three months, and if sales drop or you find the workload too heavy, we'll talk again.'

Harry grinned. 'Thanks, George. Sorry, boys.' He rubbed his hands together. 'Righto, ladies, get your purses out; the fragrance king cometh.'

Arriving at *Higson's Quality Perfumes*, Harland recognised the interest in Betty Jones's eyes, the way she subtly looked him up and down as if sizing him for the role of husband.

'Gentlemen, we rarely get buyers to the door. What may I do for you?' asked the shapely and attractive Miss Jones.

'Good afternoon, Madam. Detectives Harland Stone and Gilbert Payne seeking an audience with George Higson, please,' he announced.

'Goodness, we have never had detectives at our place of work before. Is Mr Higson in trouble?' she asked with a look of concern that Harland read as acting. Miss Jones had looked anything but vulnerable moments ago, but now she held a hand to her heart and blinked several times at him.

'Not at all, we are hoping Mr Higson can assist us with an investigation,' Gilbert assured her.

'Oh, I see. One moment please, gentlemen,' Miss Jones said, addressing Harland. She opened a door in the panelling and walked down a long hallway in a manner best described as sashaying. Within moments, she returned and motioned for them to enter. The men followed her down the dull and badly lit hallway with awards donning the walls in cheap, plain frames, until they came to the end where a large office with sparse furniture and a man who could also be described as sparse, were located.

'George Higson at your service, gentlemen. Do come in. Care for tea?'

Both men declined, and Miss Jones departed.

'Please take a seat,' George Higson said, moving to a large table in his office and sitting first, indicating that the detectives should take the two opposite seats. 'What is this about then?'

'Edward Tate,' Harland said.

'Ah, Teddy,' George Higson's face softened, and his shoulders slumped. 'I'm afraid I can't help you; he's dead. I have just broken the news to my sales team. Did you know?'

'Yes. That is the reason for our visit,' Harland said patiently. 'His death was considered suspicious—'

'Sus...suspicious?' George stuttered. 'I thought he fell, broke a bottle of perfume on impact, and it jagged him. A fine bottle it was too—Bouquet de Violette—five shillings' worth.' He shook his head at the waste, not of Teddy's life but of the perfume.

'That is all correct, Mr Higson, but it has been brought to our attention by a witness that it wasn't a fall, but rather Mr Tate staggered, possibly from illness and collapsed as such,' Gilbert explained, claiming Miss Astin as a witness of sorts.

'Collapsed?'

Harland noticed Mr Higson habitually repeated the salient point for clarification.

'Yes, collapsed,' Harland confirmed. 'Can you tell us if he was ill in the last month or took any days off for treatment?'

'Ill... no. Teddy was the epitome of good health.'

'To the best of your knowledge, might he have ingested anything that could cause that reaction?' Harland persisted.

'Oh, he ingested plenty of the good life – food, wine, romance, but none of that is fatal. Teddy was full of bonhomie, great fun to be around and very, very good at what he did. He was my top salesman.'

'Were you aware of anyone who might have threatened Mr Tate or had a grudge against him?' Gilbert asked.

George Higson webbed his fingers in front of his chest, put his head back and laughed.

'Sorry, gentlemen,' he said soberly, 'but if you were to believe Teddy, every sale involved a suitor or husband chasing him down the street away from their sweethearts. He loved a touch of the melodrama. But he's never had a genuine threat, nor has anyone come here asking him to step outside. As for grudges, he was my leading salesman and, because of that, in my top-selling zone. A few of my team begrudged him his territory, and they were keen to put their hands up to get his zone—the poor man wasn't even in the ground—but killing him... no man on staff would do that to get ahead.'

'Who got his territory then?' Harland asked.

'Harry. Harry Beaumont.'

'Might we speak to Mr Beaumont while we are here?' Gilbert asked.

George Higson shook his head. 'Detectives, if you had come earlier, yes, but he departed on the train for Toowoomba to introduce himself to Teddy's customers. He won't be back for at least a week as he'll include a stop in Ipswich on his way through. But Harry wouldn't kill a fly, let alone a man, too soft if you get my meaning.'

'No,' Gilbert said, confused.

'He's a dandy,' George Higson stated matter-of-factly. 'Harry wouldn't want a bruise on his face or a scrape on his hands. It's not good for sales.'

'I see,' Harland said, reaching for his hat and preparing to depart. 'Mr Higson, would you have a list of Mr Tate's regular clients?'

'Of course, Detective, Miss Jones can give that to you; just mention it on your way out.'

'Thank you. One last question. Do the names Miss Sophia Beaver, Miss Isla Barr or Miss Rose Ward mean anything to you?'

'Yes, indeed, I am across all my best clients,' George Higson said, surprising the detectives. 'Miss Beaver from South Brisbane is one of Higson's Quality Perfumes' biggest buyers. She has a large and regular order delivered on the first of every month, which Teddy happily takes to her in person.'

Harland noted that the date was still a couple of weeks away, and George Higson obviously did not know Miss Beaver had recently died. He was impressed Gilbert had not blurted it out; the young man was learning.

George continued, 'Miss Isla Barr from Toowoomba was Teddy's sweetheart unless he had moved on from her; it's possible with Teddy. He fell in love often and hard, and I heard Miss Rose Ward of Ipswich is a great beauty and one of our new clients. I am told she is easily convinced,' he whispered the word as if it were slightly scandalous. 'I do hope she wears our fragrance as it is a small community, but there's money there,' he said with a mind firmly focused on business. 'Miss Jones can give you their addresses if that is helpful for your investigation?'

'Yes, it would be, thank you.' Harland rose, and Gilbert hurried to his feet. 'Mr Higson, you have been most helpful. I am sorry to inform you that Miss Sophia Beaver and Miss Isla Barr are recently deceased.'

'Deceased? Good God, no. How?'

'Blood poisoning, Sir,' Gilbert said.

'Blood poisoning?' He shook his head and sat for a moment before rising. 'Surely that has nothing to do with our fragrances?'

'We cannot say, Sir, but given your length of time in business, I can't imagine it is connected,' Harland said, and George Higson visibly slumped.

'Thank goodness,' he said. 'I had best see to their accounts and cancel them before the next delivery is made. I hope Teddy got their last payments,' he muttered to himself and then seemed surprised to see the detectives still in his office. 'I will take you back to Miss Jones, gentlemen.'

The men followed him down the hallway and soon left with the promise that Miss Jones would copy the customer list and have it dropped at the station. She immediately supplied the addresses for the three ladies or their next of kin; only one remained alive to wear *Higson's Quality Perfumes*.

Chapter 9

Mr Bennet Martin, private investigator and enthusiastic suitor of journalist Miss Lilly Lewis, had not mentioned her for at least three hours, which was most out of character. He normally found some way to work Miss Lewis into the conversation, but today, he had been determined to finish an insurance case file and put it to bed. Bennet closed the file and sat back.

'Done. That is the last of them,' he declared in his crisp British accent. He placed his pen down, sealed the ink bottle and ran his hands through his fashionably cut blonde hair. 'Finished, completed and over with Daniel, the last of the insurance claims investigated and recommendations made.' He held up his hand. 'Do not persuade me to do more; do not remind me that there is good money to be made from them. I am done.'

Long-suffering and indispensable clerk, Daniel Dutton sighed and removed his spectacles to clean them.

'So be it, but—' the young man began.

'No buts,' Bennet continued. 'I know I started this business to supplement my painting until I could become a professional artist, but I did not start it to be bored into a comatose state. I must have interesting cases! Preferably cases that have me meeting Miss Lewis in her travels while reporting.'

'Ah, so that is the criteria by which I accept clients now,' Daniel said, amused. The studious and cheeky young man worked well with the pretentious Bennet Martin in the South Brisbane office with three in residence, the third being Daniel's aunt, Mrs Clarke, who served as the housekeeper. They had become more friends than employer and staff, and the atmosphere was always cordial.

'So, I should now only accept jobs if they are likely to be reported in the newspaper or are located near the offices of Miss Lewis at *The Courier*, I understand,' Daniel teased. 'In that case, you will be very excited by the request for your services I received this morning while you were painting in your attic. I have placed an appointment for this afternoon in your diary.'

'Really?' Bennet leaned forward in his seat and placed his hands on the desk before him. 'What is it?'

'A very wealthy family who believe their daughter died by foul play, but do not want to leave it in the hands of the police force. They want the investigation managed quickly and discretely.'

'Why did you not say so earlier?' Bennet demanded.

'You did not want to be interrupted for the first three hours until you finished with the insurance client.'

Bennet rolled his eyes. 'You always take me so literally.' He ignored Daniel's confused look. 'Who is the woman? Is she buried yet?'

Interrupting their conversation, the no-nonsense, mature and capable Mrs Clarke entered with a tea tray and sandwiches. 'I heard voices, so I assumed you might welcome a hiatus? A late lunch?'

'Excellent, Mrs Clarke, thank you. I direly need sustenance and am on the point of expiring,' Bennet said.

She shook her head at his theatrics. 'Fortunately, I have saved the day then, Mr Martin,' she said with a small laugh. She placed a cup of tea before him and a plate of sandwiches, doing the same in front of her nephew before departing with their thanks.

'Well, do tell,' Bennet said as he tucked into a sandwich.

'The lady's name is Miss Isla Barr, and she died of blood poisoning. She's been buried; no, she was not buried by *The Economic Undertaker* business as she lives in Toowoomba. Her father has heard of you and would trust no other.'

'So, is he staying here for a few days?' Bennet asked.

'Yes, but today is his last day, and he is free to see you at three-thirty this afternoon.'

'Excellent,' Bennet grinned, satisfied. Then, hastily thought to ask. 'Has her death been in the newspaper?'

'Not yet, but the family believe it is only a matter of time as they are well known in business and rural communities.'

'Hmm,' Bennet mused. 'I wonder if Miss Lewis has heard of it.'

'I suspect she is about to,' Daniel said drily.

Bennet glanced at his pocket watch and read 1:45 pm. 'Why don't you file my report and deliver the bill to the client, Daniel, then leave early for the day if you wish? I shall see this client and then swing by the newspaper and see if Miss Lewis knows anything about Miss... what was her name?'

'Miss Isla Barr. Perhaps read my brief first,' Daniel suggested with a grimace at his boss. 'You have sufficient time before leaving to meet Mr Barr.'

'Ah, that's a good idea,' Bennet said, waving his hand towards Daniel for the paperwork. The two worked silently for twenty minutes, finishing their tea and sandwiches, as Bennet read the file and Daniel prepared an invoice.

Rising to depart, Bennet gathered his hat and checked he was respectable.

'Are you sure you will not consider some more insurance investigative work?'

'No,' Bennet emphatically told his clerk. 'Thank them, but tell them we have demanding clients we can no longer ignore.'

'That does sound better than you are bored and want to pursue your lady love.'

Bennet sighed. 'So little respect for love, Daniel. You will lose your heart one day, and I will enjoy reminding you of this day.'

Mrs Clarke, who was passing, overheard. 'Sooner rather than later would be good, Mr Martin. His mother despairs of him. Good day to you both. See you in the morning.'

Daniel shook his head, and Bennet grinned, clipping his clerk on the shoulder as he departed with new vigour in his step.

Detective Gilbert Payne was rather pleased his superior was in love. It allowed him to depart the office several days a week at a reasonable hour as Detective Harland Stone hurried to the office of *The Economic Undertaker* to walk Miss Astin home. Having departed the office of *Higson's Quality Perfume*, Harland consulted his watch and exhaled as if facing a decision that would not work in his favour.

'Sir, Miss Beaver's family residence is quite nearby. I am sure we could go there and still have you calling on Miss Astin in time if the hansom drops you off and returns me to Roma Street Headquarters.'

'Thank you, Gilbert, but duty first,' Harland said with some reluctance, and Gilbert knew his superior was endeavouring to set a good example. 'Let us go then to the residence of the deceased Miss Beaver.'

A hansom was nearby, and they took advantage of it, giving the driver the address and settling in the back seat. The number of cabs and pedestrians slowed the journey as people made their way home after a day of toil.

'So, we know from reading the report that Miss Sophia Beaver was a respectable young lady,' Harland said, 'and none of her friends or family believe she could have been up to misadventure.'

'Precisely so, Sir. Therefore, I suspect they are looking for a person to blame.'

'I suspect you are right, Gilbert, when it might just be blood poisoning from an infection or something Miss Beaver ingested. As her father is friendly with our acting superintendent, and he has asked for the death to be investigated, they are not likely to be satisfied until someone is arrested.'

'Will the acting superintendent support us, Sir, if we find it to be a natural death?' Gilbert asked.

'Time will tell, but in my dealings with him since arriving in Brisbane, I have found him to be a fair man.'

'May I ask your impression of Mr Higson, Sir?' Gilbert asked, turning from the window to discuss the perfumery visit.

'I felt his reactions were genuine. He did not hide the fact that business was his priority, and he seemed to know his staff well. Your thoughts?'

'I thought the same. He did not flatter nor favour them. I imagine Miss Jones would have a different view of them all.'

Harland smiled, understanding his meaning. 'I suspect she has learned to manage them.'

The hansom drove up the path to a stately home with well-manicured grounds and stopped near the front entrance. The two men descended.

'Do you want me to wait for you, gentlemen? It's a busy time of the day now, and if you want a hansom, you'll be struggling for one,' the driver said, keen for a paid break.

'We would appreciate that, thank you,' Harland said, disregarding the superintendent's directive to adopt cost-effective transport usage.

Gilbert hid his delight; this would not have happened prior to Detective Harland Stone courting Miss Phoebe Astin. As Gilbert was constructing a poem to present to Miss Emily Yalden, he was keen to avoid delay and receive comments from his poetry group that met this evening.

The men took the wide stairs to the front door, and Harland used the brass knocker to announce their arrival. The door swung open, and a young lady in mourning wear asked them to wait, leaving them on the doorstep. She went inside to find Miss Sophia Beaver's father – the man with connections.

'Detectives!' A portly man with considerable sideburns and a moustache filled the doorway. 'Thank you for your attention to my daughter's case, but a man was arrested this very afternoon.'

Gilbert looked to his superior, who looked equally shocked.

'Mr Beaver, I am Detective Harland Stone, and this is my partner, Detective Gilbert Payne. On what grounds was this man arrested?'

'For murdering my daughter, Detective, what other grounds would there be?' he huffed, most offended, pulling down his waistcoat and standing taller.

'If I may ask, who undertook the investigation and arrest?' Harland continued.

'I had a private man on the case, and this afternoon, he arrived with a couple of constables at the accused's workplace and did the deed. You may stand down. The trial will no doubt see this man hanged.'

'We must run our own investigation, Sir,' Harland said. 'At the very least, review what your private agent has found.'

'If you interfere in this case, Detective, I will speak with your superior,' Mr Beaver said in his haughtiest tone.

'You must do as you see fit, Mr Beaver, as will we,' Harland said, unphased. Gilbert was enormously impressed, storing away the response and calm delivery to reflect on later. Harland Stone was a mirror of the future senior detective he hoped to be.

'Good day to you both.' The door closed firmly in their faces, and both men were pleased the hansom had waited for them.

'That was quick,' the driver said. 'Where to now then, gentlemen?'

'Please deliver me to *The Economic Undertaker* in Tribune Street and my colleague to the Roma Street Police Headquarters after that, if you will?' Harland said, pulling himself into the hansom cab.

'Right you are,' the driver said, and when both men were seated, the horses began their trot back down the long path to the street.

'Gilbert, I shall walk Miss Astin home and then return to find out who was arrested and, if possible, talk with the prisoner this evening. We shall discuss my findings in the morning.'

'Sir, I can wait and attend with you,' Gilbert offered, keeping the disappointment out of his voice.

'No need. I may not get in to see the accused today, but I will find out what I can. If the case against this accused man is solid, then it may be just a coincidence that Miss Beaver knew the deceased perfumer, Mr Edward Tate, and that she was one of his ladies.'

Gilbert frowned and rubbed his hand over his jaw.

'You don't believe it was a coincidence, nor do I,' Harland continued.

'I don't, Sir. The ladies dressed in white, their death around the same time as their perfume salesman... I wonder who this man is to be accused of her murder.'

'A scapegoat, I imagine, but we'll see. He may have played a part in the deaths that has not revealed itself to us yet.'

Within a short time, the hansom pulled up out front of the funeral home, and Harland gave Gilbert the funds to return to the station. Gilbert bid him good night and saw Mr Julius Astin exiting just as Harland arrived. The men shook hands, and then they were out of view as the hansom moved on, and Gilbert sat back, musing on the case and what to make of it all.

Chapter 10

Earlier, before departing for the evening, Julius had ventured down the stairs to Phoebe's office as the day drew to a close. He removed his jacket, appreciating the coolness of the lower room.

Phoebe smiled on seeing the brother she was most like; Julius often visited her room when he needed quiet time or an escape from the upstairs activity.

'Hello, you have buried Teddy then?'

'We have. Mr Tate is in the ground. I hope he stays there.' Julius said on reaching the bottom of the stairs.

'That's no way to speak of the dead,' a male voice said, and brother and sister turned to find Uncle Reggie sitting in the corner, relaxing, legs crossed and looking stylish in the riding outfit he died in and would always remain in.

'Uncle Reggie!' Phoebe exclaimed. 'It's been weeks.'

'No! Has it? My time flies when you are a social ghost,' he joked, rising. 'How are two of my favourites?'

'Hot and very much over summer funerals,' Julius grumbled, lowering himself onto Phoebe's couch with a sigh.

'It is so inconsiderate to die in summer,' Reggie agreed in jest. 'I'll have you know I died in late autumn.'

'Most thoughtful of you, Uncle,' Phoebe teased as she poured Julius a tall glass of water and handed it to him.

'I intend to do the same,' Julius said and thanked his sister, taking a large sip of water. 'Ambrose threatened he would have me embalmed and not bury me until winter if I died during the hot months.'

Phoebe laughed, enjoying the company of two of her favourite relatives, one alive, the other deceased. Julius liked to see her happy; he worried that working in the cool, shadowed room away from people was unhealthy for her, but she seemed to thrive in the peaceful environment. It was not that long ago that Julius would have pretended not to see Uncle Reggie, but he had exposed his secret to Phoebe and her alone. They were the only two who could see and speak to the spirits, and Julius did not want his situation to be known by anyone – family or friends.

'Where is my other nephew?' Reggie asked.

'Polishing off Mrs Dobbs's leftovers in the kitchen. Funerals make him hungry, apparently,' Julius said drily. 'Is this a social visit, Uncle?'

'Yes and no,' Reggie said. 'It is always lovely to gaze upon you both, but I have a peculiar message for you, my dear Phoebe.'

'For me?'

'Yes. A young lady said you spoke with her intimate friend by the name of Teddy... am I making sense so far?'

'Yes, Teddy is a perfume salesman who I prepared for a viewing; Julius has just returned from burying him.'

'He claims he was murdered and wants Phoebe to seek justice on his behalf,' Julius said.

'Ah, that makes more sense,' Uncle Reggie said. 'The young lady tried to appear to you but could not.'

'Some spirits are too weak once they pass to the other side,' Phoebe agreed.

'Let's hope Mr Tate is one of them,' Julius quipped, and Phoebe turned to face him.

'It is not like you to begrudge the spirits, Brother. What is it you do not like about Teddy?'

Julius chose his words carefully when speaking with his sweet, ethereal sister, who thought kindly of everyone. Dressed in pale pink today, she looked even more innocent than usual.

'I don't like his instant intimacy with you, and I have the feeling he brought this trouble, his death, upon himself.' Julius shook his head. 'Asking you to give his love to three ladies is despicable and a fair indicator he invites trouble.'

Reggie huffed. 'I have to agree with your brother on this occasion, Phoebe. I was known to be a little flirtatious in my day, but I would never have given three young ladies hope at the same time.'

'Of course not, Uncle,' Phoebe said loyally.

'The young lady who wishes to get a message to you is undoubtedly one of the man's lovers.'

'She is? What is her name, Uncle?'

'Miss Sophia Beaver.'

Phoebe gasped.

'You know of Miss Beaver?' Reggie asked.

'Yes, I can confirm she is one of Teddy's loves. Two have passed – Miss Beaver and Miss Isla Barr.'

'I haven't come across Miss Barr yet, but I will keep a lookout,' Reggie said.

'What was her message, Uncle?' Julius asked, cutting to the chase.

'She has seen her parents mourning, and her mother is most distraught, as expected. Her father is seeking answers,' Reggie said. 'Miss Beaver wants them to know there was no foul play. She was not murdered or poisoned. She was following fashion, and she hesitantly admitted she had taken a lover.'

'Following fashion?' Phoebe said. 'How odd. What does that mean?'

'Did she say Mr Tate was that lover?' Julius asked, rising now to tend to closing the business for the night.

Uncle Reggie held up his hands. 'I do not know what following fashion means, and no, she did not give me a name, but Miss Beaver believes her father is blaming himself for giving her too much freedom and has several suitors in his sight to punish. She said her only sin was in giving her love to an undeserving man. I don't know how you relay that to the family, dear Phoebe.'

'By proving she was not murdered. Harland is working on her case as we speak, and I am sure that lover is Teddy,' Phoebe said.

'Perhaps,' Reggie agreed. 'Miss Beaver said it was most important that I tell you this: "Beauty is only skin deep". There, my work is done,' he said and smiled.

'But I know that,' Phoebe said. 'Is she saying... what is she saying?'

The sound of thudding down the stairs ended their conversation, and Uncle Reggie disappeared; Ambrose arrived.

'Ah, here you are, Julius. Phoebe, you must stop providing him with asylum. Are we done for the day? I am meeting cousin Lucian. Do you want to come, Julius? Is Harland coming to walk you home, Phoebe?'

Julius sighed. 'Yes. No, thank you. Hopefully yes, in answer to your questions.'

Ambrose grimaced, thinking back to what he had asked.

'We are done for the day, thank you both. I am catching up with Bennet this evening, but we may see you and Lucian in town, and I cannot speak for Phoebe's romantic life. Phoebe, see you upstairs,' Julius said, taking the stairs with Ambrose in pursuit. He did not stop even though he saw Uncle Reggie return. He also saw the look on his grandfather's face as he arrived in reception; conversations often drifted upstairs, and there was no doubt Randolph had heard Phoebe greet Reggie.

As Ambrose went to clock the stable staff off for the day—they had been under his management since his promotion—Randolph asked his eldest grandson, 'Did my brother visit?'

Julius would not admit he saw him, and his pained expression had Randolph holding up his hand.

'Forgive me, Julius, you need not respond. I thought I heard Phoebe speak his name. I wish I could see him.'

'I am sorry, Grandpa.'

'Do not be. All is as it should be. So, are you seeing Miss Forrester this evening?' Randolph asked. 'I just saw her brother, Tom, arrive to collect her.'

'No, I am going to the club with Bennet and Tavish; Harland may get there later.'

'Good. Your grandmother and I would like you to have some fun in your life. I shall lock up; you depart while you can.'

'Thank you, Grandpa,' Julius said, reaching for his hat. Uncle Reggie appeared on Randolph's right, making Julius glance back and forth momentarily.

'What is it?' Randolph asked, looking around.

'A trick of the light,' Julius said, knowing full well his uncle was trying to force him to admit he had the "gift". 'Goodnight, Grandpa, and thank you.'

'Goodnight, Lad.'

Julius departed, the heat of the day reducing and the shadows lengthening. A hansom pulled up out front, and Harland alighted.

'You made that just in time,' Julius said with a grin and a wave to Detective Gilbert Payne in the passing hansom.

'Crime can wait,' Harland said, smiling, relieved, and the men shook hands. 'See you later this evening.'

Julius bid him farewell as Harland entered the business. Then, Julius took a deep breath and expelled it as if returning to the living after a day of working with the dead.

Harland slowed his steps as he walked beside Phoebe, her small hand placed through the crook of his arm in case she should misstep, and his body shielding her from the carts, horses and street traffic.

'What criminal is running free this evening as you make time to walk me home?' she joked.

'Oh, several are running amok,' he joked. 'No doubt your friend will write about it in the morning's paper, and I shall be hauled over the coals, dismissed, and have to shovel clean the streets to make a living.'

'How fearful. I am sure Julius could find a job for you,' Phoebe teased. 'As for my dear friend, Lilly, she is much braver than I. How she could fight every day to be seen and respected amongst all those newspaper men, I could not bear it.'

'But yet you are in an industry dominated by men and must have felt that way when training?'

'Yes, but I knew it was short term, and I would soon return to the security of my surroundings, where my family values my work. I was fortunate to have a gentleman friend who supported me during the training period. He has since passed.'

They ceased conversation as an omnibus clattered by. The noise of the horses and the people chatting within it drowned them out.

'What will your parents say of your courting a lady mortician?' Phoebe asked. 'I can't imagine they will be well pleased.'

Harland gave a small, indifferent shrug. 'My mother will be so delighted I have met someone that she would not care if you came from the moon and worked full time as a space creature.'

Phoebe burst out laughing, and he watched her reaction with delight. Like him, Phoebe was not prone to expressive shows of emotion, and seeing her laugh or a smile upon her face and knowing he placed it there gave Harland great satisfaction.

'As for my father, he will not care as long as I do well in my profession and find the right person for me. The same might not be said of your family. Julius made it quite clear to me he would prefer you not to lose your heart to a detective, and Bennet would have been his choice for you.'

He was fishing to hear that Phoebe harboured no feelings for the artist Bennet Martin, who once pursued and painted her but had now set his sights on Miss Lilly Lewis. If Phoebe complimented Harland at the same time, he would happily accept that. She did not disappoint him.

'Oh, Mr Martin is a lovely man and a good friend to Julius, but we are not a match. We look like siblings, find ourselves at a loss for conversation, and he is uncomfortable with my work. He is much more suited to Lilly; I am pleased they found each other.'

'Why is he uncomfortable with your work? Does he not want his wife to work?'

'No, I don't believe so. Lilly would never agree to that if they had a future together. No, I believe he fears the spirit world.'

'Ah,' Harland said, catching on. 'I noticed his hesitation when you spoke to your guests from the other side.'

'Guests, that is a nice way to refer to them. You don't fear them?' Phoebe asked, turning her face up to study him.

'No. I fear the people on this side more than the other.'

'That is exactly how I feel. We have that in common,' she announced as if collecting shared experiences and beliefs.

'And we both seek justice for people,' Harland said. 'We prefer roses to all other flowers, love Mrs Dobbs' fruit cake rather than her apple tart, and cannot suffer the company of others for too long before we are weary.'

Phoebe squeezed his arm. 'You have been astute.'

'It's my job,' he said in jest. 'But studying some comes easier than others.'

His words made her blush again. They moved onto the quieter streets and enjoyed the cool of the tree-lined footpath leading to Phoebe's home.

'Speaking of your job, may I tell you about a message I received today that might apply to your case?'

'Of course.'

'Uncle Reggie appeared to me; he often collects messages from the passed-over who may not wish to speak with me directly or are too weak to return,' she explained, and he nodded, not wishing to interrupt even though he had numerous questions about that statement alone.

She continued. 'The message was from Miss Sophia Beaver.'

'Miss Beaver?' he asked, surprised. 'I just called on her parents before seeing you. They have been using a private agent, and this very day, an arrest for her murder was made.'

'Oh no, that is a worry.'

'I agree, but what do you know, Phoebe?'

'Miss Beaver said – I best get this right as it is more important now,' she said, stopping to think.

'There is a bench seat up ahead under the gum tree. Let us sit a minute,' Harland suggested, in no hurry to get her home. Phoebe agreed, and once seated, she turned to face him.

'Miss Beaver was upset that her parents were in such deep mourning and that her father was trying to accuse someone of her demise. She said there was no foul play, but she took a lover.' Phoebe blushed on saying the word and looked away. 'Miss Beaver wants her parents to know she was not murdered or poisoned but that she was following fashion.'

Harland looked surprised. 'What does that mean?'

'I am afraid I don't know,' Phoebe said with a huff of laughter. 'I am not a fashionista.'

'I think you are independently fashionable,' he said, admiring her, and Phoebe gave him a grateful look before continuing to relay the message.

'Miss Beaver said her only sin…' Phoebe cocked her head to the side—adorably so, Harland thought—before continuing. 'Yes, Miss Beaver used the word sin… was to love an undeserving man.'

'Mr Edward Tate, I presume?'

'Teddy. I imagine so, even though she did not offer his name. Miss Beaver told my uncle to tell me, "Beauty is only skin deep", but my uncle could offer nothing further.'

'Beauty is only skin deep,' Harland repeated, sitting back and looking into the distance. 'Those very words were found scribbled on a piece of paper in the pocket of her dress.'

'Is that so? How odd.'

'Indeed. I saw Miss Beaver's portrait, and she was a handsome lady, but is she saying she was not as beautiful, innocent or kind as her parents thought? That she bought about her demise?'

'That is one interpretation,' Phoebe agreed. 'Or might it refer to Teddy and his charm, but in fact, he was not a gentleman?'

'Perhaps. If she was not murdered, then an innocent man is going to face a trial, and I need to prove his innocence,' Harland said without elaborating that he intended to visit the locked-up man in question after seeing Phoebe home.

'I best let you go then. I'm afraid I've made your job more difficult now.' Phoebe rose as Harland stood, offering his arm again.

'Not at all, quite the opposite. I am very pleased to know my assumption that an innocent man has been arrested is correct, and I will work more fervently to prove it is so.'

'Thank you, Harland,' she said, looking up at him as they neared her family home.

'What for?' he asked, surprised.

'For believing me and helping me. It is a terrible burden to send a soul to the next life without giving them their last wish. I am grateful that you will seek justice.'

'By nature, I will pursue justice in my line of work, but it will always be my honour to do so for you, Phoebe.'

They arrived at the gate; he opened it, saw her inside, and closed it behind her. With a small bow, a kiss of her hand, and storing the smile she gave him in his heart, Harland hurried down the street, eager to see on what trumped-up charges a young man was being held for murder. He was keenly aware, however, of the ache that increased as distance separated him from Phoebe like a band snapping and hurtling him back into the world without her.

Miss Lilly Lewis exited the building of *The Courier* at a great pace, which was, in fact, her normal speed, and she only stopped when she heard her name called. Turning, she saw Mr Bennet Martin pushing himself off the small wall where he must have been waiting for her. A smile lit her face at the sight of the handsome English man.

'Mr Martin! What brings you here?' she asked, eyes sweeping over him and noting how handsome he looked this afternoon.

'Why, you, of course, and work,' he hurriedly added. 'You look a picture, Miss Lewis.'

'A picture of what?' she frowned, and he laughed.

'A picture of loveliness in this beautiful blue gown, which brings your eyes out even more,' he said sincerely.

'Thank you,' she said with a smile. 'In a household of five brothers, I rarely get such compliments, and the ones I do get at work, I am sure, are widely used on any poor unsuspecting member of the female sex,' she said with a huff of laughter, not at all offended by the offerings of her colleagues.

'You seemed in a hurry, but might I persuade you to have tea or a drink with me? There is a case I would like to discuss, my latest investigation.'

They moved aside as a coach pulled up, and several of the journalists from *The Courier* alighted with a tip of their hats to her. Lilly returned her attention to Bennet, knowing the men from her office were glancing back to check out the gentleman she spoke with. They would rib her tomorrow, no doubt.

'You were suggesting a cup of tea to discuss a case? That sounds intriguing,' Lilly said.

'The tea, my company, or my investigation?' he teased, offering his arm, and Lilly put her hand through it.

'Definitely the investigation, but I am sure I will find you somewhat amusing, and the tea will hit the spot.'

He laughed, enjoying her teasing, and accepted her recommendation for a respectable meeting place within a short walking distance where they could order tea or a drink if they were inclined.

'I imagine you have never been turned down by a lady when making such an offer,' she said, studying the debonair, blonde man by her side. He was a mother's dream for their daughter – wealthy, of good stock, educated, good looking and charming.

'I have never offered to discuss a case with a lady, so there are no grounds for comparison. But I would like to discuss many things with you, Miss Lewis, should you favour me with your affection.'

Lilly stopped and pulled her arm from his. She turned to face Bennet, forcing the couple behind them to walk around the pair.

'I do declare, Mr Martin, are you saying you would like to court me?'

'Was it not obvious? I thought we had begun courting,' he said, looking confused.

'Perhaps where you come from, being in the same room at a dinner party counts for courting, but we're a little more direct here. I think it needs to be said.'

'Right then.' He crooked his arm again, but she did not accept it. Bennet dropped it to his side.

'Do you really want to talk with me about a case, or was that just a ruse?' She stood, crossing her arms across her body and challenging a man she held great affection for and did not want to drive away. But Lilly had to be with a man who respected her work and took it seriously first and foremost.

'I most definitely want to talk with you about a case. If I were pursuing you, I would not have come to your work but would have introduced myself to your father and asked permission to court you.'

'How old-fashioned and charming,' she smiled, appeased now, and reached for his arm, slipping her hand through it as they began to walk again.

'Is it? I am sure that is still done.'

'Perhaps, but I am a modern woman, Mr Martin. It is nearly the 20th century, less than a decade away, and things have changed.'

'Indeed they have,' he said, smiling, 'and for the better. So, before we discuss work, tell me you will allow me to court you, and I shall ask your father about it regardless of what you say?'

Lilly liked his show of strength; she did not want a man whom she could walk over.

'I believe I will, Mr Martin.'

He grinned, and she could not help but smile, caught up in the moment's excitement.

'Let us drink to it, and I shall tell you about my case then,' he said, stopping at their destination and opening the door for Lilly. 'The day has ended well.'

They were soon seated at a table by the window, where they could watch the passing parade of people and traffic. As the area was largely industrial, it soon quietened with the day's trade ceasing. Once they had ordered refreshments, Lilly invited Bennet to share his case.

'Where to begin?' he said, thinking. 'A young lady has passed away from blood poisoning, and her family believe something is afoot – something sinister.' He stopped seeing Lilly's expression. 'You know of this? I hoped you did, so we could discuss it.'

'I believe I do. Blood poisoning and a family convinced it is murder, you would not be hired by Miss Sophia Beaver's family by any chance?'

'No. And who might Miss Beaver be?'

'A case Detectives Stone and Payne are working on, and Fergus and I have the scoop,' Lilly said, looking smug. 'A dead perfume salesman told Phoebe he had three loves.'

'Good grief,' Bennet interrupted, surprised but not by Phoebe talking with spirits; he was, after all, in the inner circle. 'The poor man must have been exhausted.'

Lilly gave him a wry look, then smiled. 'I believe there was enough distance between the three that his role as a travelling salesman excused his absence.'

'I know nothing of this. Do go on,' Bennet invited Lilly to continue.

'Well, initially, it was thought Miss Sophia Beaver died from natural causes – blood poisoning, but her father would not let that lie. But then the perfumer died and told Phoebe that Miss Sophia Beaver was his love, so of course, with both of them dead, supposedly by accident, there was enough doubt to take a second look. But that is not all; the perfumer also loved two other women, and one of them is now dead, too. It is very exciting. So that is what the detectives are doing: following up! The perfumer's third love is still alive in Ipswich.'

'What a story,' Bennet exclaimed, taking it all in.

'It is. I am sure our readers will love it. I am going to see the detective in the morning. Miss Beaver's father has connections and has used them to reopen the case.

'Goodness. Was she buried by—'

Lilly cut him off with a shake of the head. 'No, they are quite affluent and did not use *The Economic Undertaker*. But she was dressed in white—like a graduation dress—and very beautiful.'

'But that is my case,' Bennet said, frowning and looking confused. 'Are you sure you have the lady's name correct?'

'Miss Sophia Beaver,' Lilly said again and nodded. 'Who has hired you then, Mr Martin?'

'The parents of Miss Isla Barr.'

Lilly gasped. 'That is one of the women that Teddy Tate loved. Miss Isla Barr was also wearing a similar dress and died of blood poisoning.'

'That is her,' Bennet said. 'This is fortuitous. I am so glad our paths will cross on this case, and we can share information. Shall we see the detectives together in the morning?'

'Why not?' Lilly said. 'I am pitching to my editor at eight o'clock, so shall we meet at Detective Stone's office at nine then? I am happy to exchange information if you are?'

'Excellent. I will be there at nine o'clock, and I will be happy to share what I know. Since you mentioned me in your articles, my profile has grown considerably, so I am in your debt. Thank you.'

They shared a smile, and Lilly felt particularly excited. She had yet to learn of the arrest that had been made and the accused young man behind bars awaiting a trial.

'It is all coming together very nicely,' she smiled, 'except for the deceased ladies, of course, they would not say that,' she mused, trying not to look too excited and failing miserably as Bennet laughed and gave a small shake of his head.

Chapter 11

HARLAND STONE WAS NOT a man people said no to very often, and he was pleased that was the case when requesting to see the man jailed for the murder of Miss Sophia Beaver. Detective Stone had garnered a reputation for getting the job done – the senior detective with the odd sidekick, Gilbert Payne, who was progressively and grudgingly earning respect in his own right. On several occasions, Gilbert's keen insights and quirky knowledge had been all Harland had needed to wrap up the case, and the pair, once laughed at, were now not so novel.

'Does this mean your case is closed, Detective?' the night officer asked.

'Not yet, Sergeant, but I'm curious to find out why the private agent believes this man guilty. What do you make of the prisoner?'

Harland liked to garner opinions from those who may have observed off-the-cuff behaviour.

'I will say the young fellow seems fairly distraught. I don't think he's familiar with a police cell. Here we are then. Detective, this is Robbie Pearce. Do you want him cuffed?'

'No, that won't be necessary, thank you,' Harland said, looking at the thin, distraught young man who had not yet reached his majority and looked bewildered to find himself caged.

After introductions, Harland sat on the edge of the empty bed opposite the wretched-looking young man and cut to the chase.

'Mr Pearce, why are you guilty?'

'But I'm not, Sir,' he sputtered respectfully. 'I would never harm Miss Sophia. She was lovely and kind. He said I poisoned her, but how would I do that and why?'

Detective Stone nodded. 'Have you access to poison?'

Robbie Pearce looked confused. 'No more than anyone else does, Sir.'

'What do you do for your trade, then?' Harland asked, keeping his voice calm, as the young man seemed on the edge of breaking down.

'I'm an apprentice to the baker, Sir. Miss Sophia often came into the bakery where I worked. Her favourite was eclairs, and chocolate eclairs were my speciality.'

'And how are you meant to have killed Miss Beaver?'

Robbie Pearce shook his head, but not a hair of his neatly parted, thin blonde hair moved.

'We had some leftover eclairs, and I had a small box delivered with the bakery's compliments. My boss said I could; they were good clients, and he liked the idea. The police and that agent said I was in love with her, and I put something in them to kill her in a fit of jealousy.'

'Did you?'

'No, Sir,' he bellowed. 'I have my own sweetheart and my work. I have my whole life planned. It was a kind deed, good for business.' Then he burst into tears. Harland sighed.

'One last question, Mr Pearce. Have you a history of gifting sweets, jealous rages or bothering ladies?'

Robbie Pearce stilled and wiped his hands on his pants. His sudden quietness had Harland's attention.

'Yes.'

Harland sat taller, taken aback. 'Would you elaborate?'

The young man's face was scarlet with shame, and he fiddled, rubbing his hands. 'There was a perfumer who used to see Miss Beaver all the time. I know because I saw them walking together, and they'd go to the teahouse across the road sometime. She always came in after to take a treat home. Once, she told me our goods were much better than what was served across the road.' He smiled.

'You were in love with Miss Beaver?'

'No, gosh, no. She'd never give me the time of day like that. I just thought she was lovely and kind and very pretty. But not for me. You should meet my girl, Louise, Sir.' He smiled, and Harland read his reactions as genuine.

'Go on. Tell me your history with jealousy and bothering ladies.'

Robbie's face dropped, remembering that he would have to admit something that did not reflect well on his behaviour. He cleared his throat and continued. 'That perfume salesman that I mentioned, well, one day, I saw him talking to my girl outside the bakery where I work. Louise came to get some bread for her ma.'

Harland nodded and encouraged the young man to continue.

'He was flirting and looking all well-dressed and uppity. Everything I'm not. But I'm an honest man, Sir, and I work hard and will always look after Louise.'

Robbie Pearce reminded Harland of a poorer, uneducated version of his protégé, Gilbert. Respectful, sincere and striving to be regarded as a good man.

'What happened?'

'He touched my girl's arm, and I raced out from the bakery and shoved him onto the street. He dirtied his suit and laughed at me when he got up. Louise begged me to go back inside the bakery, and she stood between us. He turned and left, but he looked at me like I was rubbish, and he could have had her in a minute if he had wanted.'

'Did you see this man again or harm him, Mr Pearce?'

'No, Sir, I didn't, but you asked about jealousy, and I was mighty jealous that day.'

'Mr Pearce, I believe you are innocent.'

Robbie Pearce gasped, and he began to weep with relief. 'Thank you, Sir. But how do I get out of here? Will you tell my boss and my family that you believe me?'

Harland held up his hand. 'One step at a time. Have you got good legal representation?'

'I don't have the money for that, Sir.'

Harland nodded. 'Leave it with me. I am sorry you must stay here now, but I will get you out as soon as possible.' Harland rose.

'Thank you, Sir, thank you. May I ask a question now?'

'Yes, go ahead.'

'I heard that Miss Beaver died of blood poisoning. That's not poisoning, is it, Sir? It's different. How could I do that with an éclair?'

'To the best of my knowledge, Mr Pearce, blood poisoning is about germs from an infection and not from poison in the body. I fear you may be a scapegoat, and a very bad one at that.'

Harland called for the sergeant, furious that an arrest so clearly ill-informed had been made. Waiting until they returned to the front desk, Harland asked to see the report submitted at arrest. He read through it. It had no substance.

The sergeant held up his hands. 'I only came on duty after it all happened, Detective. I can't tell you anything more.'

'Nothing here warrants an arrest except for a scenario that the private agent considered and no doubt sold to the father of Miss Beaver. I shall get this boy released as soon as possible, Sergeant.'

'Excellent, Detective. The poor lad looks like he wouldn't say boo to a goose.'

The saying brought a ghost of a smile to Harland's lips. With a tip of his hat, he departed to see if his superior was still in residence at Police Headquarters to motivate the police magistrate to free the young man and destroy the arrest warrant. It wasn't yet eight o'clock and not improbable.

Robbie Pearce wiped his eyes and face using the bottom of his shirt; he sat back on the bench. The detective's voice carried as he spoke with Robbie's gaoler—the sergeant—and they both adopted sympathetic tones. Ten minutes later, the sergeant appeared with a tray.

'Here you go, Lad. It won't match your mother's cooking, but it's a bit of supper for you,' he said, sliding the tray through to Robbie.

'Thank you, Sir. I'm feeling hopeful now; I might be able to eat after all.'

'You've got a good man on your side there. The detective will get to the bottom of this.'

'He's new, isn't he?' Robbie asked. 'Can't say I've seen the likes of him on the streets before.'

'Right you are, Detective Stone's not from around here. He was promoted from up north. His sidekick did very little time on the beat but is holding his own,' the Sergeant said as if discussing the situation with a colleague. 'Eat and try to get some sleep; I'm guessing you won't be getting out until tomorrow sometime.'

'Thank you, Sir,' Robbie said again and sat, placing the tray on his lap as the Sergeant departed. His voice drifted back as he responded to someone else in a nearby cell in a less-than-friendly voice.

Robbie straightened and exhaled when the outer door to the cells slammed shut. He gave a little chuckle, congratulating himself on his performance. He couldn't afford to lose his perfumer client, especially on the meagre bakery wages he earned. Robbie started his supper with gusto. He'd eaten worse, and if he played his cards right, it would be the first and last time he'd be eating a prison meal.

Chapter 12

LILLY LEWIS AND FERGUS Griffiths exchanged a look of surprise—a very quick look—and returned their attention to their editor, Mr Cowan. Lilly couldn't tell if the crusty, middle-aged, cigar-smoking editor was in a good mood—his mood rarely changed—or if he was too busy to deal with them at the start of his day. Or, the best outcome, he was starting to trust they could sniff out a good story. He gave them a quick nod, exhaled smoke from his cigar in their direction and waved at the door, indicating they should exit.

'Sounds like a yarn. I want the first story on my desk for the late edition no later than two o'clock!' he snapped.

'Yes, Mr Cowan,' Fergus said.

'Thank you, Mr Cowan,' Lilly added, and the pair departed, passing two senior journalists in the doorway about to enter the editor's office.

'What do you make of that?' Fergus whispered as they hurried to their desks.

'Distracted, I'd say,' Lilly said, 'but it has worked to our advantage. I am meeting the private investigator, Mr Bennet Martin, at the police headquarters to speak with the detectives at nine o'clock. Do you wish to come?'

Fergus shook his head. 'Not, I shall leave you to cover that angle. I might start on the profiles.'

'You are very good at that,' Lilly agreed. 'Where to first?'

'I will go to Mr Edward Tate's former workplace, *Higson's Quality Perfumers,* and see what I can glean about Teddy Tate. Depending on who is available, I will meet you here at midday to write up what we have. If I am quick at Higson's, I shall find out what I can about the girl, Sophia...' he struggled to recall her surname.

'Beaver,' Lilly said.

'That is her. Midday then.'

The Courier's youngest journalists departed, fired up and ready to try for that elusive lead story again.

Ambrose sat beside his brother in the hearse on their way back to the offices of *The Economic Undertaker*. Their first collection for the day had been two bodies from the Brisbane General Hospital – two souls with no one to stand up for them and afforded the cheapest of funerals paid for by the public purse. Regardless, they would be given a dignified send-off, and ladies from the local church would attend if they were available, so mourners were present.

Their route took them from Herston to Roma Street and back to South Brisbane to their offices. Ambrose favoured this route as it passed by a small office on the second floor of a dignified white building just over the bridge into South Brisbane. Ambrose glanced up at the window.

'Fifteen minutes, not a minute longer in this heat,' Julius said with a small smile, and Ambrose grinned.

'Thank you, brother, I will be brief. You may make some sales while you are waiting; keep an eye out,' Ambrose said in jest, although it was not unusual for the public to approach the men in the hearse and ask about their rates.

Julius pulled to the side of the road where he could secure shade for the horses, and Ambrose leapt from the seat beside him. He ran toward the building, giving hope to the tailor in the shop below before opening the door and taking the stairs two at a time to the next level. The handsome undertaker stopped near the top, took a deep breath, straightened his jacket and hair, and entered with a light tap on the door of Miss Kate Kirby's photographic studio.

He saw her by the window, carefully studying an image with considerable concentration. Without turning, she said, 'I'll be right with you.'

Ambrose was sure Phoebe's friend, Kate, was the most beautiful woman he had ever seen. He had not seen it before when Miss Lilly Lewis initially blinded him. Kate's auburn hair caught the light, and gold strands seemed to glint. Her skin was fair with a smattering of freckles, and she stood tall, slim, sparkling with good health and life. The cream dress she wore to best advantage was tasteful and feminine and cinched her small waist. Ambrose did his best not to look at the hint of a generous décolletage.

He wondered now what he saw in Miss Lewis when Kate was right under his nose. Lilly had been so confident; perhaps that was the attraction. But Kate was light-hearted, amusing, and a classic beauty with ambitions that did not dominate her life. A slight ache of desire, or fear or affection, rose in his chest, and he was not sure if it was a good or bad feeling, but his knuckles went to his heart, pressing there as if he could remove the pain. Then she turned.

'Ambrose!' she exclaimed with delight. 'Why did you not say it was you?'

'Hello, Kate,' he offered a small bow. 'I was passing and wanted to say hello; Julius is waiting downstairs.'

She turned to look out the window and down to the street, giving a wave and a small laugh. Turning back to Ambrose, she carefully placed the image on a small cloth.

'What a lovely surprise, and how handsome you look,' she teased.

'I can't help it,' he answered, making her laugh. 'And you look stunning, Kate.'

'Stunning? That is because I have not had my head underneath the camera cloth yet, I imagine. You seem only to see me dishevelled.'

'I saw you at Miss Yalden's dinner dance, and I wanted to dishevel you,' he teased, closing the distance between them. He sensed she did not know how to respond to that as a red flush appeared on Kate's neck, and she looked down at the street below. Ambrose silently reprimanded himself for going too far. She was a lady, and an innocent one at that, and not one of the girls who flirt with him and Lucian at their clubs.

'Are there dead people in there with Julius?' she asked, not responding to his awkward comment.

'Yes, two corpses. But they are in no hurry,' Ambrose said with a smile, making her laugh. 'Julius, on the other hand, is always hurried but granted me fifteen minutes. What have you there?'

She held up the image for Ambrose to see. 'A dilemma of sorts. I have been fortunate to attract more business clients since photographing *The Economic Undertaker* business and its staff – very good clients, by the way,' she teased.

'Are they? I heard the second son is the brains behind the outfit.'

'Truly. I wonder if he might be single. He sounds like quite a catch.'

'I believe he only has eyes for this beautiful, talented photographer he met,' Ambrose said and held Kate's gaze, ensuring his expression was warm and sincere, not lecherous, but grateful for the lovely compliment. He cleared his throat after realising they had not said anything but stared at each other for what felt like the longest time. 'I beg your pardon, you were saying?'

'Oh, yes, you distracted me, Ambrose. Do behave,' she teased. 'These two gentlemen came in to get a photograph done for their new business venture.'

Ambrose studied the shot as Kate held it up to the light.

'Very presentable.' He took in the good-looking young men, their clothes suggesting style and class.

'Salesmen, both of them and undoubtedly very successful at what they do.'

Ambrose did his best not to react to her admiration of the two men, but he was sure they tried to charm Kate, and she was sweet enough to fall for it.

'What then is the dilemma?' he asked, trying not to sound curt.

'Ah, the dilemma is that the gentleman on the left of the photograph met a terrible accident and has passed away.'

'I thought he looked familiar,' Ambrose frowned. 'Was that Mr Edward Tate? We just buried him.'

'Yes, that is him!' Kate exclaimed. 'Phoebe mentioned him at our *Vexed Vixens* meeting, and I had forgotten I had photographed him because Phoebe called him Teddy. I did not accept his invitation to address him informally, as I wanted to keep the interaction professional.'

'Teddy? He does like to be familiar, doesn't he?' Ambrose said, his rhetoric question not requiring a response, but his brow was furrowed, and his displeasure was obvious.

'Ambrose Astin, are you jealous? You cannot think I would give and lose my heart so easily just because a man can be charming. Except to you, of course,' she said and smiled at him, soothing everything.

Ambrose reached for her hand and kissed it.

'Of course I am jealous. I am jealous of every man who gets time with you when I don't. I would slap them all with a glove and challenge them if I could,' he said, play acting, and she delighted in his old-fashioned sentiment.

'You need not fight on my behalf. I am not a woman who plays with a man's heart, and I am smart enough to know that if they are charming me, they are most likely doing so with many ladies. Phoebe said as much.'

'You are right about that,' Ambrose agreed. 'This is the man who had a rather unconventional death, falling on the broken perfume bottle. Imagine if we all died by way of our trade. Perhaps a coffin might fall from the back of the hearse and finish my days on earth,' he joked.

'Goodness, I hope not,' Kate said with a small laugh. 'I would have to topple to my death while taking a photograph, or the camera could capture my soul; some believe it happens,' she said with a menacing look at the camera in the corner, and Ambrose laughed.

'Will you receive payment now for that image?'

'Oh, yes, they have already paid, but his colleague, Mr Harry Beaumont, would like me to take Mr Tate—Teddy—out of the photograph.'

Ambrose laughed. 'How?'

'That is my dilemma. Maybe one day in the future, that will be possible. Can you imagine it? We could remove anyone from our photographs if we fell out with them but liked the image of ourselves,' she said and huffed at the absurd idea. 'But I'm afraid Mr Tate is there to stay. And speaking of which, you best be off.'

Ambrose jumped. 'Goodness, yes. It has been a pleasure.'

'Thank you for the lovely surprise,' Kate said, seeing Ambrose to the door.

He placed his hat back on his head, hurried down the stairs, and turned at the bottom step to find her watching him. With a final wave, he rejoined Julius, and when he glanced back, Kate was watching from the window above. Ambrose was a happier man for the day ahead and oblivious to the fact that he had just seen a clue that would greatly interest Detective Harland Stone.

Chapter 13

It was just on nine o'clock when Harland held up his hand, and the small group comprising journalist Lilly Lewis, dressed resplendently in a fitted jacket and navy skirt, private investigator Bennet Martin, expensively suited on his father's purse, and Detective Gilbert Payne, neat and pressed, fell silent.

'As we are all on different tangents, I think it best we start at the beginning. Gilbert, will you scribe?'

'Of course, Sir,' he said, jumping up to stand by the board, ready to note anything of value to the investigation.

'Perhaps let Gilbert and me tell you what we know, including what I learnt overnight, and then if you have more information on any aspect, please elaborate.'

'Agreed,' Lilly said firmly, not that she had any choice in the matter, but Harland acknowledged her support with a nod. She had arrived with Bennet, and Harland was surprised to learn he had been appointed to the case – one aspect of it, the death of Miss Isla Barr. It concerned him that the wealthier members of society had so little faith in the police or were so wary of their results that they chose to hire private agents.

Harland began. 'In brief, we have two women found dead from blood poisoning with similar injection marks on their skin – very small, certainly not consistent with drug use. Both wore similar white clothing and believed themselves to be the beloved of Higson perfume salesman Edward 'Teddy' Tate. One had the words "Beauty is only skin deep" on her person; we are yet to hear from the Toowoomba coroner if the same message was found on his victim. The ladies died within a week of each other. Mr Teddy Tate was found dead the next week, collapsing and impaling himself on a broken perfume bottle.'

Even though the small group knew how Teddy Tate died, they shared looks of disbelief and scoffed at the irony of it.

'Initially, there were no grounds to believe the women had met with foul play, nor Mr Tate for that matter,' Harland said.

Gilbert added. 'The ladies did not have autopsies as the families would not allow it.'

'Frustratingly so, but our coroner—' Harland remembered everyone present knew Tavish McGregor socially and corrected himself, '—Tavish noted no colouring of the lips or skin to indicate poisoning.'

'Was an autopsy done on Teddy Tate?' Lilly asked.

'No. Again, there were no grounds to believe his death was anything but a strange accident. We could exhume him if the family permitted it. He's only just been buried.'

'I doubt we would be given approval to exhume the ladies,' Gilbert said.

'I agree. Since we have established a connection between the three people, the three deaths, and Teddy Tate appeared to Miss Astin insisting foul play was involved, then it does warrant investigation.' Harland felt comfortable sharing the latter information with the group, who knew of Phoebe's unique talent for talking to the dead. He told them about the wrongful arrest of Robbie Pearce.

'Gilbert and I attended the cell this morning and saw to his release.'

Gilbert nodded. 'It was odd.'

'How so?' Harland asked, turning to study Gilbert.

'It is probably nothing, Sir,' Gilbert said with little confidence. 'It is just that I had a chance to study him for a moment before he saw us, and he appeared cocky, like a street kid, and then his demeanour changed the moment we revealed ourselves.'

'That is interesting,' Harland said, his eyes narrowing in contemplation. 'Nevertheless, I believe him to be innocent.'

'Well, whether he was cocky or scared, one wonders what pressure must have come to bear on that private agent to bow to the client's request and have the young man arrested,' Lilly mused.

'Or what funds he was offered to make the case against the young man,' Bennet said more cynically.

'Maybe so,' Harland agreed, a little unsure now and with a glance to his protégé said, 'Going forward with the investigation, Gilbert and I will travel to Toowoomba to talk with Mr Harry Beaumont, who is the salesman who inherited Teddy Tate's area and is currently there introducing himself to the clients.'

'We wish to determine his relationship with Teddy Tate and if he was ambitious enough to murder Higson's number one salesman,' Gilbert said.

'And we shall visit the family of the deceased Miss Isla Barr while there,' Harland said.

'I met with Ms Barr's father yesterday afternoon so he could brief me on the case,' Bennet said. 'He was here in town, but returning to Toowoomba at first light today. He knew of Teddy Tate, claiming the man was big on talk and short on promise. Isla Barr was expecting a proposal, and her father is convinced that Teddy was complicit in her death.'

'Hmm, naturally he wants to believe his daughter's death was not from something as benign as an infection,' Harland said. 'We will visit Miss Rose Ward from Ipswich on our trip, too, as she is on the way. We'll find out about her relationship with Teddy Tate, his promises, and if she knows anything of the other ladies.'

Bennet held up his hand. 'Might I come with you both, Harland? I will make the trip regardless, so I will find suitable accommodation and hire a carriage to meet us when we get off the train. I have my client's expense account; you might as well travel comfortably.'

'We won't say no, thank you, Bennet. We will pay our way on the train and for accommodation but welcome the use of your carriage. Our superior will be pleased to reduce the bill,' Harland agreed. He told Bennet which train they were departing on so the private investigator's clerk could purchase a ticket.

'I wish I could come, but I could never get two days out of the office,' Lilly said. 'Will you update me by telegram, Mr Martin?' She asked Bennet.

'I will if Detective Stone authorises what I might share for your publication?'

'I can do so,' Harland agreed, and Lilly sighed with relief, giving Bennet a grateful look.

'We have very little to go on, Sir,' Gilbert said, looking at the names he had written on the board, the motives and the evidence.

'Yes, it is understandable why each death was marked accidental or natural causes,' Harland agreed. 'But let us pursue it a while longer until we feel we have exhausted possibilities. Miss Astin also shared some other news.' He did not use Phoebe's Christian name when speaking with others as a mark of respect and was also hesitant to tell the group of her words. Not because he didn't trust her but because Harland did not want the case to hinge on afterlife hearsay.

He turned to Lilly. 'Miss Lewis, you must be careful to distinguish what we hear from Miss Astin and what we know as fact and not cross the line in your reporting.'

'Absolutely, Detective,' Lilly assured him, her tone snappish at being identified as unprofessional amongst the group present. 'I would never put Phoebe at risk, and I am very proficient at identifying fact from an unsubstantiated story.'

'Of course, forgive me, Miss Lewis. I did not mean to imply that you were incapable,' he said humbly. 'The concern is largely mine, and it is a unique experience for me – to know something untoward did happen and to have to find the evidence to support it rather than the evidence pointing us to what happened.' He sighed.

'What else did Miss Astin say, Sir?' Gilbert prompted him.

'Ah, yes, thank you, Gilbert. Miss Sophia Beaver gave her a message.'

Bennet brightened, and Harland gave a small shake of his head in the negative.

'No, I don't believe Miss Isla Barr has spoken with her yet, just Miss Beaver. She did not appear to Miss Astin but relayed a message through her uncle.' Harland realised how ridiculous it all sounded but hurried on. 'Miss Beaver said she was not murdered or poisoned. But she took a lover whom she didn't identify as Teddy Tate but called this person an undeserving man. She then included a cryptic message that she was following fashion and said the very line that was found upon her person: "Beauty is only skin deep". That was all.'

Gilbert cleared his throat. 'Sir, I did some research on that line "Beauty is only skin deep", as it was familiar to me.'

'Go on, Gilbert,' Harland whirled to study him, hoping the fact-storing Detective Payne had something of value to offer. 'Do you think she is saying Teddy Tate was handsome but not a good person?'

'Yes, maybe,' Gilbert shrugged, looking doubtful.

'But that is not what you were thinking. Do not worry if you are wrong; tell us why it piqued your interest,' Harland encouraged him.

'Sir, a poem by Thomas Overbury in the 17th century, first introduced the terms beauty and skin-deep. The poem was called "A Wife", and the line was something like his wife's beauty is but skin-deep. That in itself is not as important as what happened to Thomas Overbury. He wrote the poem to ward off a friend from marrying a woman he did not like. He feared his influence would lessen once his powerful friend, Viscount Rochester, wed her. But she got her revenge, had him imprisoned for treason and slowly poisoned him to death.'

The room stilled as its inhabitants thought about this.

Gilbert concluded, 'In summary, she was slighted by the poet saying her "beauty was only skin deep", thus poisoned him.'

'As Miss Sophia Beaver and Miss Isla Barr died before Teddy Tate, perhaps some other lady might have felt similarly humiliated, especially if they believed themselves to be the true love of Teddy Tate, only to find he was romancing several women,' Bennet suggested.

Lilly continued, 'Or a spurned suitor had his revenge and poisoned Teddy Tate.'

'It might be irrelevant, Sir,' Gilbert added, a little embarrassed.

'Let us keep it in our mind, Gilbert. There is a reason Miss Sophia Barr got that message to Miss Astin,' Harland said. 'We will depart for Toowoomba and Ipswich this very afternoon and try to pull this case together. In the interim, I will get an exhumation order for Teddy Tate and brief the coroner, Tavish, before we depart. Let's see if he was poisoned.'

Bennet chuckled. 'Julius will not be pleased. Burying people in this heat once is bad enough.'

'True,' Harland said and could not help but smile. 'It won't win me any favours.'

'Detective Stone, can I reveal the ladies' names now and start writing about the odd perfume love triangle?' Lilly asked, and Harland thought a moment.

'Yes, I don't see why not,' he said. 'If the family is making false arrests and hiring private investigators to show us up,' he said with a small smile at Bennet, 'let the police lead our investigation on the front foot. Just don't mention Miss Rose Ward in Ipswich, as we hope she is very much alive.'

'Thank you, Detective,' Lilly said enthusiastically. With a quick farewell, she hurried off, leaving Bennet to discuss the logistics of the train trip with the detectives.

Harland turned to Gilbert. 'I hope you had no plans with Miss Yalden for the next night or two.'

'No, Sir, duty first,' Gilbert said, quoting back his superior. But Harland would miss the chance to walk Miss Astin home and knew this would be a regular occurrence they would both have to bear. He silently vowed to drop in to make his farewell before departing.

Randolph Astin thanked the young delivery man and placed the letter on the reception desk as he waited for the middle-aged couple—his first appointment for the day—to rejoin him from the coffin-viewing room. He had given them some time to wander around the coffins on display and select one for their recently deceased elderly loved one. Lucian, a nephew of Randolph, who co-owned the carpentry business with Julius, made the coffins from affordable timbers. He also apprenticed Violet's brother, Tom.

The Economic Undertaker's policy was to recommend the cheapest coffin in keeping with its business ethos, but some clients liked to spend a little more; it made them feel better about themselves. Or, they selected a coffin based on its fit with their loved one's personality – dark or light timber, white, or ornate. Today's clients did not feel the need to spend more once Randolph explained that the cheapest was the most widely purchased. No one liked to feel alone in their economic choices.

As he was writing their order, a young lady entered the premises dressed in a white formal gown as if she were making her debut.

'Excuse me for one moment, please,' Randolph said to the couple he was serving. 'May I help you, Miss?'

'Yes, please, Sir, I am here to see Mr Teddy Tate.'

'Ah.' Randolph knew Teddy had been buried the day prior but did not want a scene in front of clients. 'Perhaps you might wait for my granddaughter, who took charge of Mr Tate's viewing. She will be back from the post office momentarily.'

Mrs Dobbs appeared to assist, and Randolph gave her a grateful look.

'I am Mrs Dobbs, dear. Shall I show you to Phoebe's room, and you can wait in cool comfort? I am sure she will be here any moment now.'

The young lady thanked them and followed Mrs Dobbs down the stairs as Randolph returned to his clients, provided a receipt, and arranged a time for tomorrow's collection of the couple's grandfather; Randolph bid them a good day. He opened the letter and huffed. An exhumation order and Edward 'Teddy' Tate had only been buried one day. At least the soil would be easily turned. Randolph would need Phoebe to mind the desk while he went to the post office to telegram Teddy Tate's next of kin, an uncle. He always did so as a courtesy, even though the detective would issue a formal request. Mrs Dobbs reappeared, and he promptly forgot about the young lady waiting as Phoebe entered.

'Is everything all right, my dear?' he asked as she passed the mail to him and kept a few small boxes for herself.

'Very much so, Grandpa, thank you.' She fanned herself. 'It is very warm out there, and I'm expecting a body from the boys any minute now. I hope they don't delay, as the heat will not make it pleasant.'

'They are due back momentarily.' He waved the letter. 'We have an order to exhume your friend, Teddy.'

'Oh, good!' Phoebe said, clapping her hands together in delight. 'That means he will be tested for poison, and if there had been foul play, we will know.' She exhaled. 'I am relieved.'

'You must not take on the burden of their last wishes, Phoebe,' Randolph said. 'You always do your best, and nothing more can be asked of you.'

'Thank you, Grandpa, but it is the last wish they will ever make, and it might be the difference between resting easy or a soul remaining.'

He thought about this for a moment. 'Yes, I guess it is not unrealistic to think that if a soul has not moved on or haunts an area, they have unfinished business. But are hauntings real or our imagination?'

'I shall ask around,' Phoebe joked, indicating the spirits above. Randolph chuckled.

'Julius will not be happy,' Phoebe said.

'Only because of the heat,' Randolph said. 'He is like me. We have no issues with the exhumation process – we are paid to exhume and rebury by the requesting group. But it feels undignified for the deceased and upsetting for the family.'

'I agree,' Phoebe said with a gentle sigh. 'But in this case, if it proves somebody murdered Teddy, then he will not mind in the least.'

They heard the horses and hearse entering the back of the yard, and Randolph said, 'I must depart to send a telegram to Mr Tate's next of kin, an uncle, advising that his nephew is back in our care. I'll ask Mrs Dobbs to mind the desk until you are ready, Phoebe,' he said, noting her parcels.

'What terrible timing when I have just returned from the post office, and I could have sent it for you.'

Phoebe took her packages downstairs, and Randolph met Julius and Astin as they entered the back of the office, appearing hot and exhausted.

'It's horrendous out there, and it is not yet ten o'clock,' Ambrose complained, slipping off his hat and jacket as he walked; Julius did the same.

'I have iced lemon drinks for you both,' Mrs Dobbs called from the kitchen.

'Bless you, Mrs Dobbs, and all who sail with you,' Ambrose joked.

'I'm sorry to say we have an exhumation order, lads,' Randolph said, and Julius groaned.

'For the love of all that is holy, can they not stay buried!' he exclaimed, and Randolph hid his smile. 'Who is it for?'

'Teddy Tate.'

Julius stopped in his tracks and narrowed his eyes. 'Hmm, this is Phoebe's fault and that of her detective beau.' He smiled only enough so that his grandfather knew he was not truly angry.

'It may be,' Randolph agreed, handing the notice to Julius, saying, 'I am going to telegram the next of kin now. I shall leave you to break the bad news to your gravediggers.'

'They will be happy for the work,' Ambrose said, gulping the lemon drink. 'Delicious.'

Julius sighed and shook his head. 'I'll do so now. If they are free, they might want to get the job done this morning before the day's heat sets in.' He put his jacket back on and accepted the drink, thanking Mrs Dobbs. 'Ambrose, I will take the cart. Can you get Will to help you unload and deliver the body to Phoebe's room?'

'Right away,' Ambrose said, surprising his grandfather and thanking Mrs Dobbs as he returned the glass to the kitchen and sought a top-up.

'What have you done with Ambrose? Swapped him for a look-alike?' Randolph asked. 'Is it heat stress?'

'No. I gave him fifteen minutes to catch up with Miss Kirby as we passed her premises. He has been happy all morning thereafter. If I had known it would be so simple to get his best from him, I would have been dropping him off to see ladies for years,' Julius said drily.

'Speaking of dropping off, will you drop me at the post office on your way?' Randolph asked.

'Of course. If you wait, I'll collect you on my way back. Let's go,' Julius said, and while his grandfather fetched his hat, he glanced at Ambrose. 'Tell Phoebe to do her best not to dig up any of our other recent burials while I'm away.'

Ambrose laughed. 'At least not today.'

He shook his head, and Randolph followed right behind his eldest grandson, adding with a wink, 'Keep up the good work, Lad,' as Ambrose smiled happily and Mrs Dobbs took her place behind the reception desk, ready to greet customers as needed.

'Oh, hello,' Phoebe said, surprised to find a very attractive lady of her own age sitting on her couch and wearing a white formal dress. 'I am Miss Phoebe Astin. Are you waiting for me?'

The lady rose. 'I am Miss Astin. Your room is quite cool and pleasant, and the fresh flowers are beautiful. I am Miss Esther Lattimore. I hoped to see Mr Teddy Tate.'

'Oh, Miss Lattimore,' Phoebe said, a little confused as she studied the lady of similar age and height before her. Miss Lattimore was quite full-figured, her body more mature than Phoebe's, whose slim build looked quite boyish.

'I read in the paper that he had passed away, and that he was here. You can only imagine my shock! May I see him?'

'Miss Lattimore, I am sorry to say that he has been buried.'

'Oh, blast upon blast!' she proclaimed, surprising Phoebe with her passionate outbreak. The young lady threw her hands up in the air before placing them on her hips. 'I wore the dress he loved, and I so wished to tell him he was a cad and a rotter and that if I saw him again, it would be too soon.'

'Perhaps you will see him again soon,' Phoebe said.

'Why?' Miss Lattimore asked, surprised. 'Is he not dead then?'

'Oh yes, he's very dead,' Phoebe said, frowning and somewhat confused by the discussion. 'But you may have a chance to—

Mrs Dobbs hurried down the stairs, and Phoebe stopped mid-sentence from telling Miss Esther Lattimore that she had already spoken with Teddy from the other side, and he was most repentant. Mind you, he had not mentioned a Miss Esther Lattimore amongst his muses and paramours.

'Oh good, you have introduced yourselves,' Mrs Dobbs said and sighed with relief. 'I am sorry, Miss Lattimore. Mr Astin senior had to hurry away, but you have found Miss Astin after all.'

Phoebe's eyes widened with surprise; she thought she had been speaking with the departed.

'Oh, you are alive... that is to say, you are alive and have your whole life ahead of you, Miss Lattimore. I would not waste one more minute on Mr Tate,' Phoebe said hurriedly, covering her tracks.

'You are absolutely right, Miss Astin. Thank you both,' the young woman said, looking up the stairs at Mrs Dobbs. 'I feel such a fool. He told me I was his muse, and I found out there were quite a lot of muses. Have you ever?'

Mrs Dobbs shook her head, and Phoebe gave Miss Lattimore her most sympathetic look.

'The treachery of men,' Miss Lattimore proclaimed.

'If I may?' Phoebe began but did not wait for permission to offer her thoughts. 'You are not a fool or to blame, Miss Lattimore. Mr Tate was a handsome man and, no doubt, charming. Regardless of his affection for other ladies, I suspect he could not help but ardently admire you.' She dared not use his nickname for fear of claiming an intimacy when Miss Lattimore was distressed enough.

The attractive young woman blinked away tears at Phoebe's kindness and reached for a handkerchief buried in her decolletage. 'Thank you, Miss Astin. That is very kind of you to say so.' She took a deep breath and put her shoulders back. 'I shall heed your advice and not give him a moment more of my life. I wish you a good day.'

'I will see you out, Miss Lattimore, and relieve you, Mrs Dobbs, from the desk duty until Grandpa returns.'

With that, Miss Lattimore flounced up the stairs after Mrs Dobbs, and Phoebe followed in quick pursuit to bid her farewell. Once Miss Lattimore had departed, Phoebe said in jest, 'I shall tell Grandpa to let me know in future if the living is waiting in my office,' and Mrs Dobbs smiled and gave her a quick wink.

Chapter 14

HARLAND SLOWED TO ADJUST his hat and tie and ensure he was presentable as he arrived at the office of *The Economic Undertaker*. Slowly opening the door for fear of coming across tearful clients, he was surprised and delighted to find Phoebe alone behind the reception desk. With her halo of long gold hair and wearing a lemon dress with lavender trim, she looked like an angel waiting to console the bereaved.

'Hello!' she said, equally surprised to see the detective. 'It is safe to come in. This is an early visit for you; not yet 10.30am, and you wish to see me?' she teased.

'I would come at first light if permitted,' he said with a smile. 'But I was passing and came to apologise for my absence.'

Phoebe frowned. 'Have you been absent? Goodness, I didn't notice.'

'How that would have wounded me if I had been away,' he grinned at her, closing the door behind him and removing his hat. 'No, I should say my pending absence. Gilbert and I, oh, and Bennet too, will be taking the train to Ipswich and Toowoomba late this afternoon to speak to Miss Isla Barr's family and Mr Tate's other flame in Ipswich.' He was pleased to see the disappointment on his beloved's face but also concerned. 'I am sorry that this will happen frequently.'

'Of course. I understand, and as you are also helping me give Teddy justice, I'm grateful for your dedication. I just had a visit from another of Teddy's muses – a very much alive lady named Miss Esther Lattimore. If Teddy had not been buried, I'm sure she would have contributed to that.'

Harland chuckled and repeated the name to commit it to memory. 'Good Lord, how many did he have? We may need to talk with her down the track. She will be on the list of his clients.' Harland glanced around. 'You are not here alone, are you?' he asked, concern in his voice. He could see the kitchen, the hallway, a little of the meeting room, and the coffin sales room.

'No, someone is always in the stables out the back—Will, Claude or Charlie. But it is rather peaceful.'

'Where is everyone then?'

'Well, Julius has gone to advise the gravediggers of your exhumation order, and while I did not see him, I suspect he was not altogether happy,' she said with a smile.

'I'll have to owe him for that one. I've just told Tavish to expect the body back; I'm grateful Julius got onto it right away.'

'I am sure he'll have a word with you,' Phoebe teased. 'He will think I am colluding with you to dig up his dead,' she joked.

'Now that's romantic. Bet not many girls can say that of their beau.'

Phoebe grinned. 'True. Lucky me,' she teased. 'Grandpa is also working for you this morning, so to speak. He has gone to telegram Mr Tate's next of kin, an uncle, to advise of the exhumation order. Mrs Dobbs is next door delivering a treat to the dressmaking ladies and Ambrose—'

The back door opened, and Ambrose appeared, striding through to reception, having just delivered the body to Phoebe's room and gone with Will to clean the hearse.

'Ambrose is here,' Phoebe finished.

Harland inwardly sighed. He rarely had any time alone with Phoebe unless they were walking, and even then, they did not have a moment of privacy.

'Ah, the man who wants to dig up our freshly laid bodies,' Ambrose joked, and the men shook hands.

'I am sorry about that. Poor Mr Tate had barely a night in his earthly tomb,' Harland said.

'It would be more profitable for us if you could bump them off rather than request them back.'

'Ambrose!' Phoebe scolded.

'Well, it is true, and I am sure Julius would appreciate my business focus,' he said in jest. 'So, you are not back for someone else then?' Ambrose asked, narrowing his eyes, and Harland chuckled.

'No, you may relax. I was saying a quick goodbye to Phoebe as I am heading to Ipswich and Toowoomba in a matter of hours as part of our investigation.'

'Has Miss Rose Ward been told of Teddy's death? Perhaps she is still expecting him,' Phoebe pointed out.

'I never thought of that; we will be prepared. Although the new salesman, Mr Harry Beaumont, has taken over the area and may be calling on her as we speak. We intend to find him for a chat, too.'

'Harry Beaumont!' Ambrose mused on the name. 'That's the second time I have heard that name today in a matter of hours.'

Harland turned to him with renewed interest. 'Where else have you encountered Harry's name?'

He clicked his fingers, remembering. 'Kate–Miss Kirby—took his photo!' Ambrose said, correcting his familiarity and explaining the partnership the men had formed and that Harry Beaumont was now requesting Kate somehow remove Teddy from the photo.

Phoebe's eyes flew to Harland. 'That is interesting.'

'Very interesting indeed,' Harland said. 'I have time to drop in and see Miss Kirby before departing. I wonder what business *Higson's Quality Perfumes'* two best salesmen were setting up together and if somehow Teddy Tate was felled by his soon-to-be business partner.' Harland realised he was musing out loud and straightened.

'Thank you, Ambrose. It was most fortunate to see you this morning; that photograph could be very significant.'

'My pleasure. I am glad to have made your visit worthwhile,' Ambrose said with a nudge and a grin at his sister, who gave her brother a smirk.

Harland laughed at the pair.

'I shall look forward to your return, Harland,' Phoebe said.

'As will I,' he assured her, and then they both looked at Ambrose.

'Oh, so will I. Wait, you want me to leave?' He played dumb. 'I'll be in the kitchen for a moment or two.'

Once out of sight, and knowing they only had a minute, Harland said, 'A moment in your company made the visit worthwhile, Phoebe. Take care, and I shall call again upon my return.'

'You take care, Harland, please. There is crime afoot.'

'I will,' he assured her, and kissed her hand. Harland returned his hat to his head and, calling goodbye to Ambrose, hurriedly departed to visit Miss Kate Kirby's photographic studio and request the photo of Teddy Tate and Harry Beaumont.

'Detective Stone is departing from next door,' Miss Mary Pollard said from her seat in the dressmaking store as she hand-stitched a collar onto a mourning gown. On this occasion, the sewing work required a more delicate touch than what their state-of-the-art machines could achieve. Violet sat facing the door, and while she could only see straight ahead across the wide road, she was the first person clients saw when entering. Mrs Nellie Shaw sat opposite Mary, where she could see a little up the street, but Mary faced the direction of *The Economic Undertaker* business next door and was the source of all comings and goings.

'On police business, perhaps,' Nellie suggested as they worked quietly, enjoying each other's company.

'Goodness. He visits so often, I fear he will take them all away in cuffs,' Mary said, a little alarmed.

'Do not fear, Mary dear,' Violet said. 'Detective Stone is courting Phoebe. I am sure I can say so without being indiscreet.' Violet was careful not to mention that Phoebe saw visions that assisted the police, as the other two ladies were not to know, but it was a relief that Phoebe and the detective were courting, as it might seem odd how often he visited otherwise.

Mary looked up and smiled with delight. 'Oh, how romantic. Yet he never brings flowers.'

'He most likely has them delivered, given he is a busy man,' Nellie said.

Mary gave a firm nod. 'You are right, Mrs Shaw. I do recall some beautiful roses being delivered of late. The business gets a regular order of fresh flowers, but they usually arrive first thing,' she said knowledgeably.

'What a charming couple,' Nellie said with a smile. 'We haven't seen much of your beau of late, Violet. Are they working him to death, so to speak?' She gave a little chuckle at her pun, and Mary laughed.

'Very good, Mrs Shaw.'

'Thank you, dear.'

'It is the heat,' Violet said. 'The boys are expiring from it after wearing those dark suits out in the sun during a funeral. He does not like to come in here when he fears he may smell unpleasant.'

'Oh, we don't care about that if you don't,' Nellie said with a wave of her hand, needle and thread in tow. 'The poor man is probably pining for you. No wonder he has been visiting early in the day.'

'I, for one, don't want him near me while smelly,' Violet said seriously and, feeling the stare of the other two ladies, burst out laughing.

'I thought you were serious, Miss,' Mary scolded her manager. 'As we speak of clothes, Miss, may I update you on your wedding dress.'

'Oh yes, please do, Mary,' Violet said, keen to know how the capable young seamstress was getting along. Mary had presented a drawing, and Violet commissioned it immediately.

'I am at the stage where I would like a first fitting, please, Miss, if time permits this week.'

'Already? Oh, Mary, I hope you have not been taxing yourself after hours, but how exciting,' Violet said.

'It's my passion to make wedding dresses, Miss; it is not taxing at all,' Mary assured her.

'Bring it in, Mary, and if we have no customers, you two can disappear into the changing room, and I will hold the fort,' Nellie said. 'I'll also ensure Mr Astin does not enter and risk seeing his bride-to-be's dress.'

'That would startle him more than me, I suspect,' Violet laughed. 'I very much look forward to seeing your beautiful design come to life, Mary.'

'It is nice to be working with white fabric instead of black for a change,' Mary said and smiled. 'Some of the fabrics and laces are just dreamy.'

'Maybe one day, your future beau, should he be a carpenter, can build you a little extension to your marital home where you can have a bridal gown gallery and be Mrs Mary Name-to-be-confirmed, by appointment only,' Nellie teased.

Violet laughed at Nellie's antics, and Mary smiled while flushing to the roots of her hair.

'It would be nothing more than you deserve,' Violet said to Mary, who gave a small nod of thanks and turned her attention back to her work. She looked very pleased indeed as Violet and Nellie exchanged smiles, thinking of Tom, the carpenter apprentice who had taken a shine to Mary.

The back door opened, and then a knock was heard, followed by footsteps. Ambrose appeared hesitantly from the hallway. 'May I enter?'

'It is all clear, Mr Astin, come on in,' Nellie said.

He appeared and gave a small bow. 'Good afternoon, Violet, Mrs Shaw, Miss Pollard. I am sorry, it is only me and not my handsome brother,' Ambrose said to Violet with a wink.

'You are a lovely reminder of him, so that will suffice for now,' Violet teased him back, and Ambrose laughed.

'We were just saying he has been scarce of late,' Nellie said.

'He is grumpier of late,' Ambrose said. 'Julius has gone to organise an exhumation. Harland wants to run more tests on one of the dearly departed.'

'Why does that upset, Mr Astin?' Mary asked, curiosity getting the better of her shyness. 'Did he know the person to be exhumed?'

'No, Miss Pollard, but it is very hot, and it means we will have to bury him twice.'

'Oh, of course,' Mary said, blushing as if her question was ridiculous and she should have known better.

'At least Julius is not personally digging the poor man out of the ground,' Violet said.

'I have reminded him of the same, my dear soon-to-be sister-in-law,' Ambrose said. 'To business. A fabric delivery has arrived for you at the docks. Would one of you like to come and check the load before I sign for it and have it loaded? It will only take an hour or so.'

'Oh, good, we are running short on taffeta and crape,' Nellie said.

'I was getting a little worried,' Violet agreed. 'Would you like to go, Mary?'

'Me! Oh, yes, Miss, I would.' But then Mary saw Ambrose and seemed to freeze.

'It's a lovely warm day for a ride, and I promise I won't take the hearse,' Ambrose joked.

Violet rose. 'I shall give you my ordered list, Mary, so that you can check it off. Thank you, Ambrose.'

'A pleasure, ladies,' he said with a small bow. 'Come then, Miss Pollard. Let us go collect your fabric.'

Mary rose with a small smile that fell between terrified and excited. Accepting the list from Violet, she placed her hat on her head and hurried behind Ambrose down the hallway and out the back door.

'It will be good for her confidence,' Violet said, watching them depart.

'Absolutely,' Nellie agreed. 'She's terrified of the Astin brothers, so this may help her relax a little. Mr Astin is bound to make her feel at ease.'

'Indeed. I would never inflict her on Julius. The poor girl would be stiff with fear,' Violet said with a small laugh.

'He can be imposing,' Nellie agreed. 'I must say, now that Mary is out of earshot, I never thought the police would visit a funeral home as much as they do next door. One would think the staff has the ability to talk with the dead.'

Violet snapped to look at Nellie Shaw, and then, confident that she knew nothing and that it was just a casual statement, she gave a small laugh. 'That would make for an interesting story, would it not?'

'Yes, quite a tale,' Nellie agreed, pinning a hem.

Violet said, 'It is an odd thought. Have you heard something?'

'No, not at all. But where the dead lie, there are bound to be a spirit or two loitering.'

Violet shuddered. 'I hope my future home with Julius will not play host to spirits.'

Nellie Shaw had planted a seed of worry in Violet's mind; she needed to chat with her fiancé. It was one thing for Phoebe to see and speak to spirits, but might it extend to other family members? The thought made her quite uncomfortable, and she vowed to investigate further.

'You again,' Dr Tavish McGregor said just on midday as he stood with Julius Astin, looking down on the body of Edward 'Teddy' Tate laying on the coroner's slab.

'Do you mean me or the recently deceased?' Julius asked, and Tavish laughed.

'Rest assured, I am always pleased to see the living. But this exhumation, what a nuisance for both of us,' Tavish said.

'Indeed. Although oddly, the gravediggers did not seem to mind. Double handling pays more.'

'I should hope so for their sake,' Tavish agreed.

The door to the coroner's office opened, and private investigator Bennet Martin entered.

'Julius, Tavish, what good fortune to find you both here.'

'I am having a reprieve from the heat on the ruse of delivering a body,' Julius joked.

'Is Teddy Tate here already?' Bennet asked, eyes wide with surprise. 'Harland said he was getting an exhumation order but three hours ago.'

'This is the gentleman,' Tavish said, wrinkling his nose at the exhumed corpse.

'We don't waste time in the funeral game,' Julius told Bennet in jest and smiled. 'The gravediggers were keen to get the job done early.'

'I imagine so, most impressive, old friend.' Bennet slapped Julius on the back. 'I am just about to join the detectives to head up to Ipswich and Toowoomba by train; will you telegram him the results, Tavish?'

'I can. Where will you be?'

Bennet approached Tavish's desk and wrote the name of the accommodation where he had secured rooms in Ipswich – the North Star Hotel. 'We are here this evening.' He waved the paper.

'Excellent. You may tell Harland I shall see if any trace of poison remains within the perfume salesman. Have you been poisoned, Mr Tate?' Tavish asked the corpse.

'I believe he likes to go by the name of Teddy, although that might be just for the ladies,' Julius said. He had not warmed to Teddy – exhumed or buried.

'I imagine it is,' Tavish agreed. 'These handsome, charming men make it hard for real men like me.'

Bennet chuckled, being one of the aforementioned handsome and charming men, but Julius suspected he hadn't made the connection.

Bennet asked, 'Tell me, Tavish, in the history of your work, have you ever come across a poisonous perfume?'

'I can't say I have,' Tavish answered, 'but it's a devilishly clever idea. I've smelled a few potent perfumes in my time.'

'If there are two ladies dead and he is their salesman, deceased as well, it stands to reason the perfume could be involved,' Bennet mused.

'Yes, but you would have to restrict it to select bottles and ensure no one else had access to it,' Julius said.

'If you were a perfume salesman, that would be manageable,' Bennet said, musing on the idea. 'Except that he, somehow, was a victim too.'

'Do not race away with your thoughts just yet, gentlemen. Let us see what evidence I can find to relieve you from pondering,' Tavish said.

The door opened again, and Miss Lilly Lewis entered.

'What a day I am having,' Tavish exclaimed. 'I have never been so popular.'

'Well, on that note, I must depart,' Julius said. 'Good day to you all and you, Miss Lewis.'

'Mr Astin,' she said with a smile. 'Hello again, Mr Martin!'

'Miss Lewis, how wonderful,' Bennet beamed. 'As much as I hate to leave when you have just arrived, I must be going too,' he sighed dramatically. 'I have a train to catch. Thank you, Tavish. I shall telegram you if we have news, Miss Lewis.'

Julius held the door for Bennet, and the pair departed, leaving Lilly behind to persuade the coroner to give up his secrets for her article.

Chapter 15

HAVING LEFT THE CORONER to do his work, Lilly returned several hours later, and despite her wheedling and charms, Dr Tavish McGregor played by the rules. He could not offer her his autopsy findings until Detective Harland Stone authorised it; he was the client, after all.

'What a bother,' she fumed, but understood. Given that the detectives and Bennet were leaving on the 4pm train, Lilly raced to the Roma Street Police Headquarters and the senior detective's office to seek permission. She would not get the story in the late edition, but if she could get the scoop today, it would run in the morning's newspaper.

'I haven't got the results yet,' Harland informed her as she rushed into his office.

'They are ready, Detective.'

He chuckled. 'Lucky for you I would like them before I leave. Let us return to the coroner's office now.' He turned to his protégé, Gilbert. 'I shall go straight from the coroner's office to home to pack a small bag, and I shall see you at the station.'

'Yes, Sir,' Gilbert said as he rose to depart and organise his travel requirements.

'Thank you, Detective,' Lilly exhaled with relief and waited as Harland grabbed his hat and coat. Wishing Detective Payne a good trip, Lilly departed with the senior detective and strode up the street to the coroner's office nearby. While walking, Lilly asked, 'Would it not be helpful if you could take Phoebe with you on the trip?'

Harland considered this. 'Yes, but maybe not for her. The last time she assisted me, the persistence of a pushy spirit was too demanding and very draining on her.'

'Oh, I remember. It was that dastardly debutante,' Lilly said and wrinkled her nose. 'It would be wonderful if, in due course, I could report on the road with the detectives; what a story that would be! Phoebe could accompany me, and if she could not assist you, she could just enjoy the adventure.'

'I think you would both be very distracting for Bennet and me,' he said honestly. Lilly huffed as if that was the men's issue, not hers.

Harland held the door for her, and entering Dr Tavish McGregor's office, Lilly regaled the coroner with a grin. 'I have caught the detective before he boarded the train.'

'Miss Lewis, you are dedication personified!' Tavish exclaimed.

'Well, I think that might be the best compliment I have ever received, Dr McGregor, thank you,' she beamed.

'Here you are then, Harland,' Tavish said, handing him the results. Lilly hummed with expectation as the detective read the notes.

'Well then,' he said with a raised eyebrow at Tavish, making him laugh, and Lilly scolded him.

'What have you, Detective?' she asked impatiently.

'I have your next story, Miss Lewis,' he said with a smile, and she clapped her hands with delight. 'Tavish, will you go through your findings?' Harland asked.

'With pleasure,' the coroner said and moved to the body, removing the cloth as if it were easier to discuss if he could see the deceased. Harland and Lilly joined him, distancing themselves from the decaying corpse.

'I will spare you a detailed report on each of the organs; you can read my notes at your leisure. But I found the kidneys, spleen, bladder, and liver all quite natural. However, I found congestion of the lungs from the effect of chloroform, and if Mr Tate had not fallen on the bottle, I suspect that would have killed him.'

'Astonishing,' Harland said.

'Chloroform!' Lilly repeated. 'I have not come across that before.'

'Death by chloroform is not uncommon in the operating room,' Tavish said. 'There are a number of scientific accounts of people inhaling chloroform, often only a small amount, and not waking. It can affect some patients in different ways, but the successful use of it far outweighs the losses.'

'How quickly can it take effect?' Harland asked, glancing at the large clock in the corner of Tavish's office and mindful of the train trip pending.

'It can be very quick. I remember when I was a student studying a case of a young lady who inhaled little more than a teaspoon on a cloth and died within three minutes before the operation had even finished. In this case, however, death was caused by the glass perfume bottle piercing Mr Tate's heart, but if you were looking for a reason for his fall, then you have it. He inhaled chloroform in what appears to be a large dose.'

'So, it is murder!' Lilly's eyes lit up with excitement.

'Not necessarily,' Harland said. 'We don't know how or why he inhaled it.'

'And he would have had to inhale to such a degree that could cause him to collapse and his lungs to be congested,' Tavish said. 'That is quite a bit of inhaling.'

'It does seem peculiar,' Harland agreed. 'Could the chloroform have been put in the perfume?'

'I thought the same,' Tavish said. 'So, I retrieved the glass bottle and broken shards that were brought in with the deceased. As his death was not deemed suspicious, it is just good fortune I am a poor housekeeper, and they are still on hand.'

'Thank God for that,' Harland agreed with a smile.

'Did you find it in the bottle, Dr McGregor?' Lilly hurried him along.

He would not be hurried. 'Chloroform is colourless but smells a little like ether and has a sweet taste. But yes, Miss Lewis, it was evident in the perfume bottle and still intact spout.'

'This is excellent news, Tavish, thank you,' Harland said. 'If chloroform was in the product, I must know why and how. I shall track down the manufacturer and the lady that Teddy Tate was with when selling that last bottle of perfume. She may be able to tell me how he came to inhale so much of it.'

'She might have been one of his ardent admirers and found out she was not the only one, thus found a way to revenge him,' Lilly said.

'It could have been a ruse,' Harland mused. 'She could have put chloroform in her perfume bottle and insisted Teddy take it back and smell it, claiming that it did not smell as it should.'

Tavish sighed. 'You are both too frightening. Such sinister minds; remind me not to cross either of you.'

Lilly laughed, and Harland agreed. 'We are getting carried away. What are the chances the two deceased ladies were exposed to this chloroform?'

'And why would they be given it?' Lilly asked.

Tavish shook his head. 'Without an autopsy, we will never know now. However, I will check my Toowoomba colleague's notes and see if he noted the smell of chloroform when Miss Isla Barr's body first arrived. I shall revisit my notes on Miss Sophia Beaver as well. Ah, wait!'

Tavish rushed to his desk and returned with a file marked "Isla Barr". He opened it and waved a note at them. 'I meant to tell you; the Toowoomba coroner found the verse on the young lady, the same line that Miss Sophia Beaver had in her possession about beauty being skin deep.'

'Excellent, there is no denying now that there is a connection,' Lilly said.

'Indeed. Tavish, thank you,' Harland said sincerely. 'Miss Lewis, you may report those findings.'

'Thank you, Detective,' she said and exhaled with relief. 'Dr McGregor, a few quotes if you would be so kind?'

Phoebe's thoughts had been similar to that of her friend, Lilly Lewis; a ride on the steam train to Toowoomba would be a lovely adventure, and she might be able to assist if the spirit of Teddy or the two ladies appeared to her on the journey. She had hoped Teddy might reappear, but he had not. Perhaps his spirit was at the morgue, keeping his body company.

The idea of occasionally travelling with the detective excited her. It was possible that she might not be separated from Harland as much as he thought should their relationship develop. If he were busy or did not want her nearby, she was quite capable of entertaining herself and, even better, if she were in Lilly's company, Harland would not feel quite as responsible for her. This brought her back to Julius's discussion after he had been stabbed, about all the staff stepping up. Perhaps it was time she trained someone in her skills. Phoebe had heard Julius arrive back not long ago, but he had remained upstairs. Maybe now was a good time to discuss it.

For the next hour, Phoebe contemplated training a mortician as she finished her work on the gentleman that Will and Ambrose had delivered this morning. The idea of sharing her room held no appeal, and she was unsure she could suffer the company. Footsteps on the stairs disrupted her reverie. She could tell by the unhurried step it was Julius.

'Hello brother, this gentleman is ready,' she announced.

'Excellent, thank you, Phoebe.' He continued down the stairs, arriving at the bottom, and joined her to inspect her work.

'I hear you are having trouble distinguishing between the living and the dead now?'

Phoebe laughed, and Julius gave her an affectionate smile.

'I almost put my foot in it by exclaiming, "You're alive!" and had to get myself out of that,' Phoebe grinned with a shake of her head. 'I thought she had a strong presence; some do.'

'You are quick on your feet,' he teased. 'Poor lady, another victim of Teddy then?'

'Yes, I told Harland of her visit.'

'Did Harland tell you he will be away for a few days?'

'Yes, that was the reason he called in earlier. His train departs at four o'clock,' she said with a glance at the clock – an hour from now.

Julius walked around the body on the table. 'Your work is excellent as always. Come on up for afternoon tea; the office is empty of customers.'

'Brother, may I speak to you first on a business subject?'

'Of course.'

She read her brother's anxious look and smiled. 'All is well; do not worry so. I want to discuss training a stand-in for me, as you suggested when you were recently injured.'

'Really?' His surprise was obvious, and Julius moved back to sit on the arm of the couch. 'What has brought this on? Ah, did you want to go to Toowoomba?'

'No, no,' she hurriedly assured him, not surprised by his astuteness. 'I was not invited to go. But, down the track, should Lilly be travelling for a story with the detectives, and I could be of assistance.' She blushed as if that would be impossible and did not finish the sentence.

'It makes perfect sense to me,' Julius said.

'It does?' Phoebe brightened. 'You really think so?'

'Of course. Even if you can't assist, you might go for leisure, and if the case is closed, enjoy a day or two of sightseeing with your intended.'

'Yes, that is what I thought,' Phoebe said and relaxed. 'Thank you, Julius, for understanding. There is but one problem. I don't want anyone here.'

Julius smiled. 'Yes, that makes it difficult.' He slid down from the arm of the chair onto the couch and extended his long legs out in front of him, leaning back. 'I have an idea. Why don't you train Charlie and me?'

'You? Charlie?' Phoebe exclaimed and laughed before sobering and studying him. 'Are you serious, Julius?'

'Very.'

'But why? You have enough on your plate. Surely you cannot take on anything else, and Charlie... well, I confess he has shown great curiosity every time he and Claude deliver a body to my room.' She knew her brother well, and he was not a man of impulse. 'You have thought about this before.'

'Yes. Charlie is young and has worked so hard to prove himself and be forgiven for my stabbing. I offered similar advancement opportunities to Will and Claude when they had proven themselves with us. Will wishes to be an undertaker and has stepped up. Claude is not ambitious; he wishes to be employed and do varied jobs. I mentioned the idea of a carpentry role to Charlie, but he thanked me and said he would like your job.'

Phoebe laughed. 'Really. You did not tell me. Why?'

'He asked me not to for fear of offending you. But now, if his mother agrees, as he is not of age, you might train us both. I am not so busy since we have all shifted our roles, and it is good for our employees to be able to stand in. I cover for Grandpa a couple of days a week, which I will also train Ambrose to do. Will covers for Ambrose, while Claude covers for Will, you man the desk as needed, and even Mrs Dobbs does so when necessary. It works well should there be an absence or we are in demand.'

'It is clever business,' Phoebe agreed. 'I like Charlie; he is quiet and considerate, and you were always very good at technical drawing, but this is a little more creative.'

'Do you think Ambrose might be better at your role?' he asked sincerely.

'Good grief, no,' Phoebe exclaimed, making Julius chuckle. 'He will draw moustaches on the men and bow lips on the ladies. You might be very good at it, Brother, with your eye for detail and unrushed nature. There was a gentleman in my class when I trained of similar nature and skills to yours, and he was efficient and capable.'

'I am keen to know every aspect of my business, but I draw the line at the dressmaking,' he assured her, and Phoebe laughed.

'Violet will be relieved. The idea is appealing to me more and more. We can train over time, and I would enjoy your company, and it would be fun to train a young, keen mind like Charlie.'

'It is done then. Let's discuss it with the family over afternoon tea. This will be fun,' he said. He made to rise, but Phoebe held up her hand to stop him. She glanced up the stairs to ensure they were alone before returning her attention to Julius.

'What will you do if spirits appear and want your help?' She studied his face. 'They can be hard to ignore.'

'I won't encourage it, and I don't wish anyone to know of my, uh, skill.'

'You won't be able to help yourself, Julius,' Phoebe said. 'If a distressed lady appears, you will want to help, but how if you do not own to it?'

He gave a small shrug. 'If they appear to Charlie, he will not be able to help the spirits, so I can choose not to do so. Let us cross that bridge when we come to it.'

She nodded, and Julius rose, inviting her to take the stairs first as he followed.

'They will come, Julius.'

'I imagine so.'

As the pair left her workroom, Teddy reappeared only to find it empty.

<h1 style="text-align:center">Chapter 16</h1>

THE COURIER –MORNING EDITION
SALESMAN'S BODY EXHUMED
SENSATIONAL CORONER'S FINDINGS
DEATH OF TWO LADIES LINKED

An exclusive report by Lilly Lewis and Fergus Griffiths.

The body of Mr Edward 'Teddy' Tate, a former perfume salesman employed by *Higson's Quality Perfumes*, was exhumed yesterday morning. The burial was only the day prior by the diligent men of *The Economic Undertaker*, and after an hour and a quarter of digging, the coffin was reached and taken to the city coroner, Dr Tavish McGregor, who undertook the post-mortem examination at the request of Detective Harland Stone of the Roma Street Police Headquarters.

Mr Tate's death was initially ruled accidental when he tripped in the process of conducting a sale, falling on the perfume bottle he held that shattered and pierced his heart. However, fresh evidence led Detective Stone to open an investigation.

The coroner, Dr McGregor, said, 'After a very careful examination of the body externally to see if there were any other marks of violence which might have caused death, other than the original diagnosis, none were found.'

The doctor proceeded to open the corpse. The examination lasted two hours, and Dr McGregor had more conclusive results.

'There was significant congestion of the lungs from the effect of chloroform. While death resulted from the impalement on a broken glass perfume bottle, the cause of the victim's collapse is most likely related to the inhaling of this powerful liquid,' Dr McGregor told your journalists.

After the examination, the body was once more placed in the coffin and released to be re-interred.

The findings raise several questions and challenges for the detectives as it has recently come to light that two of Mr Tate's clients—Miss Sophia Beaver, and Miss Isla Barr, 21—both recently deceased, were dressed similar and a verse was found on each at the time of their death, reading "Beauty is only skin deep".

As revealed yesterday by *The Courier*, the ladies were being wooed by Mr Tate but did not know of each other and gave their affections, believing Mr Tate to be honourable. A third lady from Ipswich, whom the detectives have requested not be identified at this stage, was also under the impression that Mr Tate was her beau. She remains alive, but no doubt, on hearing from the detectives, she will avoid perfume salesmen and their products for the time being.

Detective Stone and his partner, Detective Payne, have taken to the road, travelling as far as Toowoomba to undertake further investigation.

With three train journey times to choose from daily, the men chose the 4pm train to Ipswich, arriving at 5:15pm. Ipswich's North Star Hotel provided a welcome meal and comfortable overnight accommodation.

Early the next morning, after breakfast, the gentlemen paid the hotel bill, leaving their luggage to be collected before the noon train, and took their seats in the two-horse, four-person carriage Bennet had organised. Miss Ward lived on a large rural estate on the outskirts of Ipswich, and the journey would take twenty minutes or so.

'The hotel was an excellent choice for the night. Thank you, Bennet,' Harland said as the horses started. He observed the scenery in all its morning crispness, enjoying the cool temperature before the day warmed up.

'I had it on authority it was the place to stay,' Bennet said. 'My clerk, Daniel, is very good at managing an itinerary. We are staying at the Globe Hotel in Toowoomba tonight; first-class rooms, hot water baths, and a porter will meet us at the station.'

Harland smiled. 'Perhaps lower your expectations a little. A first-class venue in Australia may not be as grand as the name suggests in Britain. We are heading to the bush after all.'

Bennet chuckled. 'Then I won't expect all the royal trappings.'

'I have a friend in Toowoomba, Sir, and they would not like to be considered the bush,' Gilbert said. 'They are the gateway to the bush and became a town in 1858, a municipality in 1860. His uncle is the mayor and very well off, I am led to believe.'

'I stand corrected; thank you, Gilbert,' Harland said, restraining a smile.

'My pleasure, Sir. Also, I hope I haven't overstepped, but I took the liberty of sending a telegram to Miss Yalden last evening,' Gilbert said, referring to the lady who held his heart. 'I asked if she might speak with Miss Kirby to find out if Harry Beaumont and Teddy Tate paid for the portrait using a business name or address.'

'Excellent thinking, Gilbert,' Harland said. 'If we know of their established business, it will be hard for Harry Beaumont to deny it.'

'My thoughts exactly, Sir. Hopefully, a telegram will be waiting for us at the Globe Hotel when we arrive this evening,' Gilbert said.

'Good work, Detective,' Harland said.

After a short while, Harland sighed and looked at Bennet. 'I can't imagine how you bore the trip here from England, all those days at sea. Several days of travel are enough for me.'

'It had its challenges, but it also had its charm, as all travel does,' Bennet said. 'Like last evening, that steam train trip was quite an adventure. How fast it is compared to the trusty horse and cart.'

'Thank goodness,' Harland said.

'Can we speak of the case?' Bennet asked and began without waiting for consent. 'I wonder how the symptoms might vary for blood poisoning and chloroform poisoning.'

'I did not have time to source that information, having just been told of the presence of chloroform before we departed,' Harland admitted. 'Do you know, Gilbert?'

'Yes, Sir. The symptoms are not greatly dissimilar,' Gilbert said, offering another fact from the file in his head.

Bennet exclaimed, 'You are a fount of knowledge, Detective Payne. How do you know this?'

Gilbert appeared modest. 'I assure you I only learnt of it because I read about its effects in the crime story of Mrs Adelaide Bartlett. She was accused of killing her husband, and he had chloroform in his stomach.'

'Ah, yes. That was only a few years back, in London,' Bennet recalled.

'Yes, I remember that case; she was freed,' Harland said.

'That is correct, Sir,' Gilbert continued. 'Both blood poisoning and chloroform poisoning present with fever or chills, quick breathing, nausea and vomiting. I believe the chloroform might present as a red skin irritation as well. If the doctor saw both ladies in the throes of death, then death by blood poisoning was a logical conclusion,' Gilbert said.

'Very good,' Harland said. 'We shall follow up with the doctors who signed their death certificates. Well done, Gilbert, very insightful and useful yet again.'

Gilbert flushed with embarrassment. 'I don't mean to be a know-it-all. Or perhaps you mean I am more useful today, and I have not been before,' he said, alarmed.

'It was meant as a commendation,' Harland said, and Gilbert nodded his thanks and hid his relief and delight.

The carriage slowed, and an estate with a large home that Bennet declared well-to-do came into view. Drawing up at the front gate, the three men alighted.

'Stop, Sir!' Gilbert proclaimed, and both men froze. 'Is that not Harry Beaumont at Miss Ward's front door? I recognise him from the photograph.'

'I believe it is, Gilbert. What luck that we should meet him here,' Harland squinted to study the man.

'He is either on his way to Toowoomba or on his way back to Brisbane and calling on Teddy Tate's clients,' Bennet mused.

The driver moved the carriage into the shade to rest the horses as the three men entered through the front gate and up the path to the door. Harry Beaumont stood frozen, dropping his hand after knocking on the door.

The door opened, and he turned on the charm as an attractive young woman, fair of face and hair—Miss Rose Ward, no doubt—stood in the doorway.

'Good morning,' she said, unfamiliar with Harry and expecting Teddy. Harry doffed his hat and turned as Rose was studying Harland, Gilbert and Bennet, arriving behind him.

'Gentlemen,' she said, and Harry gave them a nod of greeting.

'Mr Harry Beaumont, I presume?' Harland asked.

'Why yes. How might I be of assistance?' he asked, surprised.

'Goodness, what is going on?' Rose asked.

'We are glad to find you alive and well, Miss Ward,' Harland performed the necessary introductions.

'Where is Teddy?' she asked, looking around the men as if he might appear from the carriage.

'Perhaps we best sit down, Miss Ward,' Harland suggested.

And then a middle-aged man, rugged and tanned from the sun, appeared holding a shotgun.

'I don't think you'll be getting anywhere near my daughter. Now back up,' he snarled, and the four men raised their hands and stepped away from the door and Miss Rose Ward.

Chapter 17

Ambrose was partaking with great relish of a slice of Mrs Dobbs's pumpkin pie even though he had consumed breakfast before leaving home.

'You do not have to feed him, Mrs Dobbs,' Randolph said in jest as he sipped tea and watched Ambrose making light work of the pie.

'He does eat well at home, no matter what he tells you,' Phoebe agreed.

Mrs Dobbs chuckled. 'I am always thrilled when my cooking is appreciated. If Ambrose cannot resist it and manages to squeeze in a slice, I am not complaining.'

'There you go,' Ambrose said, indicating his family should do the same.

The front door opened, and Julius's voice could be heard. 'Just me.'

Assured it was not a customer, Randolph remained where he stood, drinking his tea.

'Good morning,' Julius said, entering and removing his hat. Within moments, he held a teacup in his hands.

'Having thought about your suggestion last night, Brother, I think it is an excellent idea for you and Charlie to train in Phoebe's trade,' Ambrose said.

'As do I,' Randolph agreed. 'Soon, we will all be proficient in every role here.'

Ambrose shook his head in warning. 'Be careful, Mrs Dobbs; Julius might have you driving the hearse soon.'

Mrs Dobbs laughed, and Julius gave her a studied look.

'I am not averse to the idea,' he said seriously and then smiled.

'Oh, you did not fool me for a minute, Mr Astin,' she said with a laugh, 'although I was not a bad horsewoman in my day.'

'I wouldn't spare you from the kitchen, Mrs Dobbs,' he said honestly. 'We would lose customers and possibly staff too.'

She blushed at the compliment, never feeling so useful as she had since coming to work with the Astin family after they buried her husband going on two years ago.

'It is true, Mrs Dobbs,' Randolph said. 'I have had many a client tell me they had not eaten since the death of their loved one, and your tea and treat had lifted them with its kindness.'

'I am so delighted to hear that, Mr Astin,' she said sincerely.

'Besides,' Julius said, lightening the mood, 'if we were to swap Ambrose into your job, we would not have a morsel left for the clients, and we could not trust him with a kettle.' He departed, smiling, as his brother Ambrose feigned shock at his lack of faith.

'As lovely as my daughter is,' the rugged man with the slow drawl said, pointing the gun at the four men present, 'if she has this many callers, then a man has to wonder what she is offering.'

'Dad!' Rose Ward exclaimed. 'How could you think such a thing!'

'Be quiet, Rosy, I'll deal with this.' With one hand, Mr Ward pushed his hat back further on his head and levelled the gun directly at Harland, the largest of the three men and likely to be the most difficult to fight.

'Mr Ward, I am Detective Harland Stone from the Brisbane Roma Street Headquarters, and these are my colleagues,' Harland introduced the men, leaving Harry to make his own introduction.

The gun lowered. 'I'm sorry about that, detectives. A man must protect his family.'

'That's why we are here,' Harland assured him. 'We believe your daughter was courting Mr Edward Tate.'

'Was?' she exclaimed, 'I still am.'

Mr Ward nodded. 'He seems like a decent young man. Works hard, a bit flash for my liking, but Rose is a good catch, and none of the country bumpkins around here are going to win her heart.'

'Thank you, Dad,' she said with a coy smile, and the man's face softened.

'Is Mrs Ward home, Sir?' Bennet asked.

'She's been dead ten years now.'

'I am sorry for that,' Bennet said. 'May we come in?'

'You might as well,' Mr Ward said gruffly, leading them through to a large sitting room filled with sunshine. They took a chair; no tea was offered. Harland noted the young lady kept a tidy home for her father, and he wanted to speak with Rose before they advised of Teddy Tate's death in case she became inconsolable.

'Miss Ward, may we ask you a few questions?' Harland looked from her to her father, and both agreed.

'Did Mr Edward Tate speak to you of his new business?'

'Oh yes, he was very excited about it.' She turned to her father. 'He was creating his own line of perfumes, Dad, and said I was his muse.'

'I bet he did,' Mr Ward grumbled.

'He wanted me to be the face of his fragrances; he was even talking about getting a photograph of me with his perfumes.'

'Over my dead—' her father stopped and held up his hands in surrender at the look Harland gave him. 'Do your interview; I will say nothing.'

'Miss Ward, did you sample the perfumes?' Harland asked.

'Yes, he brought me several bottles to try. The fragrances were beautiful. I told him so.'

'And you still have them?'

'Just one remains.'

'I am afraid we have some bad news for you, Sir, Miss Ward,' Harland said and delivered the news about Edward Tate.

'My poor Teddy,' she exclaimed, her hand reaching her heart. 'That is why you are here.' She looked to Harry Beaumont.

'Yes, and fear not, Miss Ward. I will look after your needs,' Harry said and hurriedly added as the gun was raised again, 'perfume needs, that is, from *Higson's Quality Perfumes.*'

Harland did his best to suppress a smile, and while he spoke of Teddy's demise, Rose dabbed her eyes and choked with emotion. Harland feared she would succumb to the point of no longer being able to continue. But the handkerchief disappeared on hearing of the other ladies, and her eyes narrowed.

'So, we feared for your daughter's safety,' Harland said, after telling Mr Ward about the other women in Teddy's life and their unexplained demise.

'I'm glad he's dead, the snake in the grass, and I didn't have to waste a bullet on him,' Mr Ward hissed and most likely would have spat had they been outside. The widowed father turned to Harry. 'I suggest you get going right now and don't come back. We've had enough of your type, bloody perfume salesman.'

Harry nodded and rose, not one to defend anyone's honour, not even his own, when a gun was present.

'I bid you good day then,' he said most formerly.

'We wish to speak with you, Mr Beaumont. Perhaps you could wait by our carriage,' Harland suggested.

'Yes, detective,' he said and made a hasty departure. Rose Ward's father stood as well and looked to Harland.

'Don't worry, I will not hurt him,' he said, putting the gun down in the corner of the room and departing momentarily.

Harland returned his attention to Miss Ward. 'Did you feel dizzy after inhaling any of the perfumes?'

'No, not at all,' Rose said, slightly confused. 'One smelled of rose water and the other of lavender.'

Gilbert took advantage of the opportunity to ask Miss Rose a question without her father present and said, 'Miss Ward, this might sound like an odd question, but have you required an injection of late?' He hurriedly added, 'I can tell from your state of health you are not ill, but please allow the question.'

She shuddered. 'Definitely not, Detective. I hate needles; I can't bear the sight of them and have no ailment that requires an injection.'

Gilbert nodded his thanks.

It was now that Harland wished Phoebe was with him, as impractical as that might be. They would not have been threatened at the door had she and Lilly been in their party on arrival. Phoebe could see if Teddy Tate was nearby, agreeing or denying the answers Rose Ward was giving. The ache of separation he felt annoyed him no end at what he believed was his own weakness.

Having learnt nothing of great consequence from Miss Rose Ward, the detectives and Bennet invited Harry Beaumont to travel in their carriage as they returned to the hotel to collect their luggage and make their way to the train station.

'I don't understand what has happened and why you have just lost me a very good customer,' Harry Beaumont said, looking stricken.

'I am sorry for that, Mr Beaumont. I know your living is at stake,' Harland said, pacifying him. 'But we are investigating the death of Mr Edward Tate.'

'Investigating?' Harry spluttered. 'But wasn't Teddy's death an accident?'

'Perhaps not, Mr Beaumont,' Gilbert said. 'His autopsy shows signs of chloroform poisoning.'

'Good Lord! Poor Teddy, who would want to do that?' Harry gasped. 'Do you think I'm next?'

'Why would you be?' Harland asked, studying the man who was groomed within an inch of his life and smelled strongly of a mix of fragrances on his person and from his sample bag.

'Well, if someone is after Teddy, perhaps they are targeting all perfume salesmen!'

'Unlikely,' Bennet said. 'Have you covered his area in Toowoomba already?'

'Not as yet. I head there presently.'

'Could you tell us a little about your relationship with Mr Teddy Tate, if you know a reason Mr Tate might have been exposed to chloroform, or if you have witnessed anything untoward?' Harland asked.

The handsome salesman soon realised his charm held no sway over the investigators, so he dropped the persona he normally donned for strangers and answered the detectives' questions.

'So, let me understand this,' Harland said when Harry had finished. 'Teddy and you were just friends. You admired his sales skills and acquired his territory as you were the second-best salesman within the company. You are here to call on five of his Ipswich clients, including Miss Rose Ward, whom you didn't know he was in a relationship with, nor did you know of his other indiscretions. Is that correct?'

'Excellent, Detective, that is my situation exactly.'

Harland glanced at Gilbert and nodded for him to refute the salesman's claims.

'Mr Beaumont, we understand that you and Teddy Tate were starting a business together.'

The man was about to deny it when Gilbert produced the photo from a folder he was holding.

'Oh, that,' he said and, seeing the look on Detective Harland's face, he threw his hands up in the air and declared, 'Fine then. We were starting our own line—*Perfume Emporium*—it sounds rather grand, does it not? With our sales success and a romantic new product that will have the ladies swooning, we will be bigger and better than *Higson's Quality Perfumes* ever was.'

'I see,' Harland said. 'So, you will steal the client base from Mr Higson, who has employed you these past years?'

Harry Beaumont's chin went up in defiance. 'We have clients that would have left Higson's had we not wooed them with the promise of our new fragrance and given them samples.'

'I will need the name and address of your perfume manufacturer if you could furnish it to Detective Payne,' Harland said with a nod to his partner. Gilbert took down the details, saving the name of the perfume maker to memory – Septimus Humphrey.

After supplying the name, Harry asked, 'Why do you need to see Septimus? He would not put chloroform in Teddy's perfume. They are cousins and quite close.'

'Is that so?' Harland asked with interest.

'What of the ladies then, Mr Beaumont?' Bennet asked. 'Muses, were they?'

Harry Beaumont sighed dramatically as if defeated.

'Of sorts. I knew Teddy had three ladies on the hop. I don't know anyone who'd have a grudge against him, though, except the ladies if they knew about each other. Mind you, he was a terrible flirt, and it wouldn't surprise me if he gave someone a reason to bump him off. Now, the business is mine to carry, and the workload will be too heavy. I do not know what to do,' he wailed, and his concerns fell on deaf ears. Three people were dead, and that was all Detective Harland Stone was focussing on.

<h1 style="text-align:center">Chapter 18</h1>

MISS EMILY YALDEN OPENED the door of the *Miss Emily Yalden School of Deportment* to find a young delivery boy with a large bouquet of red roses.

'These are for Miss Yal... Yalden,' he said, trying to read the card.

'Thank you, that is me.' She signed as requested and took the impressive bouquet, hurriedly closing the door to be alone with the beautiful gift. She inhaled their fragrance and hoped they were from a certain detective who had been a constant in her thoughts. Walking to her living room, she mused on what the colour of the roses meant: *red, the colour of passion and romance, of deep feelings.* Emily taught her students about such things in their lesson on being wary of men who were too forward.

As anticipation built within her, she desperately hoped they were from Detective Gilbert Payne. Emily was not a woman who normally felt desperate; she was strong, confident and a role model, but she believed she had met her match – a perfect intellectual partner, a gentleman with exceptional manners and grooming; she hoped Gilbert Payne felt the same connection.

Thankfully, her students were gone for the day, and she placed the bouquet on the table to select a vase. Seeing the card, she grabbed it. The disappointment of finding they were from someone else—a thank you from a parent or a troublesome suitor, the recent tradesman who laid the ballroom floor came to mind—would be too much to bear. Gently opening the small envelope, she pulled out the card, holding her breath.

Emily bit her lower lip as she smiled with delight and read the card.

Never would I weary

By Gilbert Payne.

To Miss Emily Yalden, from your ardent admirer.

If I were the guardian of your heart

Never would I weary of my part.

My lips would never tire of saying your name

My ears would never tire of hearing your claim.

Your hand in mine would be safe for evermore

My beloved, I will forever adore.

When poems are dust and flowers fade

Know my ardour will never sway.
So, think of me when the time does come
To give your heart and choose the one.
Know that if I were the guardian of your heart
Never would I weary of my part.

Emily needed to sit down, and although she was not prone to excessive emotion, she was, after all, a woman in love.

Having ensured everyone was present and the day's business was underway, Julius had a small window of time before he and Ambrose were required to deliver a ten o'clock funeral. He ventured downstairs to Phoebe's room to see how she felt about teaching him and Charlie her trade, having had the night to sleep on it.

'Ah, perfect timing, Julius,' she said, smiling at him. She took off her apron, brushed down her mint green dress and reached for several manuals.

'For what?' Julius asked, looking around. No spirits were in sight, and no one required Phoebe's make-up skills. He moved towards the shelves to assist her.

'I have been thinking about how we will begin our lessons,' she said.

'So, you haven't changed your mind or decided the idea was silly?'

'Quite the contrary, I think it is one of your best ideas. Another benefit is that should we need someone in the future, you can train them, and I will not have to do so,' she said, teasing him and knowing Julius was not the best of teachers.

'Hmm, we'll see.' He added in jest, 'It may surprise you, but I am not known for my patience, and training might require more than my skills can muster.'

'That does surprise me,' she said, laughing at his expression. 'Now, I believe it will work best if you read the first lesson from my training manuals, and then we apply it when I have a body in-house. We can then progress through the manual. If Charlie becomes my pupil, I will guide him through the manuals with plenty of practical examples. Will that work for you?'

'That is an excellent idea, and at that pace, it won't interfere too much with our work schedules,' Julius said. He was no stranger to academic study, having secured a scholarship for his school education, lightening the load on his grandparents' purse.

Phoebe continued. 'When I undertook my studies a few years ago, the qualification was very new, but I don't believe it will have developed too much in two years. Here is a list of our subjects.'

Julius perused the list with interest, noting topics including equipment, the best mortuary room and position, dressing the deceased person, embalming, preparing the face, hair, and nails, and selecting cosmetics.

Phoebe continued. 'I need to go to the post office to collect some samples; a company has requested that I consider their new powders, and I am happy to do so. I told Grandpa I would get the mail while I was there, so make yourself comfortable, Brother.'

'I shall, thank you,' he said, taking the first manual and seating himself on the couch.

Julius did not hear Phoebe depart, as he was engrossed in the reading material, which he thought most elementary but necessary given the delicacy of the job and family expectations. Finishing the introductory volume—he had always been an exceptional student—Julius read ahead, finding the content more interesting.

"The corpse must be completely washed. If the deceased was infected with a disease, include a sodium hypochlorite or bleach in the bathing water;

"If the eyes do not remain closed, try inserting a tiny piece of cotton directly on the eyeball under the lid to prevent it from slipping;

"To keep the mouth closed, tie the jaw with a wide band and tie at the top of the head. Remove after ten hours, which should be sufficient for rigour mortis to have set in."

While he knew of some of these processes and techniques, reading about best practices was most interesting to him, and Julius did not look up until he heard someone mutter, 'Bother!'

In fact, he tried very hard not to look up even when the spirit of Edward 'Teddy' Tate declared, 'Phoebe, where are you, beautiful? I'm guessing you can't hear me then, Sir?'

Julius ignored him.

'Bother! Bother!' Teddy said with exasperation and a dramatic sigh to follow.

'Whatever is the matter, Mr Tate?' a female voice asked, and Julius slowly looked up, glancing at the window first and then the clock to give no indication he had heard them but allowing himself to discover who was in the room. A young woman of similar age to Phoebe but a little fuller of figure, stood with her hands on hip regarding Teddy Tate. Her hair was fair, a darker blonde than Phoebe's, and piled high on her head. Her eyes were a light blue colour.

'Mr Tate, now is it?' Teddy asked. 'My darling Isla, what happened to *Teddy*? I love hearing my name on your lips.'

'Do not darling me, *Teddy*,' she warned him. 'You may call me Miss Barr. I have heard of your infidelity, and I am not here to talk with you. Where is the young lady who is a channel to the spirit world?'

'Phoebe, I am seeking her as well.'

'Phoebe! You are on first-name terms and have charmed her already.'

Julius wanted to tell them to go away and bicker elsewhere, but he did not want to reveal that he could see them.

'It is not like that. She was kind enough to assist me,' Teddy said defensively. 'Clearly, she is a good soul, as I have nothing I can offer her now, have I?'

'I wish I had not accepted your affections. To think I was injecting perfume for you and wearing those silly white clothes as if I were to be your model and muse. How foolish I feel now. How gullible.' She shook her head in disbelief.

Miss Isla Barr had Julius's attention now.

Injecting perfume?

He hoped she would continue to speak of it but did not want to ask the question, nor did he want a parade of visitors seeking his help; he was not as patient as Phoebe and never would be.

'You were not gullible; you were my muse,' Teddy waxed lyrically. 'Your beauty and grace, the perfume scent on your skin as if it coursed through your veins, and the beautiful white dress making you look so angelic.'

'I am about to become an angel for eternity, for all the good your advances did me! I should have rejected you.'

Julius noted that even in death, the young lady took a determined stand, folding her hands across her body and glaring at Teddy Tate.

'Well, I hope you become an angel forever, my Isla. I hope I may also be regarded as worthy and one day be with you again in heaven.'

Julius subtly watched as Teddy reeled her in again. His act of despair and his saddened, handsome countenance tugged at her heart, and Miss Isla Barr sighed.

'I am sure you will be an angel, Teddy. You are a kind and sweet man, even if you are generous with your affection.'

Teddy grinned. 'My darling, Isla.'

Isla was now studying Julius for the first time; he bore her attention while attempting to look as if in silent contemplation and unaware of their presence.

'My, isn't he handsome?' she asked.

Teddy shrugged. 'If you like those Byronic types.'

'Oh, I do,' she said, smiling. 'Is he the betrothed of your Phoebe?'

Julius bristled at the thought of his sister being Teddy's anything.

'She is not my Phoebe, and I do not know his connection to her.'

'So, what is she helping you with?'

'Somebody murdered me, I am sure.'

'No!'

Julius did not doubt that her shock was real.

'I am sure of it, and Phoebe said she would try to persuade the police to have another look at my case.'

'Does that mean I was murdered too?' Isla asked, and Julius looked back at his workbook, pretending to read as he listened.

'Perhaps. Do you remember how you died?' Teddy asked.

'I had a terrible fever and was very ill. I was bedridden, but I remember insisting on staying in my white dress. I was sure you would come to me, and I wanted you to see me looking my best.'

'Oh, Isla, had I known you were ill, I would have been there, I promise. But I was most likely dead myself.'

'Could the other woman be murdered too?'

'Sophia or Rose?' Teddy asked.

'Oh, you really are a rat,' she said, her hands covering her face, and with that, she vanished.

Julius raised his head as Teddy called out, 'Isla! Come back.' He huffed and looked directly at Julius, who did his best to look right through him. In moments, Teddy was gone, and Julius exhaled with relief. He rose and returned the manuals to the shelf just as Phoebe raced down the stairs.

'How did you go?' she asked with interest.

'I have read ahead a little; I hope you don't mind. It is most interesting.'

'It is, isn't it?' she agreed with a smile.

'You had visitors.'

'Oh, don't tell me Teddy returned, and I missed him,' she said, placing her new powders on the desk.

'Teddy and Miss Isla Barr. Have you ever heard of women injecting perfume into their skin?'

'Goodness no, that cannot be healthy, surely?' Phoebe shuddered at the thought.

'One would think not,' Julius agreed and told her of the conversation. 'Should I get time after the funeral, I will drop in and see Tavish and ask if that might lead to blood poisoning.'

'Oh, that is a consideration, Julius. Harland would be grateful to hear that bit of information, too.' She cocked her head to the side. 'How will you explain your question as you can't say the ghost of Miss Isla Barr was injecting herself?'

'Good point. I will say I read something of it and thought it might help the investigation, given the victims were applying new perfumes. I will let you know what Tavish says, and you can tell the detective.'

'No, it's best you telegram him immediately if possible. I have the names of the hotels where they are staying.' Phoebe blushed slightly and added, 'Harland gave them to me in case I needed him urgently.'

'I see,' Julius said with a raised eyebrow.

'Do not get overprotective and silly.'

'So, I'm silly now?' he said, and she playfully hit his arm.

'By the way, you have not started work with me yet, and you have already involved yourself in the spirits' dramas. Are you sure you will be able to ignore these guests?' she asked with a small chuckle, and Julius had the good grace to grin.

'I will tell them where you are and suggest they drop in.'

'Don't you dare!' she said, narrowing her eyes.

'We'll see,' he teased and, pocketing the addresses, departed to collect Ambrose and undertake their first funeral for the day.

Chapter 19

Julius had intended to see the coroner, Dr Tavish McGregor, earlier in the day, but work had intervened. After he and Ambrose delivered a funeral, he was required to visit cousin Lucian to sign some paperwork so more timber could be ordered; then, his bookkeeper had invoices that required signing and could not be delayed. With his grandfather, who co-signed them, the men had made their way into the city to his bookkeeper's office. It was early afternoon when he arrived at the coroner's office.

'Julius!' Tavish exclaimed on seeing him. 'I don't have anyone for you to collect, do I?'

'No, unless you want to top someone off?' Julius joked, and Tavish laughed.

'Tempting, but not today.'

'I was passing and had a quick question that I hoped you could help me with; well, it is something that might help the detectives with their perfume case.'

'Ah, you also have the stirrings of a private investigator in you. Perhaps you and Bennet could go into business,' Tavish teased, indicating a seat, and both men sat.

'I assure you I am quite happy burying the dead. The living is too much trouble.'

'It is the truth. Speaking of the living, I am taking Miss Isabelle Yalden to a piano recital this Saturday evening. I hoped to gather a party to attend,' Tavish said, his blue eyes sparkling in anticipation.

'The lovely young lady from Miss Yalden's dinner party?'

'The very one. Such a gentle beauty.' He sighed.

'A piano recital, then. As the saying goes, "Love makes fools of us all", yes?' Julius could not help but smile at the rough and rugged red-haired Scottish man with a passion for boxing.

'Yes indeed. It will be excruciating, but I shall focus on the lovely Isabelle. I hope the recital will be short and sweet. Would you and Miss Forrester care to come? I have a box at my disposal and hoped we might regather the group from the dinner party. I have been remiss in doing so, but Isabelle was speaking to her cousin, Emily, about it.' He waved his hand. 'The ladies are better at organising these things.'

'I shall mention it to Violet, thank you. Are you determined to give us all a dose of culture?'

'It will make the recital more bearable,' Tavish said in a pleading tone.

'A fine idea,' Julius smiled, 'why suffer alone?'

'Exactly so. Now, you had a question, I believe? Ask and I'll see if I can help.'

'Yes. I have come across some information about ladies injecting themselves with perfume and wondered—'

Tavish leapt to his feet and held up his hand for Julius to stop. His eyes widened. 'Yes! Those little injection marks.' He raced to his filing cabinet and pulled out the file on Miss Sophia Beaver. 'Ah ha!' he declared, pointing at his notes. 'I noted a smell of perfume around the injection site but thought she might have dabbed perfume there.'

'Could injecting the perfume lead to blood poisoning and thus their death?' Julius asked, holding his breath in the hope they might have solved Miss Beaver's manner of death and, consequently, Miss Isla Barr's.

'Yes! Yes, indeed!' Tavish, now animated, said. 'Some time ago, I read about this silly trend that Parisian women were doing. Where did I see that?' He raced to another desk, rifling under notebooks and pads, and found several scientific publications. Tavish thumbed through the pages, discarding one and then holding one high.

Julius waited, keen to put credence in what he had heard from the spirit of Miss Isla Barr.

'Here it is, listen to this, Julius: "A Frenchwoman lately found that by injecting a few drops of perfume under the skin with a subcutaneous syringe, she could scent herself in a fashion that would last for days. She tried to keep her secret, but it crept out, and presently, a perfume syringe was to be found upon every toilet table. It turns out that the practice is dangerous to the last extreme. Some perfumes are poisonous, and many are extremely unwholesome, so some of the fair ones have been to the point of death. The doctors intend to petition the legislature to stop the practice." Ridiculous! My good friend, you are definitely onto something here.'

Julius exhaled and smiled. 'Excellent.'

'It takes but a little cut or wound to risk blood poisoning, and maybe these young ladies have caused injury to the skin as well as injecting the perfume poison, thus resulting in acute septicaemia followed by a fatal termination.'

Julius stood to depart. 'Shall I telegram Harland with our finding and tell him you are preparing something for him?'

'Indeed, yes, excellent,' Tavish said, distracted now. 'You will let me know about the piano recital?'

'I shall.' The men bid each other farewell, and before returning to *The Economic Undertaker*, Julius went to the telegram office to hurriedly send a note to Detective Harland Stone at the Globe Hotel.

Detective Gilbert Payne was restless on the train journey to Toowoomba. As it departed Ipswich at noon, pulling out of the station in a cloud of steam and well-wishes from those on the platform, the young detective drifted in and out of the casual conversation between his superior, Detective Harland Stone and Private Investigator, Bennet Martin. He had given the case considerable thought overnight and felt he could confidently contribute something if and when he was challenged, but for now, his thoughts drifted to the telegram he hoped was waiting for him from Miss Emily Yalden.

He despaired she might think him presumptuous to ask for a favour – to seek information about Miss Kate Kirby's photograph. But it was an opportunity to contact her other than sending the flowers and poem. Gilbert felt vulnerable about the poem but not about his skills. He had worked on the verse for some time and invited feedback from his poetry group.

What if there were no telegram waiting for him? Would that mean she was insulted or too busy with her business to do his begging?

'Detective Payne, you are very quiet this afternoon. Will you share what is preoccupying your thoughts?' Bennet asked as he travelled backward, facing the young detective. Harland had opted to sit beside Gilbert, facing the direction they travelled. On the return journey, Harland would take the window seat.

Gilbert cleared his throat and mind of Miss Yalden and said, 'I am considering the railway and how amazing it is.'

'It is a marvel of the modern world,' Bennet exclaimed. 'The steam train and the stations themselves are rather impressive structures.'

'It makes our life easier,' Harland agreed. 'A journey of just over four hours compared to up to six days by carriage, it would be impossible to do modern policing without it. In fact, I thought you would regale me with that fact.' Harland teased Gilbert, and the young man flushed and smiled.

'It is an area of interest to me, Sir, especially for this leg of our journey,' Gilbert assured him. 'Constructing this Main Range Railway took just over two years to complete. The steep climb, sharp curves, and tunnels must have been so challenging for the crews, but, surprisingly, there have been very few accidents.'

'That is a relief,' Harland said.

'Let's hope that continues then,' Bennet said. Gilbert noticed Bennet's countenance was a little wan, and his hand gripped the nearest hand rest.

'Would you like to swap seats, Mr Martin? You look a little pale. Perhaps travelling forward would be better.'

'Thank you, Detective, most kind. But the thought of the height and the fall worries me, not the motion. Should I face the way we are travelling, it might be worse if I could see what is ahead rather than what we have successfully conquered.'

'That makes sense,' Harland said with a small chuff of amusement.

'I hope a telegram has arrived for us, Sir,' Gilbert said, revealing the source of some of his anxiety and assuming his superior would think his concern was on the case and not the emotions that he buried as best he could.

'You are not convinced of Harry Beaumont's story either?' Harland asked as the tunnel plunged them into darkness.

'No, Sir. The two men were planning to start their own business and take clients away from their employer; it is hardly honourable.'

'I agree, and I found Mr Beaumont to be very flippant about the business aspect. I believe both gentlemen have been wooing young ladies with not the best intentions in mind. If we were to investigate Mr Beaumont's sales territory, I wonder how many ladies we might find who think they are the only recipient of his affections.'

They emerged into the sunlight and braced as the train vibrated across an iron bridge.

'My thoughts exactly, Sir,' Gilbert agreed. 'Hopefully, Miss Kirby will have a business name and address registered for that photograph of the pair, and we can do a little more investigating of him.'

'Good God, what a drop,' Bennet said, looking away at the steepness below him.

'Truly amazing,' Gilbert said in awe, leaning forward to see more and spotting a tiny stream of water babbling down the hillside that he felt he could have reached out and touched.

'Do not lean too far forward, Detective. You might sway the train,' Bennet said in alarm, and Gilbert obligingly pulled back.

'Do not fear, Mr Martin, it would take more than just a few passengers to derail the carriages, I believe,' Gilbert assured him but could see he had not convinced the private investigator.

Bennet regained himself. 'Harry Beaumont did not seem greatly upset about Teddy's death.'

'He may not have liked Teddy but saw the benefit of partnering with him, or he might be happy not to share the profit in the future. But I sensed he was scared,' Harland said, 'that might be why we are not seeing his grief.'

The men leaned in as the train travelled around the curves of the mountain, revealing a panoramic view of broken ranges.

'Harlaxton!' Gilbert announced with a smile. 'The summit is 2003 feet above the sea here, Sir.'

'Truly impressive,' Harland agreed.

'I love your wonder, Detective Payne,' Bennet said, embarrassing Gilbert.

He could think of no reply, and Bennet added, 'It is a wonderful thing. Look here; from this angle, you can see into the valley of Toowoomba. We are almost there.'

Gilbert's heart raced again. He would soon know if a telegram was there. Then, he scolded himself.

If there is none, then I shall be fine. I have a case to focus on.

They travelled two more miles, and an established town and settlement with neat and orderly houses replaced the hilly landscape. The steam locomotive passenger train huffed to a stop, pulling up beside the impressive two-story brick Toowoomba Railway Station building in the centre of the town. The platform was dotted with people waiting to collect the disembarking, along with luggage-bearing passengers ready to board for the start of their journey.

The three men rose and were quick to exit. Gilbert considered walking half a mile to their hotel on the main street to stretch his legs, but the Globe Hotel porter with a buggy awaited them and several other passengers, and the lure of a telegram was too great. They arrived at the impressive hotel within a short time, the summer late afternoon light still bright and warm.

'Welcome, gentlemen,' the desk clerk said. 'I believe there are several telegrams for you. One moment, please.'

Gilbert did his best not to look too excited for a man filled with overflowing passion.

The desk clerk announced that one was for Detective Harland Stone, two were for Mr Bennet Martin, and two were for Detective Gilbert Payne.

Harland opened his telegram, but Gilbert checked his impatience and pocketed the two he had received.

'Good Lord,' Harland exclaimed, moving away from the desk. He pulled the gentlemen aside.

'What is it?' Bennet asked, joining him.

Harland looked around and lowered his voice. 'Julius came across an odd practice – ladies in Paris are injecting themselves with perfume at their own peril.'

'Do you think that is what the injection marks are on our deceased ladies, Sir?' Gilbert asked.

Harland nodded. 'Tavish believes it could be likely and fatal. He will furnish us with further details on our return.'

'I must telegram Miss Lewis as promised. Can I share that with her?' Bennet asked. 'It will put us on the front foot with the families to have a possible cause of death.'

Harland thought for a moment. 'Yes. But ensure she reports it as a lead that we are investigating unless Tavish can confirm it before her deadline.' Bennet nodded his understanding. Harland continued, 'I have a suggestion but will go with a majority vote on my proposal.'

Bennet chuckled. 'Go ahead.'

'There are still several hours of light left before sunset, and Miss Isla Barr's family live quite close to town. They are more likely to be in residence this evening than in the morning. What do you say to calling on her family now and heading back on tonight's train?'

Gilbert liked the idea a great deal.

'As the interview is the only thing we have to do in this town,' Harland continued, 'we could then return to the hotel, have dinner, freshen up in our rooms and take the midnight train. We will arrive back at 6am rather than 2pm tomorrow. I can sleep anywhere, but if you feel that is too uncomfortable and you prefer to stay the night, we shall do so.'

'I am all for it,' Gilbert said. 'The case will not be solved here, I believe.'

'I agree,' Bennet said.

'You could stay on, of course, Bennet,' Harland said.

'No, I prefer to get back and get to work as well. I shall book a carriage to take us to the Barr family residence in forty minutes and to the train depot later tonight.'

'Excellent. I shall transfer our tickets to the evening train,' Harland said. Bennet found his ticket and provided it to Harland for reissuing. 'I shall meet you back here in thirty minutes.'

'I will get your bags to your rooms,' Gilbert said, realising there was nothing else for him to do. The clerk appeared with their keys, and Gilbert followed the porter to the assigned rooms, allocating the luggage appropriately. His yearning was so intense the telegrams burned in his pocket. A few words of kindness or encouragement from Miss Yalden would be enough to satisfy him.

Greedy for the content of his telegram, he opened it the moment he entered his room and closed the door. The message was officious and businesslike.

Naturally, Gilbert thought. Miss Yalden would assume that he would give this to Detective Stone. How clever she is, he thought, justifying the business-like tone. Perhaps his insistence that she would be compensated for the cost of sending the telegram convinced her it should also be professional in its manner. He read it and tried to feel some enthusiasm at receiving the information requested – business name, owners, address:

PERFUME EMPORIUM, H. BEAUMONT & E. TATE, OF TANK STREET.

It was an impressive name and the same street location that Harry Beaumont gave him in Ipswich for the perfume manufacturer – a good street location for industry. There was no doubt that Harry and Teddy were well along with their plans. Might Mr George Higson, their employer, have discovered their treachery and brought about Teddy's demise, with Harry Beaumont next to follow? Gilbert would think about that later and discuss it with his superior.

Despondent, he opened the second telegram, expecting an update from the coroner or the sergeant. On opening it, his breath hitched.

THANK YOU FOR THE BEAUTIFUL ROSES AND THE POEM I WILL TREASURE DEAREST GILBERT. YOUR EMILY.

Dearest Gilbert. Your Emily.

Dearest. My Emily.

He would feast on those words for days.

Late that afternoon, as Julius and Violet enjoyed their customary mid-week dusk walk in the Botanic Gardens before he saw her home, Julius felt her withdrawal. He cast his mind over their last encounter to see if he had possibly offended his fiancée but could not think of anything obvious. Was he surly? Had he missed her birthday? Is she perhaps having second thoughts about their... he stopped the thought, unable to bear it.

'Did you have a difficult day?' he finally asked as she walked in silent contemplation beside him.

'No,' Violet said, surprised, looking up at him. 'What makes you think so?'

'You are very quiet this evening.'

Violet laughed. 'Goodness, am I usually such a chatterbox?'

'More so than I,' he conceded with a smile. 'I thought perhaps I had done something to distress you?'

'No, not at all, and rest assured, I would tell you, not make you guess.'

'That is a relief,' he said, his body relaxing now that he had cleared his own involvement in her despondency.

'May I ask you a question?'

'Of course,' Julius said, looking at his beloved and guiding her as they walked up a small rise, requiring her to lift her skirts slightly to avoid tripping.

'I don't wish to offend.'

'I am sure you won't.'

She gave a small nod, and they continued to walk, her arm linked through his, making a handsome couple; sometimes they drew looks from people admiring them or from those who recognised Julius from his business and heroics rescuing a young boy, Alfie, on a previous occasion in the gardens.

'Julius, can you see the spirits too?'

He stopped dead in his tracks for just a moment, so taken aback was Julius from the question. He berated himself for not preparing for it, for not discussing it with Phoebe and asking her how to handle it.

Julius fell back into step with Violet and, swallowing, asked, 'What makes you ask me now after all this time?'

'All this time?' she said with a huff of laughter. 'It is not yet a year since my grandmother died, and we met, and now we are engaged. I imagine there is quite a lot we do not know about each other.'

'Maybe that's a good thing,' Julius said and, realising what he said, hurriedly added, 'I am sure you have nothing to hide that could ever affect my love for you, but I am a man five years your senior and have done things of which you might not condone.'

'You have not killed someone?' she asked, shocked.

'No!' he said, surprised. 'Although I wanted to do so.'

She did not express surprise. 'So have I, but thoughts are not intentions. Have you promised yourself to a woman and abandoned her?'

'Never,' Julius said, slightly affronted at the question.

'I knew that,' Violet answered. 'Then whatever you have done is probably quite normal for young men – fighting, drinking, relations...'

He gave a brief nod but did not elaborate or deny it.

'Will you tell me then, Julius, do you see and hear the spirits? I have not heard that you do; it is just I thought it odd that Phoebe would be the only one in your family to do so,' she concluded as they reached the bench near the rose garden where they often rested for a short while before walking around the lake. Julius cleaned the seat with his handkerchief before Violet sat.

'Would it worry you if I did? A hypothetical question only,' Julius hurriedly answered.

'Perhaps. I do not want the departed in the house when we live together as husband and wife. I don't wish to feel their presence or see them; it frightens me a little.'

'I understand. Would you feel that way if it were your mother, father or grandmother watching over you unseen?'

'No, of course not,' she answered with no trepidation. 'I would take great comfort in that. But strangers, well, that is different.'

'How?' Julius asked. 'Spirits don't just visit Phoebe for company, with the exception of Uncle Reggie,' he conceded. 'Although I suspect he will reveal his reason for remaining soon enough. But most require help to right a wrong. Sometimes, no one is in her rooms for weeks on end.'

'So, she does not wake to find spirits in her bedroom or is frightened by daily apparitions?'

'Good grief, no. Phoebe enjoys their company for the briefest time. She feels she has helped them move on peacefully, and their worldly concerns have abated. I believe their visits are purpose-driven.'

'Do you, Julius? Do you, or Ambrose, or your grandfather see them? Will you tell me?' she begged.

'Will it make a difference to us?'

Violet didn't answer, taking his defence as an answer. She sighed and looked away to the lake, where a child was feeding bread to the ducks.

Julius read her annoyance. 'Our mother had the gift, as some call it, but for Phoebe, it is heightened because of the industry we work in.'

'Because she is exposed to death daily?'

'Yes. It is dangerous to say you speak with the dead. People regard you differently, and often, there are demands on your skills. We keep Phoebe's gift within our intimate group.'

'I understand that. But Phoebe has shared it with people she trusts,' Violet said, and the statement was not lost on Julius.

He stopped talking, afraid to look at her for a reaction, and then said, 'Only two people in our family have the sight.'

'And you are one of them?'

Julius's jaw locked as if he could not release the admission. Violet said nothing, and he turned to face her.

'I am one of them.'

'I see.'

'Violet, nobody knows except Phoebe, and I want it to stay that way.'

'Julius, you are trusting me with your heart and soul; you can trust me to keep your secret.'

He turned back to face the lake and exhaled, unhappy with having to reveal his unwanted skill to yet another person.

'Can you see anyone now?' she asked, looking around.

'Only the same people you see,' Julius said and, seeing her look of doubt, added, 'that is the truth. You are uncomfortable with me seeing spirits, as am I, but I don't interact with anyone, even when I see them. It deters them, and so they leave. Except for Uncle Reggie occasionally.'

'Would you have told me in time?'

'No,' he answered without hesitation. 'I don't want to be that person.'

'That does not bode well for a marriage,' Violet said so low that Julius just caught her words. And then she said no more about the subject.

Chapter 20

After the late edition had been put to bed and just before departing for the evening, Lilly Lewis and Fergus Griffiths stood before their editor, Mr Cowan, trying not to breathe too deeply in his hazy, cigar-filled office.

'I like your story so far,' he said in his usual gruff fashion. 'Where's it going from here?'

Lilly's eyes darted to Fergus. Fortunately, they had just received a very welcome telegram from Mr Bennet Martin with an update on the investigation.

'Well, Sir, we have a couple of new leads,' she began. 'We can confirm now that the deceased perfume salesman was starting a rival business with a colleague. As a result, that creates more suspects.'

'That's shifty of them,' Mr Cowan said with a sneer. He might have willingly reported stories of ill behaviour but did not condone the actions. 'What about the girls? Did they die naturally or not?' he cut to the chase.

'They did not have autopsies; the families would not permit it. But,' Lilly hurried on, 'we received a telegram just an hour ago from the detectives and the private investigator who are currently investigating in Toowoomba.'

'Why?' he interrupted.

'One of the lady victims was from there,' Fergus reminded him, and Mr Cowan snorted, nodding for them to continue.

'It is possible the ladies were injecting perfume into their bodies.'

'Preposterous!' Mr Cowan exclaimed, pulling the cigar from his mouth. 'Is that some new fashion?'

'I believe so, Mr Cowan,' Fergus said. 'I am going to speak with the coroner first thing in the morning, but the telegram stated it was all the fashion in Paris.'

'And that, fortunately, common sense was prevailing, and the fashion was ailing,' Lilly added.

Mr Cowan shook his head. 'Stupidity,' he muttered. 'Write about that, about the girls injecting and if you can get a quote from the coroner saying it contributed to their death, all the better. So, was the injected perfume from the rival or the established business?'

'I don't know, Sir,' Lilly said, surprised. 'We only just got the information.'

'Right, follow that up tomorrow. That's what a good investigative journalist would be asking. And good job,' he said and dismissed them with a wave.

The pair hurried from his office, and Lilly felt as if she were lacking.

'I confess I would not have thought to ask that question?' she said, berating herself.

'I doubt the coroner could tell us anyway,' Fergus said. 'One perfume would be like the other. The person to answer that question is the salesman, Teddy Tate, who is dead, or maybe the perfume maker or the other business partner.'

'Harry Beaumont. Yes, you are right, thank you, Fergus,' she said, appreciating his perspective. 'But I need to think broader. Who is making Harry Beaumont's products? What is their business name and address, if they have one? Does his boss, Mr Higson, know about the side business? I should try to obtain their client list and contact every lady on it to ask if they have been offered the new product or if they are injecting perfume into their bodies.' She sank into her chair, despairing at the enormity of it.

Fergus sat at his desk beside her and spoke in a quiet voice. 'Lilly, we are not the investigators; we are the reporters. While it is good to dig for a scoop, our job is to report on the story as it comes to light. Let us address those questions to the detectives and be the first to report their words. Also, should we contribute to the investigation in any small way, it will increase their trust in us.'

Lilly looked at him with admiration. 'When did you become so wise, Fergus Griffiths?'

He laughed. 'I have never been accused of that. Watch out, I'll start smoking a pipe soon and looking dishevelled.'

'Lord help us,' she teased. Sitting upright and feeling more buoyed, Lilly said, 'I will check when the detectives are due to return; I believe it is late tomorrow, and we will get an audience with them.'

'Excellent. Let us call it a day then, and first thing tomorrow, we will see the coroner and then determine who we will interview next,' Fergus said.

The young reporters wished each other a good evening, and as they were departing, Lilly suddenly felt a wave of longing. She was amazed to realise she missed Mr Bennet Martin. How it would have brightened her evening to see him there waiting for her with some badly thought-up plot to engage her in discussion. She smiled at the thought and made her way home.

Enjoying a late dinner after their visit to Miss Isla Barr's family—a solemn affair with a family in deep mourning—the three gentlemen consolidated what they knew, and Gilbert shared the telegram with the name and address of Harry Beaumont's new perfume company.

'They were established then,' Harland mused.

'They also were setting themselves up nicely with word of mouth from the ladies. From her portrait, Miss Isla Barr looked very much like Miss Sophia Beaver and Miss Rose Ward,' Bennet said. 'Teddy Tate liked his ladies to be blonde and fulsome.'

'Indeed. They were all very similar,' Harland agreed, sipping his red wine, enjoying the break from riding in moving vehicles and interviewing suspects. He grabbed the newly arrived telegram in front of him. 'I asked the sergeant to assign several constables to cross-check Teddy Tate's client list to ensure all the ladies were still alive and, if more claimed an intimate relationship with him. Fortunately, all clients are alive and well, and no one holds Teddy dear,' he said with an edge of sarcasm.

'Three loves were enough then for Teddy,' Bennet agreed in jest.

'Four. I have discovered another courtesy of Phoebe, but fortunately, the young lady has never injected and is very much alive,' Harland said.

'Did you get her name, Sir, and I'll note it?' Gilbert asked, reaching for his notepad.

'Yes,' Harland said, putting his head back and staring at the ceiling while he thought. 'Lattimore... but the first name escapes me.'

Gilbert opened a folded paper in his diary, found the name and announced, 'Esther. This is Mr Tate's client list,' he explained for Bennet's purposes.

'That is her. Miss Esther Lattimore. The other telegram I received I shared with you earlier – from Julius about the women injecting perfume into their bodies causing blood poisoning.'

'What women do for vanity never ceases to amaze me,' Bennet said.

Gilbert agreed. 'At least we know from our earlier interview with Miss Rose Ward in Ipswich that she had received no injections nor undertaken her own.'

'Her fear of needles saved her life,' Bennet said.

'Most likely,' Harland agreed. 'Hopefully, Tavish won't need to exhume the ladies if his notes are thorough, and he can conclude their self-injecting was the cause of their septicaemia.'

'They may have been forced to inject themselves,' Bennet said, providing an alternative motive.

Gilbert shook his head. 'They had several injection sites, so they must have done so a few times, and given the ladies only saw their beau occasionally, I suspect they were willing.'

'As do I,' Harland agreed.

'I am not familiar with this trend,' Gilbert said as if there were a gap in his education, 'but I imagine they thought the fragrance would come through their pores and last longer than applying it to the external skin.'

'Unbelievable,' Bennet said again with a shake of his head. 'I am disappointed you are unfamiliar with the trend, Detective Payne, when you are usually so well read. I know that in Paris, crinolines are rising in popularity, and the frock coat is very popular with men.'

Gilbert was at a loss for words until he realised he was the subject of the private investigator's raillery, and the young detective joined in their laughter.

Returning to the case, Harland said, 'Why did the ladies suddenly die after their last injection? Were they given a new potion to try, or had the poison been building up inside them?'

Gilbert's eyes widened. 'Sir, they might have been trialling several fragrances for the new business – *The Perfume Emporium*. Miss Ward said she had been given several to try. Something potent might have been in the last mix. Chloroform perhaps.'

'It is possible. If only her father had not tipped out all her perfumes and forced the bottles back on Harry Beaumont before we departed. Had I been aware of what he was doing while we spoke with his daughter, I would have stopped him,' Harland said frustratedly. 'No doubt Harry Beaumont will tell us he disposed of the bottles if there's suspicion to be laid.'

'My job will be done once I can prove that the injecting of perfume is what killed Miss Isla Barr and she was not murdered intentionally,' Bennet said. 'From our discussion with her father this evening, he clearly wanted to blame someone.'

'But where does the blame lie?' Gilbert asked. 'With the perfume manufacturer, or with the salesmen for supplying the product and allowing them to inject it, or with the young ladies for following fashion and injecting themselves with it?'

'It is a good question. Unless...' Harland said, thinking aloud, 'it might be possible that a jealous or spurned partner poisoned the product.'

Gilbert rubbed his temple. 'Sorry, Sir, but I need to write up our findings on the board and see it before me.'

'No apology necessary, Gilbert. I like an orderly fashion of presenting facts, too. The sooner we get back, the better. Then we can look at all our loose ends and start there.' He raised his glass, took a sip of red wine and accepted a top-up from Bennet.

'Are you sure you won't partake, Detective Payne?' Bennet asked, waving the bottle at him.

'You may if you wish; it is after hours,' Harland said, thinking the young detective might want permission.

'No, thank you, Sir. My mind is clearer without it.'

'I wish I could say that,' Bennet said, topping up his glass and huffing with laughter.

Gilbert was quite sure that Miss Emily Yalden's telegram was elixir enough to keep him buoyed for days. Although the ride through the range on the steam train was very exciting, the plan to depart home earlier was the best part of the trip so far.

Chapter 21

THE SIGHT OF THE young baker quickly soured the happy thought of working with his fragrances all day. Robbie Pearce loitered near the door as perfume maker Septimus Humphrey arrived for work. Septimus looked nothing like his cousin and business partner, the late dandy Teddy Tate – quite the opposite. A kind description might emphasise his studious nature; even his father was the first to say there was little to boast of regarding his son's looks. Septimus unlocked the door to his workroom and hurried Robbie inside. The area appeared surprisingly larger when indoors, with wall-to-wall shelves of perfume bottles, trays of label designs and distilleries full of fragrances.

As he did every morning, and today was no exception despite Robbie hovering, Septimus hurriedly removed his hat and coat and checked his glass jars filled with fresh flowers and thin layers of cotton to extract the scent. After two weeks, a batch was ready for distillation; other batches were coming along nicely, the cotton absorbing the oils to be used as a perfume.

In the corner stood several large stills he had made himself for distillation. Septimus peaked into one where he had placed petals and water and would heat it later to produce fragrant waters of lavender and rose. Satisfied that all was well, he returned his attention to Robbie, who was fiddling with a mortar and pestle.

'Leave that. Why aren't you at work?' he asked, moving to his worktable.

'I am. I'm on a delivery run,' Robbie said, pushing a box he had previously put on the table toward the perfumer. 'Some buns for your breakfast.'

'Thanks,' Septimus muttered. 'If the police see you here, you'll be back behind bars before you can say "fruit bun". They'll make the crime fit.'

Robbie laughed. 'Don't worry, I put on the best performance you've ever seen in prison. I should be on the stage, not baking. I even turned on the waterworks. I told them I liked Miss Sophia but had my own girlfriend, the lovely Louise. The detective thought there was no way I could harm anyone. Boo hoo,' he said, wringing his hands over his eyes before laughing.

Not satisfied, Septimus frowned at the younger man. 'It's only a matter of time until they come to see me. If they find out that

Teddy was planning a business with Harry and creating their own fragrances—'

'How will they find that out?' Robbie scoffed.

'They'll detect, I guess; that is their job,' Septimus said. 'They will then want to know who is creating the fragrances, leading them to me. So, what are you wanting then? Has Harry sent you?'

'Nuh, he's not back from his Toowoomba run yet. But I've got another potential lady for you. Harry told me to let you know when I find one.' Robbie looked pleased with himself, and Septimus's eyes widened with interest.

'Is she young?'

'She's just like the others in looks but snobby. Harry will win her over. She loves apple tarts and comes in every couple of days.'

Septimus smiled. 'Excellent. I'll have a perfume sample ready for her to test as soon as Harry returns and can work his charm on her.'

Robbie scoffed. 'Make sure it won't kill them this time.'

'It wouldn't have killed them last time,' Septimus snapped. 'Teddy should never have asked them to inject it. It's enough to wear it on the skin.' He shook his head. 'He always had to follow the fashion.'

'They're all like that – Teddy, Harry and the women, too,' Robbie scoffed. 'I'll be off then.'

'Good job, Robbie,' Septimus said with the first show of affection to the young man since his arrival. 'Keep your eye out for more ladies.'

'I've got an eye for it,' Robbie said and winked.

'By the way, does Louise know she's now your girlfriend?' Septimus asked, amused, and Robbie chuckled, knowing that the young lady who served behind the counter at the bakery was too worldly for Robbie.

'Nuh, but she won't say no if I need her to be.'

Septimus smiled and shook his head at the larrikin as he departed. He moved to lock the door behind him. Competitors were rife in the industry, and he should know. Septimus was one of *Higson's Quality Perfumes'* biggest threats – they just didn't know it yet. Septimus returned to his fragrances, each as special to him as a painting to its creator or music to its composer. He hoped to be known for his perfumes one day, and the thought made him hungry with ambition.

Phoebe wasn't expecting Harland back in Brisbane until later this afternoon and was surprised to find him calling her name as she approached the offices of *The Economic Undertaker* at the start of her workday.

'You are back,' she said delightedly, and his expression said he was equally pleased to see her. Phoebe halted. 'Is everything all right?'

'Fine, do not worry,' he assured her, coming to Phoebe's side and removing his hat as they entered the premises. 'We returned on the midnight train and arrived at 6:30 this morning. Gilbert and I went home to freshen up, and I am meeting Bennet at the coroner's office at ten o'clock.' Glancing at the tall grandfather clock in the oak case, taking pride of place in the reception area, assured him he had plenty of time.

'I am glad you are back safely,' she said as they stood alone for just a moment; the family's voices drifted in from the kitchen and tea room.

'In here, Phoebe,' Ambrose called, and with a smile to Harland, Phoebe led the way, and the pair entered.

'You are back!' Julius exclaimed, and Harland went through the same story again. He accepted a cup of tea from Mrs Dobbs and greeted the family. He also accepted a piece of pumpkin pie for breakfast as they sat around the table.

'It's the best,' Ambrose assured him.

'We hope our customers think so,' Randolph said drily, looking at his grandson, who laughed.

'Thank you for the telegram and your insight,' Harland said to Julius. 'It was most helpful, and I shall see Tavish this morning.'

'Has Julius been insightful?' Ambrose looked up, interested. 'Good Lord.'

Phoebe hid her smile as Julius gave his brother a wry look, and Randolph chuckled beside him.

'Occasionally, I'm useful,' Julius retorted. 'As a consequence, tell me we are not exhuming anyone today?'

Harland smiled. 'Well, I haven't been into the office yet, but I think I can safely say the dead can remain buried.'

They heard the door open, and Randolph hurriedly got to his feet to greet clients; Julius followed.

'Duty calls, thank you, Mrs Dobbs,' Ambrose said, rising without his brother's haste.

'May I have a word?' Harland asked, and Phoebe invited him to her workroom; he readily followed, feeling the room's coolness as they descended. He did his best not to watch her graceful form before him on the stairs, keeping his eyes averted to a respectable height.

'Florence looks well,' he remarked on the green plant under the top window.

'Yes. Like me, she appears to be very comfortable here,' Phoebe agreed, admiring Harland's gift.

'Are we alone?' He looked around and followed Phoebe to her empty work table.

'Yes.' She smiled, cocking her head to the side and studying the detective. 'It is wonderful that you have no fear of the afterlife.'

'I didn't say that,' he said with a small smile, 'but I have no fear of those who linger. They can do little harm, and most appear to want your help.' He moved closer and took her hand.

Phoebe yelped, and Harland immediately dropped her hand and stepped backward.

'Teddy! Do you mind?' she exclaimed, looking to her left. Harland breathed again.

'Spirits as chaperones now? Your brothers were not enough?' He rolled his eyes, and Phoebe laughed.

'On the contrary, Detective,' she said, addressing him formally in front of Teddy, 'spirits who are pests is more appropriate.'

'Come now,' Teddy protested. 'Phoebe, surely have you missed me?' he said in his usual charming fashion, a smile on his rakish face.

'Not a bit,' she teased, 'well, maybe a little. Forgive me, Harland, I was just responding to Teddy.'

'Can he assist me any further in investigating his demise?' Harland asked, 'If not, tell him to leave. I was here first,' he said with a hint of a smile.

'Oh, this is the detective on my case. A fine chap indeed,' Teddy said.

'You are a fine chap, apparently,' Phoebe told Harland.

'Of course I am. Do you not agree?' Harland asked.

She laughed and heard footsteps on the stairs. 'That will be Julius checking that you are being honourable,' Phoebe said.

Sure enough, Julius appeared moments later and looked relieved. Harland was unaware that Julius could see Teddy present and thus was satisfied they were not alone.

'I will be but a moment,' Harland assured him.

'I am not checking up on you, well maybe I am,' he conceded, 'but my visit has a purpose. Phoebe, our new clients upstairs, hoped you might call on them and prepare their mother at their home. They have booked the funeral with us,' he assured her. 'It is unorthodox, but apparently, she does not look her best—"rather distressed" was their description—and they wish her to look peaceful before mourners arrive. We will bury her once they have finished their open house.'

'I can come right now if you wish?'

'They are waiting in the hope you might,' Julius said, and Phoebe turned to Harland.

'Was there something I could help you with, Detective? Or was it a social call, which I welcome,' she added hastily with a look to her brother.

'The latter. I was on my way to the office and had just returned from Toowoomba. But I will get to work and not hold you up a moment more,' he said. 'We don't want you getting in trouble with the boss.'

Phoebe smiled. 'He can be tough,' she said, excusing herself, grabbing the small bag of cosmetics and starting for the stairs.

Harland turned to Julius. 'Thank you again for the suggestion of the injection. It was so obscure it never occurred to me.'

'Who would think of injecting themselves with fragrance?' Julius agreed.

'Don't go, Phoebe. Stay, Detective; I want to know what is going on,' Teddy wailed and grabbed for Harland.

Julius instinctively moved to block the spirit, but no contact was made.

'What was that?' Harland asked, stepping back hastily and looking around.

'Nothing. Why did you feel something?' Julius asked curiously as Teddy disappeared, sufficiently chastened.

'No. But you lunged towards me as if blocking something from touching me.' Harland stared at him. 'Do not tell me that you too—'

'No,' Julius said. 'Shall we go?'

Harland nodded and grabbed his hat. He took to the stairs before Julius, not at all convinced about what had just happened and what it meant.

<h1 style="text-align:center">Chapter 22</h1>

AMBROSE ENJOYED THE SHADE of a large tree at South Brisbane cemetery, appreciating the plot the client's family purchased, which was well placed. He donned his usual sober expression, which wasn't as respectful as Julius's permanent serious expression, but it did the job. Ambrose glanced a few times at Julius, who seemed most distracted. He had not even looked at the mourners nearby, and usually, he observed them in case assistance was required. Instead, he appeared to be frowning and staring off into space.

'What is wrong?' Ambrose asked under his breath. They were behind the mourners and far enough away from the priest and ceremony not to be heard.

Julius started, as if he had been woken from slumber, and blinked. 'Nothing.'

'There is something, I know it. You are preoccupied.'

'Business matters.'

'Care to share?'

'No.'

Ambrose studied Julius until he sighed.

'I assure you, all is well,' Julius whispered impatiently.

Ambrose let the matter lie for a short time but then could not ignore his brother's unhappy countenance. 'What is it, Brother?' He knew Julius always softened with the familiar term, and today was no exception.

Julius sighed again. 'I wonder if it is ever possible to keep a secret. If people are capable of it.'

Ambrose looked surprised. 'I believe they can. For example, I never told you that Lucian and I broke your model steam train when we were kids. We swore to keep the secret, and I guess I have, oh, until now.' He gave a small shrug.

'I knew that anyway,' Julius said drily. 'That ridiculous story you made up about a wild dog grabbing it and how you tried to get it back.' He huffed. 'Why didn't you just say it was the pair of you?'

'Because you were scarier then,' Ambrose admitted, and Julius looked ashamed. His volatility after his parents died was unpredictable, and something he had worked on since to make amends. 'What secret do you refer to?' Ambrose asked.

'Phoebe's ability to see spirits.'

Ambrose turned to face him. 'Has she been exposed?'

'No, no, quieten down,' he said, reminding his brother of their solemn duty. 'But it was once just our grandparents, you and me, that knew. Now her girlfriends know—the *Vexed Vixens*—along with Harland, Bennet, Detective Payne, and I wonder if they keep the secret or tell someone and swear them to secrecy and on it goes. It is getting dangerous.'

'I see your point.' Ambrose thought about this for a short while, adjusting his jacket and reaching for his handkerchief, subtly mopping his brow in the morning humidity before returning his hat to his head.

'You could easily deny it with a little mockery and disbelief. Who would believe such a story?' he said. 'The teller risks losing face as much as Phoebe risks being exposed.'

'Perhaps,' Julius agreed.

'Did you have a secret you wished to confess, Brother?'

'No.'

'I see. You know Grandpa believes you have the gift, the same as Phoebe. Can you see anyone here today?'

'You have been discussing me?' Julius asked, annoyed.

'Do not get cranky; we have not singled you out. Grandpa is perpetually worried about all of us. No doubt he discusses me with you.' Ambrose said and looked to his brother for confirmation. 'Somehow, I feel like the mature one in this discussion.'

Julius, caught unaware, gave a small huff of laughter at Ambrose's observation and hurriedly restored his solemn demeanour.

'Do you, Julius? Do you see the spirits, too? I don't know why I can't. How is it that you two are chosen and I am not?'

'I didn't say I saw them, and nor would I wish to be "chosen". Perhaps God has bigger plans for you in this life than seeing the ones who have left it.'

Ambrose brightened. 'Perhaps you are right.'

'The priest is finishing.'

'Yes,' Ambrose righted himself, ready to move in and lower the coffin into the ground before the diggers would return to fill the hole. 'If you do see them, Julius, your secret will be safe with me, I promise you.'

The two men moved into place, and Ambrose took Julius's lack of denial as possible admittance. Perhaps Grandpa was right, but what did this mean? Should he be worried that he was the only one who was quite normal out of the three siblings?

Dr Tavish McGregor clapped his hands together at seeing Detective Harland Stone and Private Investigator Bennet Martin enter his room.

'Ah, you are back early. Excellent. Yes, the answer is yes. The ladies could have died from the perfume injected under their skin, and it is a much more logical explanation as there was no inflammation around the injection site to indicate blood poisoning from a cut or skin rupture. Neither I nor the Toowoomba coroner believe chloroform was in the perfume as we can't recall its sickly, sweet smell. If it were present, it was not in any great quantity, so you can conclude their act of self-injection brought about their poisoning.'

'Good morning, Tavish,' Harland said, and the coroner burst out laughing.

'I forgot myself in my excitement. Good morning to you, Harland, Bennet.'

'Your excitement is contagious,' Bennet said with a grin, 'and given we have just returned from a night train trip, it is what we need to stay propped up.'

The men removed their jackets and hats, enjoying the cool respite in Tavish's room. They sat around a small meeting table in the corner of the room.

'That is a win for the case. We prefer people not to be murdered,' Harland said.

'It is good news indeed,' Bennet agreed. 'My work is done now. I will advise Miss Barr's father of his daughter's mode of death and send him my bill. Hopefully, Miss Beaver's father will also accept that and conclude his business with the other private investigator.'

'Do you not wish to discover who killed the perfume salesman?' Tavish asked.

'No. I will leave that to Harland,' Bennet said, looking smug. 'I try not to seek work unless my coffers are low.'

'Oh, the luxurious life of a kept gentleman,' Tavish said with a dramatic flair, making both gents laugh. He continued in all seriousness, 'I would have liked to have had the liberty of performing an autopsy on Miss Sophia Beaver just to confirm my findings. I believe chloroform in the perfume would have accelerated their deaths, but eventually, the result would have been the same. By the way, where is your young protégé, Detective Payne?'

'Off visiting the perfume manufacturer. We secured his name and address from Harry Beaumont while in Ipswich and thought it high time we paid a call. I believe he is quite safe to do so on his own.'

'He is a likeable but odd young fellow,' Tavish observed, rising to grab some tea cups.

'Yes, and surprisingly useful. I do not regret taking him on at all.' He declined a cup of tea from the pot Tavish kept warm, as did Bennet.

'That tea is an abomination,' Bennet said. 'It always tastes stewed.'

'That's because it is,' Tavish said. 'So where will this case lead you now, Harland?'

'Good question, and thank you for your interest, Tavish,' Harland said in jest, as the coroner was usually quick to close his cases once his work was complete. 'I was beginning to think we should give it away, and we would if it were not for the chloroform you found in the perfume salesman's lungs.'

'And except for this,' Tavish said, smiling and waving a piece of paper at Harland, thus justifying his question. 'A curiosity I stumbled across. I may yet become a detective myself.'

'Heaven help us,' Harland said and grinned.

'I had to contact the next of kin for Mr Teddy Tate to advise we are finished with the autopsy, and the body would be re-interred. It was Mr Tate's uncle, I believe?'

'Yes, Mr Orpheus Humphrey,' Harland confirmed. 'We contacted him about doing the exhumation in the first instance.'

'I knew his name but could not place it, and then when sending the telegram, it came to me like a bolt of lightning,' Tavish said, clicking his fingers. 'Mr Orpheus Humphrey was in the perfume business and split with his business partner. It was a very acrimonious split, and I heard all about it as I was seeing a lass who was a secretary for *Higson's Quality Perfumes* at the time. Plus, it played out in the newspapers like a *Penny Dreadful*. Mind you, my lady stayed to work for George Higson, as Orpheus Humphrey was supposedly a little too handy with his hands.'

Tavish noticed both men stared at him speechlessly.

'No one was murdered,' he assured them, less they should be worried, 'well, that I know about.'

Harland leaned forward. 'So, Teddy Tate's uncle, Orpheus Humphrey, was George Higson's business partner, and Teddy was setting up a rival business with a perfume maker named Septimus Humphrey! That can be no coincidence. Could Septimus be Orpheus's son or another nephew?'

'Highly possible,' Tavish said.

'Mr George Higson must now be back on your suspect list?' Bennet asked.

'Indeed. If he has heard that Teddy Tate was working in his business all this time while helping his uncle—an old enemy—settle up a rival perfumery.' Harland's eyes widened, realising Gilbert might be in danger. He rose and said to the coroner, 'Tavish, you have excelled with the dead and the living!'

Tavish laughed. 'I'd have a celebratory drink, but it is too early, even by my standards,' the Scottish doctor joked.

'I will buy you one after work,' Harland promised. 'But now I best hurry to meet Gilbert at the perfume manufacturer's premises. Something sinister might be afoot, and he is walking straight into it.' He bid both gentlemen good morning, donned his hat and jacket, and departed hastily. The station was on the way, and he would drop in first in case Gilbert was there, before proceeding to the business address that Harry Beaumont supplied for his perfume manufacturer, that of Septimus Humphrey.

If he had learnt anything from the year of tutelage under the guidance of Detective Harland Stone, it was to stop and observe before taking action. Fortunately, on this occasion, Detective Gilbert Payne did just that. It was a frightening experience on his last case that brought the lesson home; he was visiting a suspect and found himself in the street with two threatening men. If it were not for the presence of a constable, who, mind you, despised Gilbert based on his promotion, he might have found himself in great trouble. The recent feelings of being violently in love made him more cautious; there was much to live for, and he would send a note to Miss Emily Yalden later in the morning to advise he had returned and ask if he might call on her.

Your Emily.

He smiled involuntarily at the manner of her signature on the telegram and then berated himself for his lack of concentration. Gilbert stopped at the corner and studied the street. The address he was given for the perfume manufacturer was in a respectable area on Tank Street in the city, on an incline, which allowed Gilbert to study it from down the street without being observed. Most of the buildings in the street housed manufacturers, and this white two-storey brick factory had four businesses under its roof: three small offices on the lower level with separate entries and a large office area taking up the entire top floor.

Gilbert moved closer but could see nothing through the large, arched windows of the businesses on the lower floor due to the glare on the windows. Determining which of the offices was the *Perfume Emporium*, he drew back as a young boy exited, said something to a person in the doorway, and the door was hurriedly closed behind him.

Gilbert's eyes widened. That boy! It was the boy from the bakery who was arrested for Miss Sophia Beaver's murder and released. That night, he had not gone to the cell with Detective Stone, but he had seen the boy released the next morning, and it was surely him. Gilbert took off down the street, keeping a respectful distance from the boy and slipping into doorways if needed to slow his step or hide. The boy was moving fast now, most likely keen to return to work. Gilbert was pleased to reach George Street, where he could duck and weave amongst more people and traffic without risking being seen. Shortly after, he arrived on Ann Street and, sure enough, the young man went into the bakery and donned an apron.

This was most interesting, Gilbert thought, trying to reason how the boy accused of giving a poisoned pastry to Miss Beaver was connected with Teddy Tate's perfume manufacturer. Gilbert decided it was best to return to Roma Street Police Headquarters and tell Detective Stone before venturing back to the perfume manufacturer's business.

Chapter 23

THE VERY HANDSOME GENTLEMAN with the cultured British accent, dressed as if money was no object, waited at the newspaper office's reception for Miss Lilly Lewis.

'Some toff to see you upstairs, Miss Lewis,' one of the young copy runners said as he passed Lilly's desk and kept going.

'You're not dating a toff, are you, Lilly?' Frank asked, stopping mid-sentence in his writing and frowning at her.

She looked at the journalist, who was not much older than herself but rough as they came; a cigarette was always dangling from his lips, and he was no stranger to the track where he won and lost on the horses in equal amounts.

'Since you're married, Frank, I've been left little choice,' she retorted, and the men in the newsroom chuckled. They could always anticipate a good rejoinder from Miss Lilly Lewis.

Frank grinned. 'Fair enough then. Let me know if you need me to keep him in line.'

'Thank you, Frank. But you will have to stand behind my five brothers to do so.'

As Fergus had departed to speak with Miss Sophia Beaver's father, hopeful of a comment from him on his daughter injecting perfume under her skin—he was not expecting cooperation—Lilly raced upstairs, hoping Bennet would have news for her.

As always, upon seeing him, she was taken by his handsomeness and surprised that he found her of interest. She was nothing like Phoebe, whom he once carried a flame for, and certainly not the English lady she imagined he would normally charm. Lilly was also surprised at the increase in her heart rhythm. Was she truly falling for him? On seeing her, she saw the look of delight in his eyes.

'You are back and here. Do you have news?' she asked, hurrying towards him. Her eyes were bright with excitement, and she extended her hands, which Bennet accepted in his.

'Yes, I am back and here, and I have news,' he teased, clasping her hands and placing a kiss upon one of them. 'Are you pleased to see me?'

'Oh, it goes without saying,' she said, leading him outside through the large doors.

'No, go on, say it,' he nudged Lilly, and she laughed.

'Why, Mr Martin, I believe you are fishing for my feelings. All right then. I am pleased you are back, and I am pleased to set eyes on you.'

His smile lit his face. 'That was sincere, my word, thank you. And I am pleased to be back in town where you are nearby.'

They moved to a small green area where many of the journalists escaped for lunch if they were not frequenting the pub, and Bennet went to wipe the seat for Lilly, but she promptly sat down.

'I am no delicate flower, Bennet,' she said, addressing him informally now they were only in each other's company.

'Be that as it may, that does not mean I won't treat you like a lady.' He gazed upon her for a moment before starting in a serious tone. 'Lilly—'

'Oh, am I in trouble?' she frowned.

'What? No, why would you think that? I was going to say I would like to meet your father and ask to court you.'

Lilly laughed. 'How deliciously old-fashioned and formal.'

'Is it?' Bennet frowned. 'May I?'

'It is an odd time to ask me at the start of my workday and yours.'

'I know we are both busy,' he said, though his time was his own to manage, 'but having been away from you, I had to come first thing and ask. I will then be able to focus on the rest of my day.'

She smiled with delight. 'It is good to see you; I confess I missed you.'

'Did you? That is wonderful.'

'It did not feel wonderful, but I understand your meaning. So yes, Bennet, you may ask my father, but only if you ask me first.'

Bennet grinned. 'Miss Lilly Lewis, will you do me the great honour of allowing me to win your heart?'

But still, she did not respond. Instead, Lilly frowned and turned slightly to face Bennet so she was not distracted by the comings and goings at the newspaper office.

'Bennet, I know we spoke of this before, in jest, I thought, but I must clarify, I am not the dainty type.'

'But yet you are very much a lady.'

'I will not be the type of girl either of your parents would wish to see you court or marry.'

'Why ever not?'

'Well, firstly, we don't have the class system as the mother country does. I will not come with a dowry or want to keep your house.'

'I don't need your dowry, nor do I expect you to keep my house. I would like you to keep my bed,' he said racily, and she hit his arm playfully.

'Oh, good heavens! Be serious, as we will not have this discussion again.' Lilly's blue eyes sized him up to ensure he understood what he was getting in this bargain. Bennet nodded, and his countenance changed, his expression becoming sincere.

'I love my work and want to continue my career even if we should go as far as to marry.'

'I accept that.'

'Do you?' Lilly asked, surprised.

'Yes. You are resolved to marry, though, and have a family?'

'Yes, I have no objection to marrying the right man and having a family. Not a large one, though, like my own. Maybe two children, a boy and a girl,' she mused, and, seeing his amused expression, she smiled.

'Not six children then, like your own family?'

'Never,' she said and shuddered. 'The thing that I struggle with... is that you are a kept man, Bennet, and I am not sure I can accept that. And don't deny it,' she said, holding up her hand to stop him as he went to protest. 'I am from a working family; my father and brothers have trades. You told me your mother sends you funds while your father has cut you off, believing it will bring you home sooner. Your dear mother is probably missing out on fulfilling her own needs while she funds you.'

The more she spoke, the more his countenance changed, as if she had insulted him, not that it was her intention. When she finished speaking, he regarded her cooly for a few moments.

'Your disagreement with my lifestyle is noted.' His voice was curt, and he nodded and looked away.

A cold distance settled between them, and she thought of moving closer. Instead, Lilly waited, as she had learned to do in the interviews conducted for the newspaper. She did not speak, allowing him time to gather his thoughts, but she could tell she had angered him. Bennet cleared his throat.

'I have spoken too casually about my arrangement, Lilly, as I didn't realise it was of consideration. It is best I clarify my situation,' he began. 'I am not idle. I earn from my artwork and my private investigation business. I earn enough to keep my rooms and two staff. My mother is not sending me her pin money, nor would I ever allow her to go unfulfilled to support me.' He said the words with an edge of anger, and Lilly nodded.

'Forgive me, I did not think that, honestly. I am prone to say too much to make my point, or so my brothers would tell you,' Lilly said, giving him her full attention and fascinated by this different side of Bennet – serious and intense and very attractive at this moment.

Bennet softened a little and continued. 'Lilly, my parents are not lords and ladies. My father is very senior in the greater London metropolitan police force and earns a large salary. His and my mother's families were very wealthy, and that wealth was passed on to them. They have not earned it. It's old family money. I will also benefit from it, as will my children, and I feel no guilt about doing so. My mother is worried about my lifestyle here. She thinks it is the colonies, and I live in a shack and eat from a can.' He smiled slightly at the thought. 'Nothing will convince her otherwise until she comes over and sees for herself. I am sure they will do so when I get married.'

Lilly nodded. 'I see.'

Bennet shook his head. 'You don't. My mother supports several charities and gives them her time and money. Every month, Father signs the cheques that are donated to them. Among her charities is a fairly new one called "Wayward Children", of which I am the only benefactor.'

Lilly laughed.

'My father knows very well that the cheques are coming to me, and his bookkeeper no doubt tells him they are cashed in Australia. It is the funds I would be given if I lived in England and had a rightful claim to; they are from my trust fund. So, you see, my parents have a sense of humour; they are hard-working people and will admire the same in a lady of my choosing. I am not some idle fop waiting for a handout.'

Lilly looked uncharacteristically abashed. 'Forgive me, Bennet? I did not research you well enough. Not at all, truth be known.'

'I have allowed my friends to make light of my situation as it amuses them, and I accept I gave you that impression,' Bennet hurriedly added.

'You did, and you are still a kept man whether or not you like it, Bennet. A trust fund, no less.'

He shrugged. 'If the situation were reversed, would you turn down the funds?'

'No,' she said without hesitation. 'I might start my own newspaper!'

'Well, there you have it! So, shall we make this official? You and me – Martin and Lewis. Now that has a ring to it,' he teased.

Lilly smiled. 'It does. Let us then,' she said enthusiastically, her heart pattering at the thought of such a handsome and interesting suitor. She offered her hand to shake, and he turned it over, kissing her palm in a most flirtatious fashion.

Lilly pulled her hand back. 'I shall arrange an invitation for you to come and meet my parents.'

Bennet beamed. 'Splendid.'

'And five brothers.'

'Oh.' His smile faded. 'All at once?'

'Most likely. Best to get it over with in one fell swoop, don't you think?'

'Righto then, lead me to the battlefield,' he said, resigned, and Lilly laughed.

'Do not be so dramatic. So, what do you have for me?'

'Oh, a story, of course,' he teased. 'I have just come from the coroner's office with Harland, and the deceased ladies did not have chloroform on their person as far as both coroners can recall without having conducted autopsies, and Teddy Tate did. But Tavish said it is safe to conclude their death was from self-injection. And you will need to check with Harland whether you can publish this, but there's a connection between Teddy's next of kin and Mr

Higson, whom he worked for... they are ex-business partners and had a heated feud.'

Lilly gasped. 'Oh, this is too good. This story has so many ups and downs; nothing is clear cut, and I confess I'm a little disappointed that the ladies died by their own hands. I must get to the Roma Street Police Headquarters and catch the detectives immediately.'

'I shall give you a lift; I am going that way.'

'Are you really?' she asked, cocking her head to the side.

'I am now.'

With the exception of Mrs Dobbs with her tea tray—and she normally stopped on the first few steps—not many light treads made their way down the stairs to Phoebe's room.

Looking up, she thought the visitor might be Lilly, but then her future sister-in-law, Violet, came into sight.

'May I come in, Phoebe?'

'Of course, Violet, how lovely to see you.' Seeing Violet's sober expression, Phoebe hurriedly asked, 'Is everything all right?'

'Perfectly so. I know I rarely visit, but do not be alarmed,' Violet said with a smile as she reached the bottom of the stairs, her eyes going to Phoebe's work tables.

'I have no clients,' Phoebe assured her. 'I am just unpacking my kit. I have been out to make up a lady in her own home who looked distressed in death; it was sudden, and the family is arriving to pay their respects. She will be collected later for burial.'

'I didn't know you did such a thing.'

'It is rare, but we are happy to be of service when families can't manage for themselves.'

The two young ladies were quite a picture – Phoebe, fair in hair and face in a fitted white blouse and flowing navy skirt; Violet, with her dark hair pinned up and her creamy skin highlighted by a modest and professional burgundy dress.

Violet took the offered seat at Phoebe's workbench, watching as the powder cases were wiped and stored.

'Ooh, some of these powders look good enough for the living to use,' Violet said, studying one of the colours that was not dissimilar to her own skin colouring.

'I have occasionally given my face a slight sweep,' Phoebe said with a grin.

'Are we alone, you know, from the other type of clients?' Violet asked in a low voice.

'The spirits? You are the second person to ask me that today. Harland dropped in earlier and did the same,' she said with a smile.

'Ah, he is back from Toowoomba. Julius told me that the detectives and Mr Martin were taking the train. I hope the trip was successful.'

'I believe so. They decided to return on the overnight train rather than have a good night's sleep in a hotel and return the next day. He gets impatient when on a case.'

'Perhaps so, or maybe he was missing someone,' Violet teased. 'So, is it just you and me?' she asked again.

Phoebe smiled. 'I hope he misses me, and yes, we are alone. I promise you I'm not that social and don't invite company unless I can be of service.'

Violet gave a huff of laughter. 'I had not pictured you entertaining the dead down here, with a dance in swing, and drinks being served.'

'I might not be short of a partner if that were the case,' Phoebe laughed at the thought. 'So, is this a welcomed social visit?'

'No, I wouldn't dream of socialising during work hours. You have met my boss,' Violet said with a playful look of fright, and both ladies smiled at the thought of Julius, whom they loved differently. 'If I may, I hope to talk with you about the subject of spirits.'

'Of course,' Phoebe sobered and stopped what she was doing, studying her newest friend. They had become close, and Violet would soon officially be family when she wed Julius.

'In confidence?' Violet asked.

'As you wish.'

Violet looked to the stairs to ensure they were alone and spoke in a low voice. 'Julius told me he can see spirits.'

'Goodness me, did he?' Phoebe exclaimed. 'That does surprise me.'

'Don't you think he should have?' Violet frowned.

'Yes, of course I do. I am surprised because he only told me very recently, but I had long suspected as much. Uncle Reggie said he could, but Julius would not own to it.'

'Did I hear my name mentioned?' the handsome Reginald Astin appeared, draped over the chair with casual elegance.

Phoebe continued, ignoring her Uncle Reggie, as Violet wanted to be alone. She gave him a hint. 'I can understand that the presence of spirits might make you nervous, Violet, but I promise you, I have never had cause to fear them,' Phoebe continued with a subtle glance at her uncle. 'Now, Julius has told two of us in such a short time. I wonder if he will start owning to it.'

'I asked him directly. He said he would not have told me if I had not.'

'I asked him directly a hundred times,' Reggie huffed. 'Fat lot of good that did me,' he said, making a pest of himself.

'I think it is wise that you asked him,' Phoebe said softly. 'I am glad he was honest with you; that must have been very hard for him.'

'That's a good way to look at it. I was a little put out as he said he would not have told me if I had not asked.'

'Perhaps he feared he would lose you,' Phoebe suggested.

'Lord no. If she has put up with him for this long, what's a visiting spirit or two?' Reggie piped up.

'Has he lost you?' Phoebe said with a small gasp. Reggie leaned forward, now looking as concerned as his great niece.

'No, nothing like that, but it has alarmed me.'

Phoebe breathed again, and Reggie sat back with a grunt.

'He would not have told me either,' Phoebe said, 'except I was overwhelmed recently, and he stepped up for my benefit and told the spirit to leave.'

Violet's breath hitched. 'That is what I am frightened of, that we will be overwhelmed or harmed.'

'No, Violet dear, nothing like that. It was the debutante. I agreed to help her, but she pestered me because she was spoilt and indulgent and would not cease. The room I was in was hot and stuffy, and it was nothing more than that, I assure you.'

'Oh, thank goodness. So, you have never been harmed or felt fear?'

'No. On occasion, a spirit has been insistent, but I assure you, when Julius ignores them, they assume he cannot see them and soon depart. They remain with me as I engage with them.'

'Except me. He never fooled me,' Reggie said.

'That is a relief,' Violet said, her shoulders slumping as if she had been carrying the weight of the world on them. 'I feared they would hover, and someone would always be present.'

'I, for one, have better things to do than harass the living. And I saw that glance, young lady. I am not harassing you, merely giving you the pleasure of my company,' he said with a wink, and Phoebe schooled her face not to laugh.

'May I ask you some more questions if I am not being a nuisance?'

Phoebe smiled. 'You are definitely not being a nuisance, so please do. But Julius would answer you honestly if you asked him.'

'I believe he would, but given what you just said, his experience is not as broad as yours as you are engaging with them. Do you see them at home?'

'God spare me. I love Julius, but I do not seek his company after hours. He is not that pleasant during business hours,' Reggie piped up.

Phoebe shot him a menacing look before responding to Violet.

'I rarely see anyone at home and do not encourage that. I am not a psychic, nor interested in conducting seances. I lend my services only to those at the end of their journey who cannot rest in peace because of unfulfilled business in this life. Most appear in my workroom beside their bodies in their final moments.'

Violet nodded, taking in Phoebe's words.

'Do not fear. You will not wake to find spirits in your house or find yourself in danger. And you know how Julius loves you; he will always protect you.'

'Thank you, Phoebe, I feel much better,' Violet said, feeling more reassured. 'Are we still alone?'

'No, there's a queue of seven people waiting to speak with me.'

'Really?' Violet looked shocked.

'No.'

Violet laughed and playfully hit Phoebe's hand. 'Very naughty of you.'

Phoebe grinned. 'My Uncle Reggie has dropped in to visit.'

'Oh, he is the handsome one, your grandfather's brother? I saw his portrait when your grandmother gave me the tour of your home.'

'I like this charming young lady. I think she might be my favourite.'

Phoebe laughed. 'He likes you above all others.'

'As it should be,' Violet agreed with a small laugh. 'Thank you, Phoebe, for being so honest with me. I guess if you can give people peace and justice, that is a blessing too.'

'I like to think so.'

The sound of footsteps thundering overhead and heading to Phoebe's room had her rolling her eyes.

'That will be Ambrose in the lead and Grandpa behind him,' she said, making Violet laugh at her tone. Her grandfather's footsteps stopped to the right, where the reception desk was located. Ambrose's pounding continued towards them.

'What does Julius sound like, since you can tell them all apart by their footsteps?'

'Very quiet. Sometimes, he appears without my hearing him. And no, he is not a ghost,' Phoebe hurriedly added.

'You had me spooked for a moment,' Violet laughed.

'Ladies,' Ambrose said, hurrying down the stairs. 'Such beauty in one spot, and you too, Phoebe,' he teased.

'Hello, Ambrose,' Violet said with a smile and a grateful nod for the compliment.

'Reggie is here too,' Phoebe said, indicating the chair where he sat, which remained empty to the naked eye.

'Ah, the handsome uncle I've been told I take after. Hello, Uncle Reggie. I would ask if you are well, but that's a moot point, isn't it?' he joked and returned his attention to Phoebe. 'Pray tell, where is Julius? He was troubled at this morning's funeral, and now I have lost him.'

'I have no idea. I assumed he was with you.'

Violet shook her head when Ambrose looked her way. 'I have not seen him since our evening walk in the park.'

'Did he not enter the office when he returned with you?' Phoebe now looked worried.

'No, we departed at the cemetery; he said he had to attend to something. I drove back alone. Do not concern yourselves; Julius may have paid a visit to his bookkeeper or Lucian,' Ambrose said as tension filled the surrounding air.

'But he always advises us if he intends to do so,' Phoebe said, beginning to worry.

'I fear he may be upset,' Violet said, biting her bottom lip. 'We had… a different view on a matter,' she explained to Ambrose.

Ambrose gave a low moan. 'He was very contemplative at this morning's funeral and looked as if he had not slept well. We have a funeral in an hour. I'll have to… I'll sort it out and find Julius,' he said with a wave and departed just as noisily as he arrived.

'I am sure there is no cause for alarm,' Phoebe said.

'I hope you are right,' Violet said, her voice edged with emotion. 'I will return to work. Will you please let me know if he arrives, Phoebe? If he comes in through the back entry, Mary won't see him to alert me.'

'Of course.' Although she was concerned herself, Phoebe tried to remove the worry from Violet's countenance; it was out of character for Julius. 'Before you go, would you like to try a little of this powder? It is your shade.'

'Boring. I'll go find your brother,' Reggie said, and with a cheeky smile to his great-niece, he disappeared.

Chapter 24

Julius occasionally visited the graves of his parents, rarely during a working day, but he needed to think and get away. Leaving Ambrose and his incessant questions, he went to the far side of the cemetery, out of sight, to where his parents rested. He had not slept for fear of losing Violet. She had not liked his truth; he didn't particularly like it either, but it could not be denied, and it would not go away. He saw the spirits like Phoebe did, like his mother before him and her father before her. There appeared to be no rhyme or reason as to who inherited the gift, and he hoped by refusing it, it would go away; it didn't.

Julius loved Violet from the moment he had set eyes upon her, standing on the stairs when he arrived to take away her grandmother for burial. Vulnerable, beautiful and strong, all at once. She was the embodiment of his desire. No one had stolen his heart before, and he could not lose her; the thought was unbearable. But last evening, she had looked at him as if he were a different person, as if she feared him. Her hand felt limp on his arm; she was distracted, and her eyes did not meet his. Julius was firmly convinced he should not have mentioned his unwanted gift to anyone, including his future wife.

He sat on the edge of his father's grave, his jacket and hat resting on his mother's grave next to it. Why had he never been able to see or talk with his parents? If he must be subjected to this curse, why must he put up with visits from people who are meaningless in his life? Except for Uncle Reggie, of course.

He took a deep breath. There was no point in dwelling on it; what will be, will be. If Violet left him now, then he would ensure she kept her role and was not exposed to him. How the future would look for him, he could not say; it was too bleak, too dark to contemplate.

'Everyone is worried about you.'

Julius jumped and turned to see his Uncle Reggie lounging on the grave.

'You nearly scared me to death,' Julius grumbled.

'Then you are in the right place. The ladies are worried, as is your grandfather.'

'Ladies?'

'Yes, your fiancé and sister.'

Julius received this information with some relief. 'I shall return now.'

'What is wrong, nephew? I am a good listener even if I cannot bodily help,' Uncle Reggie said and then disappeared. Julius turned to see what had caused him to depart and saw a man walking toward him.

'Hello, are you all right there?' The man called, and Julius rose just in time to stop a large, shaggy black dog almost landing upon him, the man following some distance behind. The dog sat promptly before Julius as if it had been ordered to do so.

'Hello there, you're a big boy,' Julius said cautiously. Extending his hand, he found it still intact without a bite. He patted the large dog before reaching down for his coat and hat.

'Oh, it's you, Mr Astin, beg your pardon; I didn't mean to disturb you,' Mr Redford, the senior grave digger, said, his son not by his side as he normally was during the workday.

'Hello, Mr Redford. You did not disturb me; thank you for your concern. I was paying a visit to my parents.'

Mr Redford looked behind Julius. 'Ah, they've been gone a while then,' he deduced from the weathered colours of the gravestones as he could not read. He did all right without the need to do so. 'I'm sorry for that.'

'Seems like a very long time. Fourteen years now. Is this your handsome dog?'

'No. The wife will not allow a dog; she has two cats.' The word "cats" was said with a slight hiss and a lack of enthusiasm. 'He's a fine fellow, and I'd prefer him over the cats, that's for sure. He's here most days. I suspect his owner has turned up his toes.'

'You are a fine-looking fellow,' Julius agreed with Mr Redford and, still speaking to the dog, added, 'you should have a good meal and a master to walk beside.' Julius rested his hand on the tall, lean dog's head. He always wanted a dog but never seemed to organise himself to get one. 'Do you know his name?'

'No, can't say that I do. He needs a home. You might suit each other; he's only a young dog by the looks of him.'

'Perhaps he's happy here,' Julius said, looking around. 'It's a peaceful home.'

'Well, if he follows you, you'll know. I best get going; my lad's waiting for me. We've got one of your funerals in under an hour.'

That stirred Julius into action. 'Good Lord, what time have you, Mr Redford?'

The man held out his timepiece for Julius to read.

'I'll be in serious trouble when I return.'

'Aren't you the boss?' Mr Redford asked, confused.

'Yes, but some days, you would never know it,' Julius said in jest, feeling better for the human and canine company.

Mr Redford laughed and, bidding Julius farewell, continued on his way.

'Well then, young fellow, I am heading to work. Is this farewell then, or shall I hail a ride that will take us both?' He put on his jacket and hat, tipping it at the dog, who immediately stood and walked beside Julius.

To see them, one would have thought they had always been together, perfectly in step for a hurried return to the office of *The Economic Undertaker*.

Harland exhaled with relief on finding the young detective in the office. 'Gilbert, excellent. I was worried I had sent you into danger. I have learnt—'

'Sir, I saw something we should discuss, something that made little sense—'

The two detectives talked over each other as Detective Harland Stone hurriedly entered their office in the Roma Street Police Headquarters. They both stopped.

'Sorry, Sir, you were saying?' Gilbert asked, rising from behind his desk.

Harland removed his hat and threw it onto his desk. He moved to the board and studied the names that Gilbert had written up – the list of players in their mystery.

'Dr McGregor has just mentioned an extraordinary connection between the deceased – Teddy Tate, his next of kin uncle Orpheus Humphrey, and Mr Higson from *Higson's Quality Perfumes*.'

Gilbert moved to the board, arming himself with chalk to write up the connection. 'That is very suspicious, Sir. Especially as the perfume maker is Septimus Humphrey, a cousin of Teddy, and he may be Orpheus Humphrey's son unless there are more brothers.'

'My thoughts exactly. You know the old saying: revenge is best served cold. No doubt the Humphrey clan was planning to compete with Higson, and the salesmen were well on their way to siphoning Higson's customers. But is there more afoot? What have you got, Gilbert?'

'I saw the young man who was released from the cells coming out of the address where Septimus Humphrey manufactures his perfume.'

Harland muttered an oath.

'A similar thought to my own, Sir,' Gilbert said with uncharacteristic humour. 'I didn't go in and came straight here.'

'Excellent, Detective,' Harland said, amused by his protégé's small joke. He grabbed his hat again. Gilbert swelled with the praise. To be called Detective by his superior was a glowing endorsement. 'I am glad you took that lesson on. Let's go there now.'

Gilbert gathered his belongings. 'It was not one I will forget, Sir. Being cornered by two men who were no strangers to fighting was not my best day on the job.'

They hurriedly departed to visit the Perfume Emporium's premises and meet the perfume manufacturer, Mr Septimus Humphrey.

On arrival twenty minutes later, the men could see little resemblance between Septimus and his cousin, the deceased Teddy Tate. Teddy was a handsome man who spent time on his appearance and dress. Septimus looked more like an absent professor who would forget to comb his hair if left to his own devices.

'I wondered when you would find your way to me, Detectives,' Septimus Humphrey said in a refined British accent. He held the door open for them to enter.

'Why is that, Mr Humphrey?' Harland asked.

The man shrugged. 'My cousin was killed. Inevitably, you would have discovered his burgeoning side business if you investigated his death, and here I am at the helm.'

'And was it your father who is Teddy's next of kin, the uncle?' Gilbert asked.

'Orpheus Humphrey, one and the same,' Septimus confirmed, his tone crisp and professional with no hint of endearment to acknowledge his paternity.

'Are you the perfume maker for this new business, a chemist perhaps?' Harland asked.

'I am a perfume manufacturer, Detective. My father, who was in the business before me and is now retired, inspired me. Mind you, he did not manufacture perfumes but, during his time, was one of the most successful salesmen in the field, as he is bound to tell you if you should make his acquaintance. Take a seat if you wish,' Septimus said, indicating the high stools near his workbench where he stood on the other side. The detectives took up the offer.

'What is the biggest challenge for your new business, Mr Humphrey?' Gilbert asked with curiosity. 'Is it finding a unique fragrance?'

'Surprisingly, no, Detective. Most fragrances are versions and variations of each other. But how it is presented is big business. My father used to ask his ladies to be his muse because he always said, "Ladies talk and talk some more, and the prettier they are, the more everyone wants to be like them, wear what they are wearing, and smell as they smell".' He shrugged. 'Teddy took this on board and used the same technique mixed with his own charm.' Now, Septimus smiled, and his features softened.

'Did you ever see him apply this technique?' Harland asked.

'Oh yes. When I started, I wanted to see the ladies' reaction to my perfume, so I went with him on his house calls a couple of times. He tempted the ladies. He used to sniff the perfume, roll his eyes in rapture, tell them all about it, sniff again, and continue. They are panting for it by the time he allows them to try it.'

Harland looked to Gilbert, as he often did when he wanted his protégé to note something important. In this case, Septimus confirmed Teddy had inhaled the perfume numerous times. Given that chloroform was in the bottle, that might explain why he collapsed, but was it enough to fell him?

Septimus continued, 'There will always be women who like the comfortable fragrances, handkerchief perfumes we call them, like Colgate's *Cashmere Bouquet Perfume*, but many young ladies want to make their own mark in the world.'

'It is a big market, I imagine,' Harland said.

'Always was, always will be,' Septimus agreed. 'Thank goodness for the vanity of women.'

'Beauty is only skin deep,' Gilbert said, and impressed his superior. Clearly, the young detective was fishing for a reaction to the line found in the deceased women's garments. Septimus's eyes widened.

'I could not agree more, Detective. To find a beautiful woman who is also kind and clever, now that would be a feat,' Septimus said with an edge of bitterness.

Harland left that well alone. The ladies in his acquaintance whom he regarded as beautiful, displayed no vanity, only modesty – Miss Phoebe Astin came immediately to mind. 'Mr Humphrey, why would someone wish to kill your cousin?'

Septimus shook his head. 'I cannot fathom, Detective, and now Harry and I are at a loss how to proceed with the business. We may have to recruit another salesman, but we are not in a position yet to pay staff.'

'Surely you can see how this is unethical, Mr Humphrey?' Gilbert asked, surprised.

'Oh no, Detective, quite the opposite, if you knew our family history.'

'Let's have it then,' Harland said. 'Tell us why you, along with your cousin—the late Mr Teddy Tate—and your colleague, Harry Beaumont, are keen to rival Mr Higson.'

'It's a long, sorry tale.'

'Be brief and succinct if you will,' Harland said and added 'please' as an afterthought.

Septimus did not look pleased at having his pending performance clipped and began his tale with an exaggerated sigh.

'My father, Orpheus, met George Higson when they were boys. Their parents were on the same ship sailing to Australia, and their families remained close friends. George had an outstanding mind for business, and my father was exceptionally handsome and, like his namesake, Orpheus, could charm all living things,' Septimus said with pride.

'In Greek mythology, Orpheus had the skill to charm, but the name itself means "darkness of the night",' Gilbert mused.

'Is that so, Detective?' Septimus asked. 'Well, I assure you, my father was like a light, a candle to moths when it came to women. So, George and my father made a good team, and with the help of their parents, they bought a struggling perfume business and made it their own. It was very successful. My father headed sales, and George Higson managed the business. George still does.'

'When did it all fall apart?' Harland asked.

'It does me a disservice to air the family business, but as it is an investigation, I shall elaborate,' Septimus said as if he had a choice. 'The partnership collapse was reported widely at the time. You have undoubtedly discovered that the men had a very public feud.' He did not wait for their response. 'My father fell in love with Mrs Higson, and she with him. She was a beautiful, accomplished woman who came from a wealthy family. While George Higson was not a handsome man in appearance, I imagine he won her hand with his kindness, clever mind, and the promise of a very comfortable life. But then she met my father. Their love was mutual, and George Higson agreed to divorce her if, and only if, he was given the business completely.'

'Quite a trade,' Harland said. 'Then he put it in his name?'

'Yes, but Father was sure he could build another business, and he and Mrs Higson were in love. Being self-made, George Higson had refused her dowry, and my father hoped he might get it. He did not, as the divorce scandalised her parents. But ever confident, he agreed to hand over the business; she divorced and married

Father, and Mrs Higson, now Mrs Humphrey, gave birth to me and, several years later, my sister. But the marriage was soon in trouble. My mother accused him of having a wandering eye, and he reminded her it was his job to charm in order to sell and keep her in the comforts she expected and deserved.'

'It didn't last then?' Harland asked.

'No. My mother sailed to England to be with her family and took me and my sister. George Higson would have nothing to do with my father despite his pleas, apologies, and requests to reform their partnership. *Higson's Quality Perfumes* went from strength to strength. My father does not have a mind for the administration of business and remained a salesman on a wage.'

'I can't say I blame George Higson. What would he gain by taking your father back?' Harland asked.

'The best salesman in the business, an old friend he might reunite with, a man who knew the business inside and out. A better man would have forgiven him,' Septimus said, and neither detective looked convinced.

'How did you come to be here in Australia and reunite with your father, Mr Humphrey?' Gilbert asked.

'When my mother died, I had reached adulthood, so I came here. My father was not keen to reunite with me and blamed my mother and his old business partner for all his woes. To say my father is bitter is an understatement. But I became very close to my cousin, Teddy.'

'A bitter father cannot be easy to live with,' Gilbert said.

'No, and that is why my cousin, Teddy, and I wanted to build our business. For him, for us. We had a plan and thought it might restore his sense of worth. My father is still attractive and could sell to a mature market, while Teddy and Harry captured the young ladies.'

'Why would Mr Higson employ Teddy Tate? Did he not know the connection to your family, that he was Orpheus Humphrey's nephew?' Gilbert asked.

'No, isn't that too good to be true?' Septimus said and chuckled. 'Teddy always expected to be called into his office and dismissed, but Higson never found out. But there is nothing illegal going on, so you need not get your cuffs out. I am creating new fragrances for us, and we are not stealing them. While Teddy and Harry might convince some of Higson's client base to try our new products, they are still selling Higson's perfumes to them.'

'If George Higson did not know that Teddy was his enemy's nephew, then it is unlikely that he had a reason to harm Teddy unless he learnt of your business,' Harland said. He rarely offered theories to those he interviewed, but a desire to see Septimus's reaction won out.

'I don't know how he would have heard of us, and there are other perfume manufacturers besides us in business. Anyway, Teddy said George Higson never did due diligence on competitors, focussing only on his own products. Given Teddy was his top salesman—just like Teddy's uncle, my father, once was—Teddy could do no wrong.'

Harland was less than convinced. 'The young man Detective Payne saw departing earlier this morning, what is his connection to you.'

Septimus looked surprised and hesitated as if looking for a lie to explain the sighting, but he sighed, his shoulders slumping when he could not.

'Robbie is an innocent boy. Thank you for releasing him. He had nothing to do with the death of those women, but he is working for us.'

'Doing what?' Harland asked with obvious suspicion in his voice. He had let the boy go, and his instincts had told him at the time the boy was innocent; it would be a setback to think he got it wrong.

'Robbie works in the bakery. He's street smart and got a smart mouth, but—'

Harland interrupted. 'Are we talking about the same boy? The one I met was nervous and tearful?'

Septimus laughed. 'He can perform as needed, that boy; he said he had you convinced.'

Harland was not amused or impressed.

Septimus sobered on seeing the detective's countenance and continued. 'Robbie grew up on the streets. He got one over on you, Detective, but he's no criminal, and he wouldn't harm anyone.'

'Who is he to you and the business then?'

'Harry, our other salesman…'

'We've met Harry Beaumont in Ipswich while he was covering Mr Tate's route,' Gilbert said.

'Right, well, Harry's father owns the bakery,' he said, explaining the connection between the remaining salesman and the boy. 'One night, Harry's father was set upon when heading home with the day's earnings in his pocket. The boy helped him; he's a good little fighter. Mr Beaumont offered him an apprenticeship and a room to live in at the back of the bakery in return for the good deed. Robbie's doing quite well, I believe.'

'I see. What does he do for you?' Harland asked again.

'He's a spotter for want of a better term, and Robbie earns a few extra dollars for his labours. He tells us if he meets a young lady who could be a perfume muse for us, what she likes and when she comes into the bakery, and Harry just happens to be there on that day to charm her and get her on board. Harry's dad, the baker, is happy to support that, as you can imagine. He's mighty proud of Harry and wants the perfume business to succeed. Besides, we're just flattering them and offering them perfume. No crime in that, or we would all be locked up.'

The two detectives exchanged a look, and with that, Harland thanked Septimus for his time.

'Do you have any leads, Detective? Anyone you think might have killed my poor cousin, Teddy?'

'Nothing we can reveal at this stage,' Harland said on departing. Once outside, he mumbled, 'Nothing at all, in fact.'

Gilbert sighed. 'Back to the chalkboard, Sir?'

Harland stood for a moment, surveying the area and thinking. 'No, Gilbert. We have nothing. So, we shall do what I always suggest in these circumstances.' He looked to Gilbert, expecting him to know.

'Start over, Sir.'

'Precisely. Let's go back to the beginning. Let's go to the site where Teddy Tate died and talk to the young lady he was selling perfume to when he had his collapse.'

Gilbert opened his notebook and thumbed through the pages, finding the address. With that, the men departed with no new leads and no suspects.

Chapter 25

Julius was accompanied by a large black dog when he entered through the back of the business.

'Where have you been, Lad?' Randolph asked, relieved to see him and then annoyed. 'We were worried. Will put on his suit and filled in for you. He and Ambrose left thirty minutes ago for the funeral, and Phoebe and Miss Forrester were beside themselves.'

For just a moment, Julius's anger flared. It had been a long time since he had been quick to anger, and it was irrational. But he didn't feel like answering to anyone or being reprimanded like an employee of the business he had created.

Behind him, Phoebe raced up the stairs, and the front door opened. Violet rushed in.

'I was so worried about you,' she said, throwing her arms around his waist and hugging him without self-consciousness.

'Julius, you are very inconsiderate to make us worry,' Phoebe scolded him, and seeing their faces, his anger was diffused.

'Thank goodness you are all right, Mr Astin. I'll put the kettle on,' Mrs Dobbs said, appearing in the doorway, her hand on her heart, and disappearing just as quickly.

Violet released him and stepped back. 'I am sure I have aged ten years.'

'I have only been gone a few hours,' he said, frustrated at the dramatics.

'According to Ambrose, you were most distant and then ambled off without a word and have been gone three hours now,' Phoebe pointed out. 'He waited a while and then returned.'

'And you missed a funeral. Most out of character, and enough to raise concern,' Randolph added.

Julius took a deep breath, his hand resting on the head of the large dog beside him as if observing a scene from a stage production.

'Oh my, who is this beautiful dog? Have you got a dog now?' Violet asked, her eyes alight, and his heart melted for her. She leaned down and hugged the dog, who gave her a lick with an enormous tongue. Julius never gave consideration to the thought that she might not want a dog, and given that his fiancé and her brother, Tom, would soon reside with him, it was an oversight. But truth be known, he had not thought about anything except his own pain this morning and was not even surprised when the dog followed him. It was as if he had been waiting for Julius to collect him.

'I am sorry to distress you all, and thank you for your concern,' Julius said. 'I was visiting Mum and Dad at the cemetery.'

'That's all right, Lad,' Randolph softened, knowing Julius would only do so if he were worried about something. 'It was just out of character for you, and we thought you might have come unstuck.'

'It won't happen again. I shall get word to you. I apologise,' Julius said, now feeling churlish and selfish for his actions. 'And that was where I met... I don't know his name, but the gravedigger, Mr Redford, said he needed a home. So here we are. He seemed quite happy to accompany me.'

'Oh, wonderful,' Phoebe said. 'He can keep me company when you and Ambrose are in service.'

'I am sure he will provide comfort to some of our clients as well; dogs have the ability to do that,' Randolph added.

'I have always wanted a dog. So has Tom,' Violet agreed happily, which Julius found reassuring as she talked as if she would reside in the same abode as the dog – Julius's house. 'What will you name him?'

The dog looked at all the faces around him and did not protest to receiving a new name.

'You must do the honour. What do you have in mind?' Julius asked Violet, their eyes holding each other's gaze, and he desperately tried to read her state of emotions or if she had just been worried given his absence.

'Rufus,' Violet said without hesitation. 'I have always wanted a dog called Rufus, which is a name for a strong, clever dog just like this fellow.'

'Perfect,' Phoebe laughed.

The large black dog looked quite content with his new name.

'Rufus Astin it is then. I best make amends to Ambrose,' Julius said with a glance at the clock.

Randolph shook his head. 'Have a cup of tea. Will is with him; they'll get the job done.'

'I had best get back to work,' Violet said. 'Will you walk me there?'

Julius nodded and excused himself while Mrs Dobbs declared she had a bowl of water and a treat for Rufus; the remaining family ventured into the kitchen.

The young couple exited through the back of the office, as the walk was a little longer, and they would have privacy. Her hand on his arm felt stronger in its grip than it did on their last walk, as if reinforcing the connection between them, and he felt Violet studying him.

'I took the liberty of speaking with Phoebe this morning, and she patiently answered many of my questions.'

'I see,' Julius said.

'Forgive me, Julius. I was just frightened, and I had to consider Tom as well. I am not frightened anymore.'

'I would never put either of you in danger,' Julius said.

'I know, and I did not mean to distress you; it was quite a shock,' Violet said, speaking quickly.

'Of course. It was for me too,' he said almost in jest.

Once down the stairs, outside, and away from Claude and Charlie in the stables, he said, 'I do not want this ability, I assure you.'

'I know.'

He stopped walking and turned to look down upon her, into her blue eyes and familiar face, the face he wanted to see every day for as long as he walked the earth.

In a low voice, Julius said, 'I will understand if you want to walk away, Violet, but if so, do so now. I promise you, your job and Tom's will not be in peril, and you need not see or deal with me, but do not torture me,' he said, pushing a hand through his hair and standing tall as if he were bulletproof, when inside, he felt quite the opposite. He could not recall a time when he had shown his vulnerability to anyone as he did at that moment.

'Julius, I do not want that,' she said, reaching for his hands and grasping them both. 'I could not bear the thought of life without you. Last evening, I needed time to think through it all. That is how I handle things; we will learn that about each other in time. But I do not run away so easily.'

'We are not speaking of a hidden secret like a past love or a financial mishap. This is a flaw in my character.'

'It is neither a flaw of your character nor that of Phoebe's; I believe you are both perfect. Some consider it a gift, but it is our secret now, and it will not take me from you, Julius.'

He exhaled with relief, exhausted from the time spent in heartache. Now, in a matter of moments, it was as if Julius could not recall the grief he had known overnight. His world was bright again, and he had the beginnings of his own family – a fiancée and a dog named Rufus.

Phoebe took her lunch break out of the office, intending to return the business photograph of the deceased Teddy Tate and his business partner, Harry Beaumont, to Kate. Harland had given it back to Phoebe, and while Lilly hoped to publish it, the detectives requested she wait, given that the business was still operational despite Teddy's death.

On entering Kate's photographic studio, Phoebe was surprised to find another *Vexed Vixen* present, Emily. She laughed; all three ladies were dressed in blue.

'Goodness, aren't we coordinated?' Emily exclaimed as the ladies hugged each other in greeting.

'We are, and excellent timing, Phoebe,' Kate exclaimed. 'I was about to break for lunch, and Emily just arrived to collect her students' photographs, and here you are!'

'I commission a photograph of all my graduates, and Kate takes it,' Emily explained. 'I include it in their fee,' she grinned.

'Good on you, Emily. It's a nice keepsake and good for boosting Kate's business,' Phoebe nudged Kate.

'Absolutely,' Kate agreed, storing the photo of the *Perfume Emporium* men back in her drawer.

'It is good for the young ladies to see women making their mark in untraditional occupations; Kate will inspire them,' Emily said, and Kate's expression showed that she was genuinely touched.

'So very true,' Phoebe agreed, studying the photo of the two men before the drawer closed. 'It is such a good photo of Harry Beaumont. What a shame Teddy could not be cut from it.'

'Can you imagine?' Emily said. 'It would be like erasing a part of your life. Quite sad, really.'

'I agree,' Kate said, and then, seeing something else in her drawer, bit her lower lip and lowered her eyes as if in consideration.

'What is worrying you?' Phoebe asked.

Kate threw caution to the wind and pulled a framed photograph from her drawer. She held it up to show Emily and Phoebe, waiting for their reactions.

'It is you and Ambrose! Oh my, how adorable!' Phoebe said with a delighted laugh.

'Look at the pair of you playing up with his hat on your head and Ambrose holding the umbrella,' Emily said.

Kate smiled happily, turning the image to look at it. 'I love it.'

'Why is it not on display?' Phoebe asked.

'Because I am a serious businesswoman,' Kate said, putting it back in the drawer. 'I don't want people thinking my work is all a bit of a lark!'

'Understandable,' Emily agreed. 'Lilly and both of you are in male-dominated industries. On the other hand, I have never had a male counterpart wish to teach young ladies about deportment.'

'It would be a brave man indeed,' Phoebe said.

'They would probably focus on housekeeping and how to make a man's life comfortable,' Kate said, and the three ladies laughed at the thought.

They agreed to have lunch at a small teahouse nearby, where they could enjoy a modestly priced sandwich and pot of tea in a quaint atmosphere.

Once seated, Emily asked, 'How is Julius progressing with learning your make-up artist skills, Phoebe?'

'Very well indeed,' Phoebe said, 'although I should not be surprised. He is very disciplined, and if he has the will to do something, he will achieve it. In fact, as he missed a funeral service with Ambrose this morning, I have left him to start work on his first deceased client.'

'Good Lord,' Kate exclaimed. 'What if you come back and his work cannot be repaired?'

Phoebe laughed. 'I have chosen an elderly gentleman, so a little grooming and a light powder will suffice. He was not injured; that is when it proves challenging. We also have instructions from the family on how our client wore his hair when he was alive, and Julius read well in advance of his lessons.'

Emily shuddered. 'I hate the thought of someone touching me when I am dead.'

'But you'll be dead,' Kate said matter-of-factly.

'Exactly. What if I don't like them and they are brushing my hair?' Emily said and shuddered again.

Phoebe and Kate exchanged small smiles.

'Best you die fully made up and in the repose position then,' Kate said, patting Emily's hand. Emily brightened as if that were something she could manage. 'And what of the lad?' Kate asked.

'Charlie. He is keen to learn my trade. Julius and I are meeting with his mother later this week to discuss his future.'

The ladies looked up as a couple approached their table. An exceptionally attractive blonde lady wearing a most stylish pink dress that flattered her voluptuous figure glanced to the very dapper gentleman with her and then back to the ladies.

'Please do forgive the intrusion, ladies, but I fear I left my silk handkerchief on the table. I assure you it was unused, but as my grandmother did the stitching, it is very sentimental.'

'Of course,' Phoebe said, and the three ladies lifted their cups and the platter of shared sandwiches, but nothing revealed itself.

'Oh, what a shame. Then, I must have lost it elsewhere. I am sure you would have noticed the scent if I had left it here; it is the latest from a new perfume manufacturer.'

'Oh, do tell,' Kate said, most excited.

The attractive woman smiled as if she had a secret and leaned forward slightly, blocking the gentleman from sharing her confidence. In almost a whisper, she said, 'All right, but do not tell too many of your acquaintances, as the less that wear it, the more exclusive it is – the fragrance is called *Amour* and will soon be available from select chemists and the *Perfume Emporium*'s door-to-door perfumers.'

The three ladies inhaled sharply at the brazen name—*Amour*—and the manner in which it was so informally mentioned as if speaking of romance with a stranger was an acceptable lunchtime conversation.

'You have been most gracious, ladies. Thank you, and we apologise for the interruption,' the gentleman said, lightly touching the woman's arm to lead her away. He was unaware of how Miss Phoebe Astin regarded him, and no doubt took her curious look to be that of admiration.

They bid the couple goodbye.

'Well, what do you think of that?' Phoebe said, most excited.

Emily straightened. 'I think they need to come and spend some time at my school of deportment and etiquette.' Seeing the blank looks on both ladies, Emily elaborated, 'While she was most gracious, the lady should have introduced herself and then asked our permission to introduce her gentleman friend to us, especially as they were interrupting our discourse. Whispering should be avoided, most unseemly, as was leaning in when we have a display of food on the table. To speak of something as personal as a choice of perfume to three ladies she has never met is quite distasteful. I could go on, but I won't.' Emily shook her head.

'Goodness,' Kate said. 'I cannot imagine how often I must offend your sensibilities, dear Emily, when I am in your company.'

'You do no such thing, and we are well acquainted,' Emily assured her. 'And, yes, I accept my views are a little old-fashioned, but it is better I teach classic rather than modern manners. It was most odd.'

'I wholeheartedly agree with you, Emily,' Phoebe said, and Emily smiled with relief. 'But not because of the display of manners as I bow to your wisdom, but because it was staged.'

'Staged!' Kate exclaimed, looking around, hoping no one had heard her outburst.

'Ah, that explains the impropriety then,' Emily said.

'What do you mean by "staged"? Why would they select us? Are we in danger now?' Kate said, ensuring she still had her purse, lowering her voice and looking around.

'Not at all. Did you not recognise the man you photographed with Teddy? That was his business partner in the perfume company – Mr Harry Beaumont,' Phoebe said.

'No,' Kate said, confused, and strained to see out the shop's front window, looking for the pair. 'But he looked different.'

'I believe his moustache was gone,' Phoebe said, 'but I've no doubt it was him, and I suspect he recognised you but played along.'

'I guess it could have been,' Kate agreed. 'I didn't look at him to any great extent because he was slightly behind me, and she held me captive.'

'Indeed, and that was her plan,' Emily said, understanding the ruse now. 'She was selling us perfume.'

'Exactly. That is very clever. I, for one, was most curious to know more about the perfume, *Amour*,' Phoebe said.

'Me too,' Kate said. 'I was going to try to get it before my Saturday date with Ambrose.'

The ladies shared a smile akin to naughty schoolgirls.

'A girl has to appear at her best advantage,' Kate said.

'That was so very interesting,' Phoebe said, sitting back and sipping her tea. 'I will tell Harland what we were just part of and see if it is of interest to his investigation.'

'She was wearing an engagement ring,' Emily said, 'so we must assume that she is engaged to Mr Harry... what was his name?'

'Beaumont,' Kate finished. 'Harry Beaumont. Unless he is related to her. Do find out more, Phoebe, and let us know.'

'I shall, ladies. And if you buy the perfume, Kate, let me know if it works,' Phoebe said with a small laugh and then her eyes widened. 'Oh, you best not since it will involve my brother.'

'My lips are sealed,' Kate said, looking mischievous.

'What is the world coming to?' Emily asked with a sigh and a shake of her head.

'I don't think that kind of selling will work for the death industry,' Phoebe said in jest as the ladies finished their lunch and the subject received much more discussion.

Unbeknown to them, the young, handsome couple had moved on to another venue to repeat the episode, while Detectives Harland Stone and Gilbert Payne knocked on the door of the premises of the lady who was there when Teddy took his last breath – she was not home as they were one and the same.

Chapter 26

Turning the horses and hearse into the backyard of *The Economic Undertaker*, Ambrose pulled up at the stables and descended quickly, handing the reins to Claude, who stood nearby with young Charlie, waiting to care for the horses and clean the carriage.

'He's back and seems in good stead,' Claude said, and Ambrose exhaled.

'I shall kill him then for worrying me,' Ambrose said to the chuckles of the surrounding men. 'Thank you, Will, for stepping up.' He departed, hurrying up the back stairs and bursting into the office building.

His stride—rather noisy at the best of times—said he meant business, and Mrs Dobbs hurriedly appeared from the kitchen, placing her finger on her lips and pointing to the meeting room.

He stopped, acknowledged he had received the message loud and clear and continued, glancing into the room where low voices could be heard.

His grandfather grimaced, and Ambrose nodded at the elderly couple present.

'My condolences,' he offered, removing his hat and continued. He recognised the look of disparagement they gave him. It had been a regular feature on the faces of his teachers over the years when Ambrose had made them aware that he was not his studious brother or his dutiful sister and never would be.

A glance around told him Julius was not at his usual post, and thus, he took the stairs down to Phoebe's workroom, coming to a halt halfway down at the sight of Julius combing the deceased's hair.

'Ambrose, you are back. Did it go without a hitch?' Julius asked, ceasing his work and coming around from the body on the table before him.

Ambrose strode toward him, not harnessing his rising anger at seeing his brother so relaxed; his jaw locked in frustration, and Julius stepped back. A large black dog leapt off the couch nearby and stood before Julius.

Ambrose looked at it, then at his brother, and hissed, 'I am not going to hit you.'

'Really? Because you looked as if you might.'

'I wouldn't be so stupid; we both know you could lay me low.'

'But I would not raise a hand to you. And I know I deserve your anger,' Julius said, holding Ambrose's gaze. 'I am sorry to worry you; it won't happen again.'

'That's the thing, isn't it?' Ambrose said. 'If it did happen regularly, it would not be an issue. We would assume you were busy on other matters and all step up. But you are so disciplined, Julius, that when you disappear on me, and I hear of a disagreement with Violet, who is here wringing her hands in concern, we naturally waste our time worrying about you. I waited for you before deciding you must have run an errand. But for the last two hours, I have been distracted with concern, hurrying to get back here to see if you had returned,' Ambrose's voice had risen considerably during his address, and then he exhaled sharply, shook his head and looked at his brother as if just seeing him. 'Is everything all right now?'

'Yes. Yes, it is, thank you. I am sorry, Brother.'

'Do not "brother" me with that sincere tone,' Ambrose said, trying not to smile. 'I am getting weary of being the responsible brother.'

Julius flashed a rare smile. Ambrose looked at the dog in front of his brother.

'How do you do, Sir? I am the brother of this ill-behaved individual you seem to have adopted.'

The dog moved toward Ambrose, licking the out-held hand.

'This is Rufus Astin. We met earlier in the cemetery, and he has joined the family,' Julius said, introducing the pair.

'Rufus, welcome,' Ambrose said. 'We shall be firm friends.' He patted the dog's head and looked at his brother with understanding, assuming the late morning visit was paid to the graves of their deceased parents. 'You could have come to me; I am alive. But I would have re-tried the cemetery had you not been here now.'

Julius nodded. 'It was thoughtless of me. My apologies.'

'It is done. Now, I must see what Mrs Dobbs has to eat in the kitchen. I am sure I have lost weight from worrying about you.'

Julius scoffed. 'Wait, and we'll come with you. I am finished here; hopefully, my first effort will be to Phoebe's satisfaction.' He carefully covered the body, and with a nod to Rufus, the three took the stairs, and life returned to normal in the funeral home of *The Economic Undertaker.*

Phoebe had only just returned to the office of *The Economic Undertaker* when Lilly Lewis arrived.

'I wish you had come earlier, and you could have joined us for lunch,' Phoebe bemoaned Lilly's absence as the ladies made their way down the stairs.

'I would have liked that but could not have spared the time. My editor has a bee in his bonnet, or perhaps that should be a fly in his cap; regardless, he is cranky about deadlines and expects us to have a story backed up as soon as we file another. Fergus and I have written up the story of the ladies injecting perfume, but now there is nothing new on the case. The detectives will not let me write about the business connection to *Higson's Quality Perfumes* yet, and poor Fergus is writing a story about obscure deaths, such as impaling yourself on a perfume bottle like the deceased Teddy Tate.' She sighed with frustration, having delivered quite a mouthful.

'I may have something for you if you can find an angle. I will tell Harland as well, but it will not make or break his case; it may be irrelevant,' she added for fear of exciting her friend too much.

'I am sure I can make something of your news. Do tell, Phoebe,' Lilly said with a mixture of pleading and anticipation.

'At lunch, a strange ruse was played out to sell us perfume,' Phoebe said and explained about the couple approaching to retrieve a handkerchief.

'Where was this?' Lilly asked, and Phoebe described the small tea house near Kate's photographic studio.

'Most interesting. I can see how that persuasion could be very effective,' Lilly said, tapping her chin as she thought. 'I wonder if that is how Teddy Tate recruited the two deceased ladies.'

'Recruited is a very good term,' Phoebe agreed. 'I did feel a little like I was meant to go forth and spread the word.'

'I am sure I can make that stick to the case and warn ladies of the subtle art of subterfuge. Yes, Phoebe, I think there is a story in that. Thank you,' Lilly said and smiled with relief. 'If I find the detective, can I tell him of your encounter and the information you hoped to share with him? He may give me a comment.'

'By all means, thank you, Lilly.'

'No, thank you, Phoebe, yet again.' She kissed Phoebe on the cheek and hurried up the stairs, departing as quickly as possible while maintaining dignity in the funeral business premises.

Phoebe smiled, watching her excited friend depart. She moved to the body in the corner and removed the shroud; a small smile graced her lips.

'He has done a good job, don't you think?' A mature male voice said. Phoebe did not look toward it but instead carefully studied Julius' work before her. Satisfied, she responded, 'Yes, Mr Gould.' She turned to the spirit in the corner and smiled, 'I believe he has you looking most dignified, and we would have it no other way.'

The elderly man chuckled and clasped his hands in thanks before disappearing from Phoebe's sight.

As Harland and Gilbert started down the path of the home where Teddy Tate took his last breath on the doorstep, a neighbour called to them from the fence; they paused.

'If you are looking for the young lady, you missed her by about an hour, and her mother left early; she works at Finney's in the city,' she said, approaching the gate to meet them. While Harland perished the thought of having a neighbour who knew his every move, as a detective, he appreciated when the community assisted them. He could tell by the look of the lady approaching that they had struck gold.

'Thank you, Madam,' Harland said, meeting her at the gate.

'She was with one of those salesmen again. I've seen this one before, but I can't tell you his name. She is helping them to sell ladies' fragrances, or so she told me. Have you ever?' The portly lady, well endowed everywhere but in height, pursed her lips as if something distasteful had taken place. She wore a simple floral house dress and an apron that blended in; her brown-grey hair was pinned up into a large bun at the back, suggesting her hair would be quite long when freed.

'May I ask the purpose of your visit?' she said haughtily, and Harland thought it was a bit late for that, given she had already revealed quite a bit about her neighbour to two strangers. Had they been thieves, they would have learnt the coast was clear for pilfering the house contents.

'Detectives Harland Stone and Gilbert Payne, Ma'am,' Gilbert said, stepping up.

'Oh, you are here on police business, and fine work you do too, if you don't mind me saying. My husband was a police officer but retired years back; he's been dead for ten years now.'

'Then you have both given of yourselves to the community, Ma'am,' Gilbert acknowledged her, allowing his superior to now address the matter at hand.

'Mrs Mabel Newman,' she said. 'And you are here to see Miss Spooner then?'

'Yes, Mrs Newman, assuming that is the young lady who recently purchased perfume when the salesman collapsed at her feet?'

'It certainly was Miss Amy Spooner, but that's not quite how it happened, Detective,' she said, raising her chin knowledgeably.

'Please continue, Mrs Newman, we would value your observations,' Harland said, encouraging her, not that she needed any to continue her story.

'Well, I was gardening at the time, but I soon hurried inside and continued to watch from the kitchen window,' she said, waving towards a window with a lace curtain flapping in the breeze and offering a perfect view of the front of Miss Amy Spooner's abode. 'A perfume salesman arrived, mind you, he never calls at my house.

He's a regular visitor to her, and there she is, all in white, flirting terribly with him when she's engaged to another gentleman. Mind you, she flirts with every good-looking young man.'

'Did you see what happened next, Mrs Newman?' Gilbert asked, moving her along.

'I certainly did. The next minute, her fiancé was hurrying up the path and not looking at all happy. There were raised voices, and I went inside then.'

'Did the men appear to know each other?' Harland asked.

'Oh yes. They greeted each other by their first names. Teddy, I think, was the name of the salesman, and the fiancé is Mr Humphrey.'

'Mr Septimus Humphrey?' Harland asked, surprised.

'The very same. Do you know him, Detective?'

'I met him during the course of the investigation, but he failed to mention that he was engaged.'

'Is that so?' Mrs Newman mused and no doubt stored away that piece of information for further use. They waited momentarily as a horse and carriage went down the street, interrupting the peacefulness of the neighbourhood, and when it had passed, Mrs Newman resumed. 'Once safely inside, I watched from the window and the fiancé, Mr Humphrey, sent Miss Spooner inside. She closed the door, but I suspect she watched from inside, like me.'

'What happened then, Mrs Newman?'

'Well, they were very quiet, as if speaking through gritted teeth,' she said, 'and then Mr Humphrey pushed the salesman, and he fell backward. He jumped up quickly, and the strangest thing happened.'

Both detectives leaned in slightly, keen to hear the next instalment of Mrs Newman's tale.

'The fiancé grabbed the salesman from behind; he had a neck hold on him and then held a bottle under his nose. It looked like a perfume bottle. I was amused at first because it reminded me of my mother washing my mouth out with soap when I gave her cheek, and I could not imagine why he was doing it. Perhaps trying to punish him by making him smell his own perfume. Most odd.'

Harland's mind was racing.

'But then, the salesman collapsed to the ground, and Mr Humphrey leant down, and he was sneering. I stood back from the window; he looked very angry, and I didn't want him to see me witnessing their fight.'

'And all this time, Miss Spooner was inside?' Gilbert asked.

'Yes, but moments later, she hurried out, scolded Mr Humphrey, and was down on her knees trying to rouse the salesman.'

Mrs Newman stopped now and looked around before continuing her story. She lowered her voice. 'Miss Spooner cried out that he wasn't moving, and Mr Humphrey stood and began to pace; he looked anxious. I left then and rushed to lock my doors and windows in case they came over to me. I heard the sound of breaking glass, and when I came back, Miss Spooner was with the salesman, who was still lying on the ground, and Mr Humphrey was gone. I'd assumed he'd gone to fetch the police, but mind you, the policeman came, but no one accompanied him.'

'Did you tell the police about this, Mrs Newman?' Harland asked.

'Of course. They even took my name and address and thanked me. But you are the first police officers back here since then.'

'Do you know if Miss Spooner received recompense to help the salesman?' Gilbert asked.

'I could not say, Detective. But she was full of her own importance; she used to call herself his muse.' Mrs Newman scoffed at the thought.

'No one came onto the premises or left during the argument?' Harland asked.

'No one.'

'You have been exceedingly helpful, Mrs Newman; we thank you,' Harland said, and she preened with delight.

'It's a citizen's duty, isn't it, Detective?' she said, smiling smugly.

'If only all citizens were as conscientious, Ma'am,' Gilbert said, and the men tipped their hats as they departed.

When they were far enough away, Harland looked at Gilbert. 'Well, that's a whole different story now, isn't it?'

'It certainly is, Sir. Shall we try to find Miss Spooner or go back to see Mr Septimus Humphrey at the perfume factory?' Gilbert asked.

'Both and if possible, I would like to speak with Miss Spooner first and hear her version of events. Mr Humphrey must have had chloroform in that bottle, or he had some on his person, but did he come with murder on his mind? He certainly managed to hide his actions.'

'He must have been worried when we started investigating,' Gilbert said. 'If he loved his cousin, Teddy, as he says, then something more than perfume sales must have been going on between his fiancée and Teddy for him to act so ruthlessly.'

'Yes, and while there were no witnesses to the act, Mrs Newman heard that bottle break after Teddy Tate was on the ground. Might Septimus have broken the bottle, pierced the heart of his cousin and made it look like an accident?'

'Ruthless,' Gilbert said. 'But I could not bear it if another gentleman flirted with Miss Emily Yalden.' His comment was an open admission of his feelings, and Gilbert coloured, realising what he had said.

'Nor could I bear the same,' Harland said, appreciating the young man's trust. 'But we are unlikely to kill over it.' As Gilbert did not reply, Harland glanced at him. 'Are we?'

'Oh, no, Sir, definitely not, but I would not be upset if they were harmed, as uncharitable as that might be.'

Harland chuckled. 'I prefer to believe they will have their comeuppance, as tempting as it might be to hurry it along.'

Chapter 27

LILLY HURRIED FROM THE premises of *The Economic Undertaker* and stopped, torn about which way to go. The detectives might be at the station, but if she were to spend a fare to get there, and they were not there, Lilly would have to spend more to return to the newspaper with nothing to show for it. Nearby was the office of Mr Bennet Martin, and despite a pressing deadline, Lilly started there hurriedly on foot. After all, Bennet might be en route to somewhere or accompany her if he were idle and assist with the cost.

'He is not here, I am sorry to say, Miss Lewis,' Bennet's clerk, Daniel Dutton, said, greeting her at the door. 'He will be disappointed to have missed you. Would you care to wait, or can I take a message?'

'No, but thank you, Mr Dutton,' she said. 'I am on a deadline, so I shall head to the police station.'

'I am going in that direction to drop off a report to a client. Would you care to share my hansom?'

Lilly's eyes lit up. 'That would be excellent, thank you, Mr Dutton, and a great time saver.'

The young man told his aunt that he was heading out for a few hours and to lock up should she leave if Bennet had not returned. Grabbing the report and his hat, Daniel followed Miss Lewis to hail a ride, which they immediately did.

'This is very kind of you, Mr Dutton,' Lilly said as he handed her up into the carriage. Not that Lilly was the type to need assistance, but she did not want to be rude when the offer of a ride was so gratefully accepted. Sitting opposite each other as the journey began, Lilly studied her companion, who appeared to be of the same age, wore a conservative suit and glasses, and looked very much like the bookish type.

'The pleasure is mine, Miss Lewis; I am going that way after all. I'm sure Bennet will be most annoyed that I got to enjoy your company, and he didn't.'

'Do you think so?' Lilly huffed with laughter. 'He is a complex man sometimes.'

'Yes, on that, we agree. I have refused so much work for him I cannot bear it. I would get a private investigator licence and do the overflow if I were not occupied full time as his clerk. But without meaning to be indiscreet, he does not need the funds.'

'I can't imagine it,' Lilly said, and Daniel laughed.

'Nor can I.'

The pair became as thick as thieves in moments with their shared outlooks and mutual connection with Bennet Martin.

As they sat back comfortably, enjoying the breeze from the moving hansom, Daniel asked, 'Are you still working on the perfumer's death story? I've read your reports when I can wrestle the newspaper off Bennet.'

'Yes. It is a most frustrating case, and it is understandable that the police thought the deaths were not suspicious when all the time the young women were injecting themselves with perfume and bringing about their own poisoning.' She shook her head. 'We are silly creatures sometimes.'

Daniel chuckled. 'Love, vanity, religion... the things we do, the persuasions we allow.'

'Indeed,' Lilly agreed, appreciating his comment. 'As for the perfume salesman, well, he looks like he died by someone's hand, but...'

'But what?' Daniel asked, curious.

'Well, don't repeat my words, but it does make for a dull story when people die of natural causes.'

Daniel burst out laughing, and Lilly laughed softly beside him. 'Well, it's the truth.'

'Good Lord, I pray that I am a dull story when my time comes to turn up my toes.'

When they sobered, Daniel said, 'There was something on the file that might interest you, Miss Lewis. Bennet was only hired to find the murderer of Miss Isla Barr, and once he could show it was death by natural causes, his bill was paid. But we received some information—'

'Oh, anything would help. I would be grateful,' she cut him off.

'It may be nothing. It was an anonymous letter sent to us only a few days ago, and Bennet was in Toowoomba then. But the stamp mark was from the West End of town.'

'You are observant; perhaps you should ask Bennet if you might train under him.'

Daniel did not mock the idea. 'Hmm, perhaps. Anyway, the letter I kept was only a few lines long, and it said, from memory, "History repeats if lessons are not learnt. The son is being punished".'

Lilly repeated it back, then grabbed her notepad and pencil and wrote it down.

'That's not a direct quote, but near enough,' Daniel said as the horses slowed and the Roma Street Police Station came into view.

'Mr Dutton, you are a gem,' Lilly said. 'Have you still got the letter?'

'I do. I can have it sent to your office. Silly me, I'm sure Bennet would like to deliver it.'

'Thank you, that would be appreciated, at his convenience,' she said. 'Would you say it is a feminine hand that wrote it?'

'No. It is a hurried scrawl, and the paper has no scent and is of poor quality.'

'My, that is interesting. We are here. Thank you again, Mr Dutton. Allow me to contribute to the fare,' she said.

'Absolutely not. I was going this way anyway.'

'Thank you,' Lilly said, relieved, and did not argue.

'Allow me,' he said, swinging down to the ground and offering his hand as she descended.

'Thank you again. Oh, and there are the detectives now!' Lilly said, seeing them departing the building. She called out as loud as she dared, but the detectives did not turn.

Daniel Dutton gave a loud whistle, and both men turned towards the sound. Lilly waved and, with a laugh and thanks to Daniel Dutton, raced to meet the men with only a few hours until her copy was due.

Allowing the reporter, Miss Lilly Lewis, to accompany them in order to hear her latest insights, the detectives saw her into another hansom and the three headed to the perfume manufacturing residence of Mr Septimus Humphry.

'So you see, detectives, the message, "History repeats if lessons are not learnt. The son is being punished", might indicate that Septimus Humphry's life is mirroring history – his father ran off with the business partner's wife, and now, as you have just advised, Septimus confronted his cousin, also his business partner, who was flirting with his fiancée.' She stopped to draw breath. 'I don't know how he is being punished except by a broken heart, perhaps.'

'And who is doing the punishing?' Harland mused. 'A West End postmark. *Higson's Quality Perfumes* is located in the West End.' He shook his head. 'A sordid affair and one I would rather not be involved in,' Harland said under his breath.

'Family feuds are always disappointing,' Gilbert agreed, 'but are not most murders about money or passion?'

'Very observant, Detective Payne,' Lilly said, 'I agree.'

The small party of three wasted no time exiting the hansom when it arrived at the Tank Street office. Gilbert offered Lilly his hand, but she had already hurried out and was keen to see if Miss Amy Spooner was on the premises, given she had been seen at work with Mr Harry Beaumont. They were in luck.

'Detectives!' Septimus said, surprised, 'you are back.'

'Mr Humphrey, Mr Beaumont,' Harland said, acknowledging the perfume seller Harry Beaumont as well, whom they had met at the house of Miss Rose Ward in Ipswich.

'Hello again, Detectives. I should get going then,' Harry said.

'Please stay,' Harland said, but it was not a request. 'This is Miss Lilly Lewis from *The Courier*. We have invited her to accompany us, as she shared some valuable information. This young lady must be Miss Spooner?'

Amy Spooner looked surprised that the men knew her.

'Yes, allow me to present my fiancée, Miss Amy Spooner,' Septimus said. 'Shall we take a seat?'

'No, we are comfortable standing,' Harland said, speaking for himself and Gilbert. 'Miss Lewis, if you wish,' he indicated a seat, which Lilly took so she could take notes.

'Perhaps we should start at the beginning, Mr Humphrey,' Harland suggested.

'I do not know what you mean, Detective,' Septimus said and chuckled as if the idea was absurd. He glanced at Harry and Amy and then back to the detectives looming in front of him.

'Your father is not Orpheus Humphrey but Mr George Higson, is he not?'

And now all eyes turned in shock and surprise to Detective Harland Stone.

Chapter 28

Miss Amy Spooner sat down abruptly, and Harry Beaumont did the same. Harland knew he had played a wild card, but seeing Septimus Humphrey's reaction, he realised he had discovered the truth. There was a resemblance between George Higson and Septimus Humphrey, and he suspected George Higson had sent the anonymous note to Bennet. It might have been an act of compassion by Higson. Harland gave his protégé a slight shake of his head not to ask how he knew and proceeded with his questions.

'How long have you known about your parentage, Mr Humphrey?'

Septimus glanced at his fiancée before answering. Then, as if accepting that denial was futile, he said, 'Since I was about twelve.'

'Goodness,' Amy Spooner said, her hand going to her heart.

'To avoid confusion, we shall continue to call Orpheus Humphrey your father. Do you have any objections?' Harland asked the perfume manufacturer.

'I could not care either way.'

'What happened when you were told the truth?' Harland asked.

'I found out; no one told me,' he said. 'My parents were fighting, and my father called me his bastard son. It was not as shocking as you might imagine. Even then, I had been a disappointment to him.'

'Why is that, Mr Humphrey? You are obviously scholastic,' Gilbert asked.

'Ah, that didn't interest my father, Detective. Orpheus Humphrey is charming, handsome, and desired by women. Just ask him,' Septimus scoffed. 'He made his success on his looks, including stealing his business partner's wife. When Mum divorced George Higson, she was pregnant with me. She didn't know that at the time,' he hurriedly added. 'But it was obvious as I grew up that I was not my father's son, and the resemblance to George Higson was obvious, to me at least.'

'I see it now that you mention it,' Harry said, looking at his business partner. 'Good Lord, to think all this time that Teddy and I were working for George Higson and you were his son. It explains Orpheus's animosity toward you. He was always so horrid,' Harry said to the detectives.

'Oh yes, my so-called father, Orpheus, loved to praise Teddy, his nephew. Handsome, charming Teddy, so like him, the son he should have had instead of me. Why couldn't I be more like Teddy instead of burying my nose in a book?' Septimus's eyes narrowed at the memory of the constant slings.

'Not all value vanity above intelligence and integrity, Mr Humphrey,' Harland said.

'Thank goodness,' Gilbert added. He was no oil painting, as he had heard from his own father on occasion.

'But why are you working with Mr Beaumont and the deceased Mr Tate to compete against your real father? Why could you not join the Higson manufacturers?' Lilly asked, confused, and Harland looked impatient. He would ask the questions, although he allowed this as it was information he wanted to know.

Septimus exhaled, and his shoulders slumped. 'I approached George Higson and said I believed I was his son. His response was, "What do you want?" It was not how I'd pictured it going, the reunion and the bond we shared, our interest in science and business. But I persisted and asked to work with his manufacturing team. I presented my qualifications and ideas for new fragrances, and he laughed at me. He took pleasure in reminding me he once provided for my mother and wouldn't provide for me as well. He said he wanted nothing to do with the Humphrey family ever again, including me, as I bore the name if not the blood.'

'Surely, he must have been shocked to know you were his actual son?' Amy spoke up for the first time, surprised to find her fiancé was not the man she thought him to be. He was, in fact, the son of a very enterprising businessman and possible heir to a perfume empire. 'Might he have come around?'

'No, he knew all that time. George Higson took pleasure in telling me that when my mother left my father and returned to London, she asked to come back to him, but he would not have her. She told him then that I was his son, and he believed her to be lying but conceded from our similar looks that I probably was his firstborn. He's a bitter man too. So, I thought I would show my two fathers what I could do.'

'Might he have compassion for you?' Harland said. 'Could he have sent a note to warn the private investigator that you were being punished as history repeated itself? It was postmarked from the West End.'

Septimus looked surprised. Even hopeful, Harland thought, studying the young man.

'I...I... could not say,' he stuttered, as the thought made him a little emotional.

'But then history did repeat itself,' Harland continued. 'You found out your cousin, Teddy, was wooing your fiancé. Father and son both lost out to the Humphrey family – Orpheus and his nephew.'

Amy flushed with humiliation as all eyes turned towards her. 'We never meant—'

Harland cut her off. 'Miss Spooner, the affair is of no interest to me, only the loss of Mr Tate's life on your premises.'

'Teddy turned out to be just like my father, Orpheus, in more ways than one,' Septimus said, spitting out the words. 'Thinking he could have anyone and anything he wanted and no loyalty to me. We were like brothers.' He shook his head in disgust. 'I would have done anything for him. I loved him.'

'He clearly persuaded you to be one of the partners,' Lilly concurred.

Septimus nodded and smiled ruefully. 'He was one of my biggest supporters. He'd say nothing to defend me in front of my father, but the moment we were alone again, he'd assure me of how important I was, how clever, how much he needed me and what excellent partners we were. And I always believed him because I wanted to think he was on my side. I was so desperate for a word of encouragement and love. Pathetic.'

'Even though you knew he had several women he was wooing for business, you did not berate him for that?' Gilbert asked.

'Hardly,' Septimus declared. 'Did you hear that, Amy? You were being wooed for business purposes? Did you even know Teddy, whom you so admired, was saying sweet things to other women?'

'When did you find out about Teddy and your fiancée?' Lilly asked, and Harland gave her a look to remind her this was an investigation, not an interview. She gave a nod of understanding, dropping her eyes to her notes.

'Months ago, but I didn't believe it until I arrived to find him flirting with Amy. He told me they were planning something special for my birthday.' He looked at Amy. 'You must have both been laughing at me; what a fool I was to believe you.' He returned his attention to Harland. 'But he got what he deserved, and so did my father and those women whose vanity allowed them to be so easily wooed.'

The sneer on Septimus Humphrey's countenance made him look frightful. The room stilled, and Harland motioned for Gilbert and Lilly to remain silent.

'And you two,' Septimus glared at Harry, then Amy. 'With your sales tricks trying to manipulate young ladies to buy perfume, with that ridiculous lost handkerchief act,' he scoffed.

'Oh, you were the pair who approached my friends at lunch,' Lilly exclaimed and glanced at Harland to make the connection. He did.

Septimus continued. 'How long until you succumbed to Harry's charms, Amy, now that Teddy is gone?'

Amy gasped. 'How dare you?'

'How dare you!' he yelled back before expelling a hiss of laughter and addressing Harland again. 'I showed them. Who's laughing now?'

'Did you put chloroform in the perfume samples for Miss Sophia Beaver and Miss Isla Barr?' Harland asked.

'No! I wouldn't dare risk that. Those samples could have been given to any lady.'

'But you put chloroform in the salesman's bottle, in Mr Tate's bottle?' Gilbert asked, but Septimus shrugged, choosing not to respond. Gilbert continued, 'Did you know of the ladies' demise?'

Septimus gave a small smile. 'As soon as I heard from Teddy that they were injecting themselves, like the ladies in Paris, I knew enough about blood poisoning to know they would meet their end.'

'But you did not prevent it?' Amy said, shocked.

Septimus shrugged. 'Their vanity brought about their demise, as did his. Teddy didn't even notice a verse I tied with ribbon around each bottle's neck that read, "Beauty is only skin deep". It was my warning to them not to be taken in by Teddy's handsome face. They ignored it. Women are all ugly under the surface.'

Amy rose and headed for the door. No one stopped her.

'He asked you to wear white too, and you did, just like the other ladies,' Septimus called after her. 'But I forbade you from injecting yourself. You have me to thank for your life, not him.'

She departed with a slam of the door. Then Septimus seemed to realise he had been boasting, and he looked at Harland and added, 'Except Teddy's death was an accident, wasn't it? Teddy fell on his perfume bottle; how sad, and my real father could not resist the manly fragrance I created, highly recommended by his precious nephew, Teddy.'

Harland nodded to Gilbert, who quickly and quietly left the room to visit Mr Orpheus Humphrey and check on his health.

'You'll never prove otherwise, Detective,' Septimus Humphrey gloated.

'I will, Mr Humphrey,' Harland said calmly. 'You see, I have a witness who saw you that day with Mr Teddy Tate. They saw you hold him in a strangling hold and push the bottle to his nose. It was laced with chloroform. The witness saw Mr Tate collapse and heard the breaking of glass long after Mr Tate had fallen. You stabbed him to make it look as if he had fallen on the broken glass. The coroner also confirmed chloroform was congested in Mr Tate's lungs. Should anything have happened to your father now, you have just admitted to that in front of all of us.'

With that, Septimus grabbed the bottle in front of him and hurriedly drank its contents.

Chapter 29

THE COURIER –MORNING EDITION
POTENT PERFUME LACED WITH CHLOROFORM
GENERATIONAL FEUD IN PERFUME FAMILY
FOUR DEAD IN SENSATIONAL CASE
An exclusive report by Lilly Lewis and Fergus Griffiths.

A sensation was created in the city last evening when the most challenging of cases came to a head, and a murderer took his own life in extraordinary circumstances. At the centre of the case was a generational feud of bitterness and jealousy, resulting in the death of two young ladies, their perfume salesman and the perfume manufacturer.

But this story did not begin with these innocent ladies' deaths as reported by *The Courier* and first believed to be of natural causes. Nor did it start when a perfume salesman was found dead, the jagged remains of his perfume bottle perforating his heart. But it ended last evening when Mr Septimus Humphrey admitted to Detectives Harland Stone and Gilbert Payne of the Roma Street Police Station that he had committed murder. He then rashly swallowed the contents of a bottle containing chloroform.

A doctor was called, and he arrived promptly, but despite all attempts at resuscitation, Mr Septimus Humphrey died two hours later.

The readers of *The Courier* will be shocked to learn this story began thirty years ago when Mr George Higson of *Higson's Quality Perfumes* agreed to divorce his wife, Catherine, so that she could marry his boyhood friend and business partner, the charming, handsome, Mr Orpheus Humphrey. But a child was already in the womb—

Harland stopped reading, threw the paper down onto his desk, and turned to face his protégé Gilbert, private investigator Bennet Martin, and reporter Lilly Lewis, who were gathered in his office at the police headquarters at the start of a new day.

'A very nice job, Miss Lewis. I would continue reading, but I am familiar with the case and its outcome,' Harland said in jest.

Lilly laughed. 'I imagine you are quite tired of it, Detective, but thank you again for allowing me to report it.'

'It is another case where the murderer might have got away with it if not for Miss Astin having a request from the victim himself to investigate,' Gilbert said. 'Credit must go to her.'

'True,' Harland said. 'However, there were troublesome circumstances before then, such as the ladies bearing the written verse about beauty being skin deep.'

'And they wore white and bore a striking resemblance to each other, which was unusual and not to be dismissed,' Gilbert agreed.

'It was fortunate that the parents were insisting the truth be revealed and were in a financial position to hire me to determine if their daughter, Isla, was murdered,' Bennet said, also claiming some of the success for himself.

'Will you have to refund them, given you advised it was death by natural causes?' Lilly asked Bennet.

'Not at all. I investigated and concurred with the police and coroner that she had been self-injecting, which caused the blood poisoning. Thus, she was not murdered, and that was the assurance they sought. Septimus said no chloroform was added to their perfumes, and we will never really know if he spoke the truth, given we could not perform autopsies. But if they had not self-injected, they would be alive,' he said matter-of-factly.

'You were also onto something, Gilbert,' Harland said. 'We should have investigated who gave the note bearing the words, "Beauty is only skin deep", to the ladies.'

'Thank you, Sir, but it was an obscure clue at best with many interpretations,' Gilbert said humbly.

'What did Mr Orpheus Humphrey say when you arrived last night to see if he had succumbed to the potent perfume, Detective Payne?' Lilly asked Gilbert.

'He was true to character – disparaging of his son Septimus. Mr Humphrey said a small sniff had proven unsatisfactory. Despite what Septimus told him, he did not believe his nephew Teddy wore the fragrance and said Teddy had better taste and preferred a sandalwood fragrance, like himself.'

'Poor Septimus,' Lilly sighed.

'A father who would not even try a gift from his 'step' son. That is telling of their relationship,' Bennet said. 'I am sure I created many things as a child that my parents had to say were well done, or taste, wear or bear, when in fact they weren't very good at all.'

They all smiled, having experienced a shared memory.

'Well, we can all relax now, and detectives, you can enjoy the recital knowing you have wrapped up the case,' Lilly said, rising. 'I am sorry we can't attend, but Bennet is coming to dinner to meet my family. I will not be wearing any perfume.'

Her declaration made everyone present laugh.

Chapter 30

Bennet Martin wished he were escorting Lilly to the music recital with his closest friend, Julius, along with Harland, Tavish, Ambrose, Detective Payne and their partners. He enjoyed a good recital, and the prospect of dinner with Lilly's five brothers, father, and mother had given him indigestion before he had even arrived. Still, it was best to get it over with, and hopefully, he would not be rejected by the family as Lilly welcomed his advances.

Bennet had always been a confident man. The only son, he was raised in love, adored by his parents and younger sister, and enjoyed the companionship of good friends during his private schooling years. He surprised himself and his parents when he decided to make the move to Australia to break out and stand on his own two feet. He had long been thinking about it, and after another heated argument with his father, who harped at him continuously to consider a career in his footsteps in the British police force, Bennet strode to the ticket office and booked his sea passage.

Had he acquiesced to his father's wishes, his career would have been on a similar trajectory to that of Detective Gilbert Payne – promoted promptly through the ranks due to connections; he felt an alliance with the young man. But he never wanted that lifestyle. Art called to him – the desire to capture and relay what he saw in his mind's eye as he stood in front of his easel, brush in his hand, with the freedom to create. It was all he wanted, and with his trust fund and private investigator business, he would not be a starving artist. He hoped Lilly's father would find that satisfactory.

Tonight, he had decided to be himself. Love him or hate him, it was pointless to put on a persona that would please Lilly's family when he would not do that for his own family. He had always been considered a good catch and never had to work for the love of a woman before, but he was serious about Miss Lilly Lewis, and if they were to spend a life together, he could not keep up the act of being anything but himself for very long.

He arrived on the front step of the modest home in a neat and respectable street. An observer from his old life would be quick to point out that it was nothing like the large estate Bennet hailed from, but he did not care for that. He wore his best suit, carried a bouquet for Lilly's mother, a good port for her father, and hurriedly offered a prayer to the Lord to survive the evening before taking a deep breath, raising his fist, and knocking on the door. It was as if the family stood on the other side of it, and it opened immediately.

'Mr Martin, welcome,' a stern and serious man said, who was most likely wearing his best suit too. He was slim and of similar height to Bennet, with a good mop of greying hair and a thick moustache to match. Behind him was a petite lady who looked very much like an older version of Lilly, and beside Mrs Lewis were five young men, all taller than their father. Lilly stood at the end of the line with a smug look, as if challenging him to run the gauntlet.

'Mr Lewis, Mrs Lewis, thank you for the kind invitation,' he said, offering the gifts that were happily received, and he was bustled into the living room.

'Nothing for us then?' Cyrus, the eldest brother of similar age to Bennet, asked with a small smile. He shook Bennet's hand, introducing the rest of his brothers—James, Elijah, Ethan and Samuel—adding, 'All good biblical names. But you'd know that.'

Bennet looked surprised but did not show his ignorance of the Bible; he was, after all, attempting to win Lilly's mother over, so he said, 'What a coincidence. My name, Bennet, means blessed – the church's Latin name is Benedictus.

'Of course. How lovely,' Mrs Lewis smiled approvingly as if Bennet's mother was a woman of great merit for selecting such a name.

Bennet gave Cyrus a side glance. One point for himself if the eldest brother intended to score, but Cyrus just gave him a wink and a grin.

Mrs Lewis, who, like Lilly, was diminished by the surrounding men, said, 'Let us dine straight away. That way, we can be comfortably seated and talk at leisure. Lilly, take Mr Martin's hat and coat.'

'Yes, Mum. Here, Mr Martin, oh blessed one, hand it over,' Lilly teased, and he shot her a grin.

'Thank you, Miss Lewis.' He subtly touched her hand as he passed over his possessions, given it might be the closest he got to her all night.

'Miss Lewis,' Lilly's youngest brother scoffed in a sing-song voice, and Bennet saw the next in line give him an elbow to the rib.

Were they warned to be on their best behaviour? Bennet mused. *That could make his life easier.*

Surprisingly, Bennet found himself seated next to Lilly, and the evening did not go as he expected, not at all. They passed around the meat and vegetables, cooked superbly and much to Bennet's taste, given he rarely had a roast meal these days, and told Mrs Lewis just that.

'Oh, you must come more often then; there's always room at the table.'

There wasn't. With eight already permanently seated for each meal, the addition of a ninth diner limited everyone's elbow room, and one brother appeared to open his mouth to suggest that. He was offered a large slice of bread and a stern look.

'I do hope, though, that you are not intending to return to Great Britain and take our Lilly with you,' Mrs Lewis said.

'I assure you, Mrs Lewis, I have no intention of returning to my foggy, wet, and cold homeland. I am rather enjoying the warmth and brightness of my new country.'

That pleased Mrs Lewis, who appeared only to have the one question to satisfy her requirements, but Bennet braced himself as Mr Lewis cleared his throat.

Here come the inevitable questions about my job prospects, my intentions, and my abode. But they did not come.

'You realise our Lilly is quite unconventional, Mr Martin?' Mr Lewis asked.

'Please call me Bennet, and yes, Sir, she is that. Very spirited.'

'It is not from want of trying,' Mr Lewis sighed. 'She had the best education, and her mother is a very gentle soul and a wonderful role model, as you can see. But having five brothers... well...'

'I am right here, Dad, and Bennet is not buying a horse. He does not need to hear about my pedigree. Perhaps you wish to ask about his intentions or prospects?' Lilly suggested drily.

Bennet suppressed a laugh and realised that they were hoping he would court Lilly; this might not be as difficult as he thought.

'We didn't think anyone would put up with her,' the middle boy, Elijah, said and was nudged by his sister for his frankness.

'I assure you, I think your daughter and your sister,' he said, including the brothers, 'is wonderful, and I am here to seek permission to court her, Sir.'

'How terribly old-fashioned,' Lilly said drily.

'Be that as it may, I still wish to have your father and mother's blessing,' Bennet said firmly, which seemed to impress her parents and amuse Lilly. Mrs Lewis smiled with delight now, looking at her daughter as if her dreams had come true.

'If you are hoping to modify her behaviour and to make her more suitable for wifely duties, I fear you will have your work cut out for you,' Mr Lewis continued.

'Oh, for the love of God,' Lilly said. 'He's not asking for my hand in marriage, Dad, just to take me to a show now and then.'

'I certainly hope to tame her, Sir, and am up for the challenge.'

Lilly huffed. 'I would like to see you try.'

'Good on you, Bennet,' Cyrus said, hitting him on the back. 'And if you can't?'

'Well, luckily, I think she is perfect just as she is,' Bennet said, looking at Lilly beside him, and she flushed with happiness, even though he suspected she did not want to in front of her family.

'Did you hear that, dear family,' Lilly said smugly, 'perfect as I am.'

'You are,' her brother of closest age, Samuel, said; they were particularly close, and she regarded him affectionately.

'It's a miracle,' Mr Lewis said, winking at his daughter. Raising his glass, they toasted everyone's health and a long life for Mr Bennet Martin.

As the ladies arrived in their dresses, looking very glamorous for the recital ahead, they huddled to admire each other's appearance and the exciting atmosphere in the Centennial Hall. The men did the same, shaking each other's hands and not looking quite as excited as the ladies.

'You look splendid too, Julius,' Harland said in jest.

'Do you think this tie brings out my eyes?' Julius asked, and Tavish chuckled beside them.

'It brings out something,' Harland agreed with a huff of laughter.

Ambrose arrived, greeted the men and reluctantly released his hold on Kate, who hurried to the ladies' side.

'I hope it is a quick recital,' Amber said under his breath. 'These things bore me to tears.'

'Ironically, the only one of us who would truly enjoy it is not here,' Julius said.

'I don't envy Bennet meeting the parents and five brothers,' Tavish shuddered.

'They'll think him a good catch,' Harland said. 'If it were my daughter, I'd welcome him as you did for your sister once,' he reminded Julius.

'I still would prefer him for Phoebe, but it is too late now,' Julius said with a sly smile at Harland's expression to show he was not serious. 'Here's the last of our party, Detective Payne and Miss Yalden. He might enjoy a recital.'

'I am sure he will,' Harland agreed. 'Gilbert has quite cultured tastes.'

Emily greeted the gentleman and went to join her cousin, Isabelle, and the ladies of the *Vexed Vixens*, minus Lilly.

'Sir, Doctor, Mr Astin and Mr Astin,' Gilbert said in greeting.

'We are glad you are here, young Gilbert,' Tavish said, 'as I suspect you are the most cultural among us. I will follow your lead, clap when you do, and be silent when you are.'

Gilbert smiled. 'I'll do my best not to mislead you, Doctor. I am not a musical expert, but I've attended many recitals with my mother. Some can be wonderful; others are... trying.'

'Very diplomatic,' Harland said to his protégé.

'What is your favourite piece on tonight's repertoire?' Tavish enquired. 'I only ask so I might boast the same if I am put on the spot.' He chuckled.

'I've only briefly perused the programme, but I always enjoy Chopin's Ballade Op. 23. It is conducive to thinking in some parts and rousing in others. You will be pleased to know, Doctor, it is only about ten minutes long.'

'Blessed be,' Tavish exclaimed, 'I like it already.'

'The last number is always my favourite,' Ambrose said in jest, and the men were quick to laugh and agree.

'I believe congratulations are in order to you both, Harland, Detective Payne,' Julius said. 'Another case closed.'

'Thank you, an odd one indeed,' Harland said. 'It would have been very easy for the murderer to get away with it if he had been a little more careful.'

'Or clever?' Julius suggested.

'Yes indeed,' Gilbert agreed. 'Surely, it is not hard to plan a murder.'

All four men looked at him in surprise.

'Perhaps you should give up the poetry study and become a mystery novelist,' Tavish suggested, and to his surprise, Gilbert nodded.

'I shall give it some thought, Doctor. You would be a wonderful source for the novel.'

'Do not give my detective ideas, thank you, Tavish,' Harland said, frowning at the coroner. The small party laughed as Harland's gaze sought Phoebe again.

Phoebe did her best not to look at Harland, but they had so little time together, and she relished the chance to see him socially. He looked most handsome in his dark suit, and she was sure he had visited his barber for the occasion. Harland did not go unnoticed by other lady guests, nor did Julius, but Phoebe was not so insecure that she found that distressing. Quite the opposite; she studied him through their eyes and knew he was an excellent catch.

'They all look most handsome,' Violet said, startling Phoebe, and she returned her attention to the ladies.

'Don't they just?' Phoebe agreed.

'It is so easy for men,' Kate sighed. 'They do so little and look so good. I've been having my hair tugged and twisted for hours.'

'It was worth it,' Emily assured her, 'you look lovely.'

Kate smiled. 'Thank you, dear Emily. But it puts one off going out.'

'Not me. I love dressing up and preparing for a night out,' Violet said, surprising them. 'My mother always said anticipation was the best part of any event.'

'Yes,' Phoebe mused, 'I am sure there is truth in that. I have been looking forward to this for days. We will have to plan our next outing so we have more to anticipate after this.'

A bell sounded, and the ladies joined the men of their party.

'Is it time?' Tavish asked, looking at the lovely Isabelle and offering his arm. 'Splendid.'

'We don't want to miss a minute,' Violet added, smiling at Julius, whose attempt at looking as if he agreed failed miserably and relayed that he would be happy to miss quite a lot of it. Violet poked him. 'Not convincing,' she said, and he narrowed his eyes at her, making her laugh.

Moving slightly away from the group, she whispered, 'Do you see anything odd here?'

'Plenty,' he said, 'but that's human nature.'

Violet pursed her lips at her fiancé, knowing he understood her meaning and was being obtuse.

'I am referring to anyone who... you know... says "Boo" rather than hello.'

Once he got over his momentary surprise, Julius laughed, and several of the group turned to look at him; it was a rarity, and both Violet and Phoebe admired the handsomeness of his face at that moment.

'I shall give you boo in a minute,' he whispered, making her giggle.

'Stop with the love talk, you two,' Ambrose said behind them. 'You are causing a scene, and Kate and I are embarrassed.'

Ambrose's comment earned him much ribbing, knowing that was far from the truth and that Ambrose would prefer to be the one making the scene.

'Shall we?' Harland asked, offering his arm to Phoebe. He whispered, 'Or shall we pretend to follow them and then detour for a walk?'

'Do not tempt me, Harland. Let us at least wait until there is a recess; maybe we could slip away then. I quite like a good piano recital, but an hour or so will more than suffice.'

'Good Lord, yes,' Harland said. 'But if we disappear, your brothers may come looking for me.'

'Not if they beat us to it,' Phoebe said, making him smile. 'We are a terribly uncultured lot.' They entered the box that Tavish had booked for the evening. 'I prefer a more intimate setting for a recital, such as dinner in the company of friends.'

'As do I,' Harland agreed. 'But let us just hope there are no major crimes tonight. I would rather suffer a piano recital than a call to arms.'

'I have been at some recitals where being called to work would be a welcome alternative,' Phoebe said, and Harland grinned.

'I shall bear that in mind. Bravely then, we shall go forth. Are you wearing a fragrance?' Harland asked as they took two seats nearest the exit.

'Yes, Teddy recommended it to me.'

Harland turned hurriedly to look at her.

'I am teasing you.'

He hit his heart with his hand as if restarting it. 'Miss Astin, teasing a detective is a fragrant violation of the law,' he said, making

Phoebe laugh and groan at his play on words. As the music began to swell, she allowed Harland to tuck her hand through his arm. They sat back to enjoy the time in each other's company, somewhat oblivious to the recital underway and to that of their six friends nearby.

On stage, only Julius and Phoebe could see the ghost of a mature woman standing behind the young performer, beaming with pride.

THE END

Author's notes:

Miss you, Mum (Merle Goltz), 1941-2022.

Thank you for taking another trip back in time with me and the Astin family. Unbelievably, in the early 1890s, Parisian women were injecting perfume with syringes. The trend soon stopped when septicaemia (blood poisoning) occurred.[1] The doctors seeking to introduce legislation to stop the practice was also true.[2] Although we inject fillers and all manner of things into our skin these days, perhaps we haven't changed over the past century and a half.

As for chloroform, it was a very powerful and potent fluid and quite experimental in use in the 1890s. In a small village in England, poor Hannah Greene, 15, died from inhaling no more than a teaspoon of chloroform on a handkerchief administered by a surgeon in order to remove her infected toenail. An inquest found the surgeon was not to blame.[3] However, it had many successful uses in the 19th century, especially on the battlefields, which outweighed the small number of tragedies experienced.

The case that Gilbert mentions was a real case. It was known as The Pimlico mystery or The Pimlico poisoning mystery. In 1886, Adelaide Bartlett was tried for her husband's murder and acquitted. His stomach was full of chloroform, but it could not be proven how it was administered. Plenty can be found online if you wish to read further.

Like Septimus's brutal end, there was a terrible death from drinking chloroform[4] in 1890, the year before I set my book. The gentleman who drank it was a young doctor determined to take his life. He ingested it when visiting another doctor friend and could not be revived – a terrible waste of life.

The hotels that the detectives and Mr Bennet Martin stay in while visiting Ipswich and Toowoomba were considered very good accommodation in the day. They both exist today but have been rebuilt and refurbished over the decades.

I sourced a train timetable from *The Toowoomba Chronicle* in 1890 to base my times upon. However, I did embellish a midday train to Toowoomba to get the detectives moving. The times were not quite as convenient.[5] Brisbane to Ipswich: 7.25am, 4.10pm or 6.55pm; Ipswich to Toowoomba: 9am, 5.15pm and 8.10pm, which arrived at 12.40am!

The incredible feat of laying the railway to Toowoomba through and up such a steep range is an amazing story. I was also fortunate to find a tourist guide written in that era. If that is your passion, the link is below in my references.[6]

I love writing in this era and love doing the research, but occasionally, I'll make a few allowances for fiction. We are so lucky to have Trove (the National Australian Library) to check terminology and facts. I wanted to say that the perfume salesman could sell ice to the Eskimos, but no such luck in 1891! In fact, I had trouble finding any slang to support this. Let me know if you know of any.

And just a little information on the death industry. If you read my novel when the Astin family was first introduced to readers–*The Mortician's Clue* in the *Miss Hayward and the Detective* series—you will recall my note that dying was a big industry in the 19th century with elaborate mourning rituals followed. Most funerals were conducted at home, and the body was washed, dressed and placed on display for mourning. There were exceptions. For example, in the mid-1880s, when a bachelor died suddenly, the mortician charged the estate ten shillings for completing this duty in the absence of family. Another exception was the hospital burials. Many of the hospitals in the mid-to-late 19th century had contracts with funeral directors to prepare and bury patients who died in the hospital and had no one to claim them. For some undertakers, it made up over fifty per cent of their business, and I have claimed some of this business for *The Economic Undertaker*. So, Phoebe receiving a deceased person to prepare for a viewing who had very few family members or the family, for various reasons, could not house the body, is plausible.

However, by the end of the 19th century, the undertakers had stepped up in duties; thus, they began calling themselves funeral directors and morticians rather than undertakers. Their role expanded to include preparing the corpse, shaving the men, combing their hair, and arranging ladies' hair to appear as they did in life. At the start of the 20th century, some funeral homes also offered a private room for the family to gather. I have taken the liberty of *The Economic Undertakers* starting this practice a little earlier than most – 1891. Let's call them trendsetters!

As the services of undertakers or funeral professionals developed, they often held several jobs to sustain their earnings – they might be carpenters or builders, made coffins, or provided carriage service that doubled for hearses as needed. Thus, Julius has his side businesses of carpentry with his cousin, Lucian, and the mourning wear where Miss Violet Forrester works. In the decades to come, the wearing of mourning clothing would change, and department stores would produce more readily available clothing. But we will come to that as the years roll on.

Not long into the 20th century, the full-service funeral director/mortician became the normal model. It must have been a relief for relatives who preferred to have a funeral director undertake the work due to the heat or having few family members in Australia.

As for training, from the 1890s onwards, the funeral industry became more structured and training and certificates were offered. Phoebe was a qualified professional.[7]

Thank you for reading *The Potent Perfume*. I hope you enjoyed it and will continue the journey with me. More to come.

Also by Helen Goltz:

Murder at the Carnival

The Artist's Missing Muse

Mystery at the Asylum

The Mortician's Clue (introducing Phoebe and staff from The Economic Undertaker)

Murder in Bridal Lane

The Clairvoyant's Glasses (paranormal/romance)

Volume 1 – A vision unexpected

Volume 2 – Time has a shadow

Volume 3 – Love knows no bounds

Volume 4 – Fate comes to call

Volume 5 & 6 – The Raven's Son

The Jesse Clarke series (cosy mystery):

Death by Sugar

Death by Disguise

Death by Reunion

The Mitchell Parker series (crime thriller):

Mastermind

Graveyard of the Atlantic

The Fourth Reich

Writing as Jack Adams (mystery suspense):

Poster Girl

Delaney and Murphy childhood friends' series:

Asylum

Stalker

Cult

Hitched

Carnival.

Writing as Ally Adams:

The Saints team (contemporary romance):

Team Lucas

Team Tomas

Team Niklas

Team Alex

Stand-alone titles:

The House on Findlater Lane (mystery/romance paranormal)

The Forgotten House (historical romance)

Three Parts Truth (mystery suspense)

Morphers (middle grade fiction)

With journalist Chris Adams:

The Grave Tales series (non-fiction) x 9 titles:

Grave Tales: Brisbane Vol.1

Grave Tales: Great Ocean Road – Geelong to Port Fairy

Grave Tales: Sydney Vol.1

Grave Tales: Bruce Highway

Grave Tales: True Crime Vol.1

Grave Tales: Queensland's Great South West

Grave Tales: Melbourne Vol.1

Grave Tales: Queensland's Scenic Rim & Surrounds

Grave Tales: Tasmania.

Grave Tales: Cold Cases (an amalgamation of stories from existing titles)

About the Author:

Helen is a hybrid-published, Amazon best-selling author. After studying English literature, media, and communications at universities in Queensland, Australia, and obtaining a Counselling Diploma, Helen has worked as a journalist, producer and marketer in print, TV, radio and public relations. Born in Toowoomba, she has made her home in Brisbane, Australia, with her journalist husband, Chris, and Boxer dog, Baxter. She is published by Next Chapter, Podium Entertainment, and her own imprint, Atlas Productions.

Connect with Helen:

Website: www.helengoltz.com

BookBub: www.bookbub.com/authors/helen-goltz

Facebook: www.facebook.com/HelenGoltz.Author

Instagram: https://www.instagram.com/helengoltz1/

1. Injecting Perfume into the Blood. (1891, October 9). *Petersburg Times (SA : 1887 - 1919)*, p. 3. Retrieved April 13, 2024, from http://nla.gov.au/nla.news-article110271032

2. Advertising (1890, September 16). *The Avoca Mail (Vic. : 1863 - 1900; 1915 - 1918)*, p. 2. Retrieved April 13, 2024, from http://nla.gov.au/nla.news-article203006820

3. DEATH BY CHLOROFORM. (1848, July 12). *Launceston Examiner (Tas. : 1842 - 1899)*, p. 4 (AFTERNOON). Retrieved May 3, 2024, from http://nla.gov.au/nla.news-article36255117

4. GENERAL NEWS. (1890, August 30). Adelaide Observer (SA : 1843 - 1904), p. 28. Retrieved April 30, 2024, from http://nla.gov.au/nla.news-article159551760

5. Railway Time-tables. (1890, January 16). *Toowoomba Chronicle and Darling Downs General Advertiser (Qld. : 1875 - 1902)*, p. 2 (SUPPLEMENT TO THE TOOWOOMBA CHRONICLE). Retrieved April 5, 2024, from http://nla.gov.au/nla.news-article218320334

6. Meston, Archibald, Queensland railway & tourists' guide, compiled under instructions from the Queensland Railway Commissioners. Gordon Gotch. Retrieved 11 April 2024 f r o m http://www.grantonline.com/grant-family-genealogy/Tipperary/Family-Charts/acc-richard/railway.htm

7. Maclean, Hilda Erica, *Funerary consumption in the second half of the 19th century in Brisbane, Queensland.* A thesis submitted for the degree of Doctor of Philosophy at The University of Queensland in 2015.

www.ingramcontent.com/pod-product-compliance
Lightning Source LLC
Chambersburg PA
CBHW020300120726
47904CB00001B/282